THE
PURPLE

D O O R

DISTRICT

Welcome to the District!

Erin

D1264040

[signature]

ISBN: 978-1-7329450-0-5

Dedicated to anyone who feels alone and needs a community.
Welcome to the District.

Acknowledgments

Dozens of people were involved in the making of this book. Most notably is AE Kellar, my fellow author-in-crime. Much love goes out to my editor, Leona Bushman, and my proofreaders, Shakyra Dunn and AE Kellar. Artists Gabriella Bujdoso and Oni Algarra brought my characters to life through beautiful portraits. Sara Cunningham and Amanda Bouma helped develop marketing materials. "Les" made the incredible cover. This book is about community, and that's what you see here. Thank you, everyone. I couldn't have done it without them, or you, the reader!

Forward

The world of *The Purple Door District* started out as the stubborn brainchild of AE Kellar and myself. We have spent years writing together, researching, brainstorming, and developing characters and rules governing our parahumans and worlds. Our main series, *Fates and Furies*, is still in production but occurs in the same urban fantasy setting.

When we started to design the District, I latched onto it and suddenly had ideas blossoming in my head about creating one in Chicago. Plus, as a birdmom of seven feathered kids, it gave me the chance to professionally write about a werebird, even if I still get the side eye. With AE's blessing, I wrote *The Purple Door District* to introduce you to our world and insanity.

We jokingly say that AE is the brain and I'm the heart, but I think it's very true. While AE fills our books with well-researched facts and logic, I add feeling, creativity, and literary flair. I couldn't have done it without my walking encyclopedia. All you see here exists because of our love for storytelling and our incessant need to get fewer than 8 hours of sleep a night.

Keep an eye out. *Fates and Furies* is on the horizon.

About AE Kellar

AE Kellar works as a professional wingman by day, while by night pretends to write by hiding behind a laptop and listening to a well-crafted, shuffled playlist. With a penchant for dark humor and plenty of snark, AE writes urban fantasy with a smattering of sci-fi and Paranormal thrown in for spice.

Serving as the creative consultant on Erin Casey's *The Purple Door District*, AE is also co-creator and co-author of *Fates and Furies,* an as-yet unpublished fantastical urban fantasy series upon which *The Purple Door District* is based.

In addition to the world of *Fates and Furies,* AE has written a sci-fi short story called *Remember Nevada,* with hopes to publish before Mars is colonized.

Chapter 1
On the Run

Bianca

"Where to, kid?" the driver grunted.

Bianca fell back against the taxi's worn seats with a bone-weary sigh. The lingering scents of perfume and cheap vodka wafted through the compartment, courtesy of the drunken couple stumbling towards the next bar.

Bianca sneezed.

She hated drunk people.

As she ran her fingers through her tangled hair, she noticed the driver watching her from his rear-view mirror. His eyes roved up and down, taking her in, though there wasn't much to see. Then again, when did that ever matter to a guy? Gaunt cheeks, tattered clothes, and dark bags that swallowed her green eyes weren't exactly what she would call sexy. But his gaze became less hungrily appraising and more concerned.

"Where to?" he repeated, less gruff this time.

"Huh? Oh…um…" Bianca bit her lip, thinking. It wasn't a simple answer. She tried to breathe him in to see *what* he was, but the cacophony of scents in the taxi made that near impossible. Bianca had trusted the wrong people before, even if he did seem genuine, and the idea of ending up at the end of a Hunter's gun almost made her add her own vomit to the list of unpleasant smells.

"*Well?*"

"The Purple Door District."

The man turned and glanced back at her with a frown. "Never heard of it."

Her heart sank. It was probably stupid to assume she'd find another parahuman.

Bianca shook her head in frustration then reached into her pocket, pulling out a $20. "Take me as far as this will get me."

The man eyed the bill. "You in trouble, kid?"

"*No.*" Bianca shook it at him. "Look, can you just drive me somewhere or not?"

The driver stared a moment longer then turned back around with a shrug. "Yeah, sure. Buckle up, kid."

Bianca snuggled into the backseat, trying to ignore the spring poking her in her thigh. It didn't matter. Anywhere was better than being drenched out in the cold. The heat hissed as it turned up another notch. Her hands gravitated towards it, drinking in the warmth as it thawed her frozen limbs. As her tension ebbed, her eyes started to flutter.

How many days had passed since she'd slept for more than a few hours? Most nights, she rested in the park, on a bench, and sometimes on top of a roof when she changed forms, one eye always open. Shifting for a werebird like her came as easy as breathing, unlike for other parahumans. But with an empty belly, it left her feeling weak and helpless. And right now, she couldn't afford to be helpless.

She reached into her mind and touched her sleepy caracara. The bird, a reflection of her soul, shuffled around and twitched her dark wings as she got comfortable. Bianca sensed every movement, like the way she tucked her beak into her wing, and the exhaustion from spending so many nights out in the open, exposed to the elements. No other lycan had such a connection to an inner animal. She was the bird, and the bird was her. The bond made avians special; it made them feel a little less alone.

But it had its drawbacks, too. When you went from having your bird and another avian's bird in your head—flying, preening, and comforting your soul's connection—to *nothing*, it created an abyss. Sometimes Bianca thought she could hear the haunting echo of her sister's caracara in the depths of the night, but then she'd wake up to the ghostly sound, alone. She'd cried more tears than she'd care to count over the repeated heartbreak.

Bianca opened her eyes to a watery vision. She scrubbed them stubbornly then slipped her fingers into her tattered jacket and pulled out her phone. The sudden bright light made her blink rapidly until she could focus on the home screen.

Two warm beige-skinned Latina women smiled at her in a partial embrace. The picture brought back memories of an art contest Bianca had won a year ago. They wore matching purple necklaces with a silver feather charm, a necklace Bianca still wore. Her sister Nora looked so proud, her green eyes gleaming, her rosy cheeks full of life.

Her caracara keened in grief, shaking Bianca to her core and threatening even more tears.

Bianca's stomach twisted, and she closed the phone, turning to the sights out of the taxi window for distraction.

The Chicago skyline gleamed beyond a window rippled with rain. The glow of street and building lights soothed her. She didn't want to fall asleep, but between the light, the warmth, and the soft seat, her eyes fluttered, and she dozed off.

***

"Riccardo called about a missing avian. Yeah, you have a description of her?"

Bianca didn't open her eyes as the voice stirred her awake. The car jostled beneath her. Her seatbelt was fastened, and the heat still on, so she hadn't been moved. The taxi driver spoke quietly, but she had better hearing than most humans. She swallowed hard and hid her trembling hands in her pockets.

"Uh huh, that's what I thought. No, Riccardo told me to watch out for a kid around this area. Said she was of interest...said he'd pay good. Uh huh." He shifted, and Bianca gave a little snore. "Yeah, looks like her. Yeah...yeah, okay, not far from the drop off point. Look, don't get blood in my cab this time. Hard to explain that, okay? I'll be there soon. Tell Riccardo he better have the money."

Bianca's heart pounded in her chest as she heard the call end. Dear Mother, they'd found her again. She thought she'd been careful this time! It had been days since the last encounter, and she'd even traveled to a different state.

She swallowed a lump in her throat, every muscle sparking with stress. She'd come this far; she refused to let herself be captured by a *human* taxi driver. Would running help? Or was it better to fight her way out? Why couldn't she be a weredog or werecat? They were stronger than werebirds! But no, she had wings, not teeth.

At least avians had speed.

She cracked open an eye. Streetlights flickered past, and she could see townhouses and apartment complexes on the side of the road. Shops and eateries were few and far between.

Bianca reached slowly towards her seatbelt. She clicked it free then froze, waiting. But the driver said nothing. He played a quiet song on the radio, which would have lulled her back to sleep if her heart hadn't been jackhammering in her chest.

The taxi's brakes squeaked as they pulled up to a red light. Bianca counted to three, pulled the door handle, and shoved it open.

"Hey!" the driver shouted.

Bianca fell out of the car in her haste, gashing her knees on asphalt. The driver slammed his door behind him, but she didn't look back. She scrambled to her feet and darted through the cars, running faster than a human possibly could. Landmarks blurred past her, and the wind whipped her face as if she soared through the night sky.

She didn't stop running until her legs began to burn with the effort. Bianca slowed near an alleyway, gasping for breath. Rats skittered out of dumpsters and waddled through the rain puddles. Each sound sent another jolt of adrenaline through her, but still, she couldn't bring herself to continue.

She sank to her knees, her entire body trembling from exhaustion. If her sister couldn't outrun Hunters, what hope did she have? She couldn't even trust a taxi driver!

"Stop it," she snapped at herself, her caracara squawking in agreement.

She wasn't a quitter.

Bianca gripped the rosary-like necklace and ran her thumb over the purple glass beads several times. It helped her draw on the strength of both the saints and the Blessed Mother. She remembered spending nights memorizing and reciting the prayers alongside Nora. Their first communion and their acceptance into the church. It had always brought her comfort, grounded her at the hardest times.

Nora wouldn't want her to give up.

Bianca rocked back on her heels and looked around. There was no sign of the taxi driver or any of the men who had been following her for weeks.

Bianca grabbed the side of a brick wall and pulled herself up. Water dripped from her bloody knees and left a small trail as she headed down the alley. Rain pattered on her head and made the dumpsters smell even more rancid than the cab. As she ran, she searched frantically for a purple door or anything that might signify safety for a parahuman.

Nora said I could find one somewhere here. Where is it?

And if the men knew she was looking for it, would they surround all of the Purple Door District buildings?

She pressed on, moving through the nearby streets. The shops were all locked up with iron bars or grates over the windows and doors. Some buildings bore broken glass and for sale signs that had lost their color over the long months of waiting for a new tenant. It was *not* a good part of town. Just her luck. But she wouldn't expect Hunters to live somewhere good.

The minutes and rain ticked and dripped on as she slowed to a walk on her sore feet. Water ate through her shoes and made her blisters ache. By the time she reached the next intersection, she started to limp.

Bianca sighed and pulled out her phone. Not for the first time she typed in, "Purple Door District in Chicago" into the search engine. Nothing of consequence came up until she clicked on the images and saw a picture of a little Airbnb with an iconic purple flower pot hanging directly over the same-colored door. When she checked the link, she saw it had been posted by a woman named Gladus with the letters (PDD) following her name.

Purple Door District.

Bianca couldn't help but hesitate. She smelled a trap. What if the Hunters were lying in wait?

Do I have much of a choice? she wondered.

She checked the address and put it in the maps feature. She almost sobbed with relief when she saw that it was only a few blocks from where she currently stood. Locking in the location, she started to run.

Running soon turned to hobbling.

Cars zipped past and splashed her with water, but she didn't care. She watched the little icon on her screen move closer and closer to the Airbnb.

Ten minutes.

Five minutes.

Bianca looked up and caught sight of the purple flower pot in the distance. A warm light in the front window beckoned her, promising safety and reprieve. Even if the beacon didn't belong to a District savior, hopefully the owner would be willing to let in a bedraggled stranger, just for a—

Something hit the back of her leg, cutting through fabric and skin. Bianca pitched forward with a cry of surprise and collapsed. She smacked hard against the sidewalk, her phone cracking as it struck the corner of the curb. She reached down her calf, whimpering, and fingered a dart in her thigh. She barely felt the pinprick mark over the ache of poison inside it.

Henbane. A toxin meant to render avians helpless.

Her vision blurred. Her leg burned like a hundred red ants were burrowing into her veins. She looked over her shoulder and saw two men running towards her—the same two Hunters who had been tracking her for the past three weeks. The larger of the two was a broad-shouldered white man with a brown beard flecked with frost. His thinner Hispanic companion bore dark hair and eyes as sharp as a raptor's despite being human.

"No," Bianca groaned.

She cast aside the dart and grabbed the light post beside her. Grimacing, she pulled herself up and hobbled towards the building. The pain in her leg burned worse, and her vision faded in and out, pulsing black at the edges to the tempo of her heartbeat. The flower pot. She had to reach the purple flower pot.

Bianca hit the steps and struggled up to the door. She pounded on it with both fists. "Help! Please!" she screamed.

She looked back as the Hunters closed in. The bearded man pulled his gun out again and aimed it at her.

The door wrenched open.

A tall woman with beautiful ebony skin stepped out onto the porch where Bianca huddled. She stood nearly six-feet tall, her chin raised with pride and strength. The colors of the rainbow swathed her body, her hair pulled up in layers of purple and crimson cloth. Her gaze swept to the man with the gun, and she held out her hand.

"She's on my property now, gentlemen. PDD."

But the men didn't listen and approached the stairs. "We want no trouble," the bearded one said. He took another step forward.

The woman moved in front of Bianca and raised her hand. A wall of water suddenly sprang up between the Hunters and their prey, driving them backward.

Bianca rolled onto her back, watching in wonder as the rain coalesced into a waving, living creature. It arched over the men and formed into a clawed hand. Water dripped from the fingers like venom.

"I won't tell you again," the woman growled. She flexed her fingers, causing the watery apparition to do the same.

The bearded man hesitated, but the second trained his gun on Bianca.

The woman waved her arm.

The watery hand snatched both men in its cold embrace. The fingers closed, squeezing them. The second man's gun clattered to the pavement. She lifted them several feet into the air, winding the water around them until only their eyes and noses were exposed. "You come back to my home, and I'll bring Legion down on both of your heads."

With a jerk of her hand, she sent the two men flying across the road. They hit the ground with a painful thud which could have broken a rib, just as they had done to Bianca not moments ago. Bianca felt no sympathy for them.

In fact, she hardly felt anything at all as the henbane consumed her senses like a hungry beast and the cold blanketed her body.

She looked up at her rescuer and slumped down on the porch, her strength fading with each passing moment. She caught a glimpse of the woman reaching for her and then darkness descended.

Chapter 2
The Purple Door District

Bianca

Bianca stepped through a wooded field filled with barren trees. Sunlight gleamed between splotches of clouds, but a purple haze embraced everything around her. Twigs snapped beneath each footstep. She turned her head slowly and glanced around. At first, the area was quiet, but as she walked further, she heard the familiar beat of flapping wings that prompted her to look up.

Three majestic birds circled her. A golden eagle looked down at her and opened his beak in a muted call. A barn owl, her feathers speckled like a starlit night, swooped beneath him on silent wings and screeched. Behind them flapped a small ring-necked dove with silver-tinged wings. Bianca could barely make out the little bird's gentle coo.

Bianca thought she should have been comforted being surrounded by fellow avians, but her heart pounded, and her hands trembled with a steady chill that spread through her body, warning her something was amiss.

A piercing screech startled her. She whirled around as a red-tailed hawk flew towards her, his wings outstretched, the sunlight glinting off of his glorious feathers. She could make out every dark bar on his red tail and the bared talons meant to crush the head of his prey.

Bianca twisted around and fell to her knees as the bird zoomed over her head. When she looked up, she saw the hawk crash into a large shadow reaching out for her. Shadow and bird twisted together in a horrendous display of feathers and darkness. Bianca shouted for the bird to get away, but the shadow consumed him with gnashing fangs.

It turned its dark face towards her. As Bianca scrambled backwards, it snatched her up in a clawed hand.

***

Bianca woke with a gasp. She bolted upright, sending something tumbling off of her. Images of the birds whirled in her mind. And the shadow; that dark, hideous essence still reached for her even though she was awake.

She swung her legs over the edge of a couch and staggered to her bare feet. A chill passed through her body, reminiscent of the one in the dream, as a wave of dizziness almost brought the floor to her knees. Where was she? She remembered the Hunters and running through the rain. After that, her memories fizzled, muddling everything in an ugly color. Her damp clothing hugged her body, so she hadn't been out long.

Bianca ran her hands over herself, checking for wounds. Scuffed knees and swollen flesh on the back of her leg where she'd been hit with the dart were paltry injuries and a victory in her mind. The henbane remained in her system, if her dizziness and confusion were any indications. Maybe the toxin had fueled the dream. But her wrists and ankles weren't bound, so the men hadn't succeeded. Or were they trying to lull her into a false sense of—

"Oh! You're awake."

Bianca spun around with a yelp, her bird echoing her cry of alarm. They started to merge, her nails shifting into vicious talons that could rend skin. Her pupils dilated and became more birdlike, her sharp gaze zeroing in on the tall woman standing nearby. The bird yearned to launch out at the intruder, but Bianca held her back in her mind, fearful that once she departed, they'd be separated forever. That didn't stop her from hissing.

The tray tumbled out of the woman's hands, sending a teapot, cups, saucers, and food crashing towards the ground. With a quick flick of her wrist, the woman caught the items in a blue aura. They levitated in front of Bianca's eyes, even the liquid tea. The woman calmly picked the tray back up and used her magic to fill it, placing each piece delicately. She reached for the pot and held it aloft until the last drop of amber tea flowed back inside. "Hello to you, too," she said with a half-smile

Bianca slowly lowered her hands. She didn't shift back yet. The woman still had a natural weapon after all, but she no longer went on the attack. "Who are you?"

"My name's Gladus." She set the tray down on a nearby end table. "I'm the priestess of the Oakfield Ward and Violet Marshall of the Purple Door District. Well, in this area of Chicago anyway."

"You're a water magus," Bianca added, remembering the liquid wall that had protected her. "Or do you know how to use multiple powers?"

"I do, but I prefer water." Gladus gestured to her, as if encouraging her to respond to the question in kind.

Bianca narrowed her eyes, not quite willing to divulge that information yet. "Those men... Are they—"

"Gone," the woman replied. She sank down in a creaky chair next to the tea and smoothed out her colorful skirts, making herself look less of a threat.

Bianca knew better.

And yet, her arms slowly relaxed. The adrenaline started to ooze out of her, replaced by the buzzing pain of the henbane. If the magus had wanted to hurt her, she would have done it already. "Thank you. Are you sure they won't cause us trouble?"

"They won't get through my door. And if they try, Legion can have them."

Legion.

The adrenaline spiked again like an energy shot. Bianca took a step away from Gladus, which turned into a stagger. Being on her feet was *not* a good idea, but encountering Legion would be worse. She couldn't bring them into this. They had eyes and ears everywhere, a little too *1984* in her opinion.

The woman eyed her. "Legion?" Gladus asked, mistaking Bianca's panic for confusion. "The organization that keeps Hunters and parahumans in line."

"I know who they are," Bianca said. They were supposed to be the police of the parahuman world, but Nora had warned her not to go to them. They weren't safe. If this woman associated with them, Bianca could be in real trouble. *Like I'm not already in trouble*, she thought. "You aren't going to call them, are you?"

The woman offered a concerned look. "I should inform them about Hunters running loose in the Purple Door District. I'm a Marshall; it's my duty to keep the parahumans safe."

"*Safe?*" Bianca laughed dryly. "No one's safe with *them* or with Hunters lurking in the shadows ready to pounce." She shivered in her damp clothing. Nora had said the District would be safe, but she'd never mentioned anything about the Marshall being connected with Legion.

This was a mistake.

"I shouldn't be here." Bianca limped towards the door. As she moved, lights started to sparkle on the edges of her vision. An odd sensation coursed through her body, as if it couldn't quite obey her thoughts. The henbane reared its nasty head, threatening to devour her again.

She grabbed the door and yanked it open.

Rain had turned to snow and sleet. White powder dotted the grass and sidewalks outside. Falling crystals sparkled like shattered diamonds in the street lights. It would have been beautiful if it hadn't filled Bianca with such dread.

"It's supposed to get worse out there tonight," Gladus said quietly, still nestled in her chair. "I'd hate for you to fall ill or freeze. If you don't want Legion involved, I won't call them. You're not going to find a much better or safer place than this to spend the night."

Bianca glanced over her shoulder reluctantly.

Gladus motioned to a pile of clothing and blankets. "I have clean clothes for you."

Bianca's arms slumped, and she closed her eyes. Her bird stirred restlessly in her head as she thought, *Who am I kidding? I won't survive the night out there like this.*

Bianca shut the door and hobbled over to the offered clothing. As she gathered up pink PJs decorated with cats and hearts, she muttered quietly, "Thank you."

***

Bianca didn't know how long she slept, but when she awoke, the dizziness and pain in her leg had both fled.

The gentle medley of piano, harp, and guitar roused her from her sleep. She breathed in deeply, her nose catching the scent of something floral. Jasmine maybe? It permeated the room along with the soothing smell of fire crackling on wood. She squirmed sleepily in a warm nest of blankets and pillows. Someone had wrapped a thick downy blanket tightly around her. It smelled comfortingly familiar—a morbid thought since it was probably made from the plucked feathers of dead birds.

For a moment, Bianca allowed herself to rest and not fly into action. Her bird huffed a quiet sigh as Bianca fiddled with her feathered necklace. She ran the smooth glass beads between her fingers, counting the times they spun. It was the last thing connecting her to Nora and her home. Everything else was probably under police custody or smashed on the street outside.

Bianca shuddered and counted the beads a second time. Getting worked up wouldn't help her. She'd been given a blessing, so she said a silent prayer to the Mother, the avian matriarch, thanking her for the reprieve. The threat of Legion and the Hunters still hung in the air, but she could deal with that storm later.

Bianca dozed for another hour or so before her snarling stomach jerked her out of another purple dream. She sat up reluctantly, brushing her hands along the smooth fabric of the red couch. A fire burned merrily near her. Shadowy flames flickered on the black and beige rug covering the hardwood floor. The dark walls surrounding her bore pictures of dried plants, but also of famous musicians, some of which Bianca knew were parahumans. How else had Elvis eluded the paparazzi for so long? The King definitely wasn't dead. He'd just taken a break.

Gladus had suggested Bianca take an upstairs bedroom, but she'd chosen the receiving room instead. The fireplace provided warmth and comfort and reminded her of the one her father used to stoke on cold, winter nights while her mother sang sweet lullabies.

The receiving room also provided a clear exit to the door if trouble ensued.

She swung her legs over and planted her feet on the rug.

"Ah, stay down," Gladus said as she walked into the room. She carried a fresh tray of two mugs, a teapot, a plate of sandwiches, and…were those homemade cookies? Bianca's mouth watered in anticipation. "That henbane might be out of your system, but you still need rest."

"How long have I been asleep?"

"Almost a full day." The magus poured tea into the two mugs

and handed one to her. Bianca raised her hand to ward it off, but Gladus shook it, exasperated. "You need to eat and drink, girl. You're half withered away as it is."

"Uh, actually, where's your bathroom?" Understanding dawned on the magus' face. Gladus pointed towards the hall. Bianca slipped off of the couch and went to do her business. Walking still hurt, but not nearly as bad as before. Even the dull ache in the back of her leg had eased.

Bianca nearly ran back to her warm nest, muttering, "cold, cold, cold," as her bare feet slapped across the wooden floor. While she settled on the couch, Gladus handed her the tea and placed a tall glass of water on the table. She half expected the mug to have a floral pattern on it. Instead, the phrase, "I'm a bear before morning coffee. You've been warned" was scrawled across it. It made her smile; she could sympathize.

Bianca drained the water but took the tea slower. She picked up one of the beef sandwiches and took a hearty bite. Spicy Dijon mustard danced on her tongue and turned her growling stomach into a beast. She threw all decorum out the window and tore into the dainty sandwich like a vulture into carrion.

"So," Gladus said after a time, "you haven't told me your name yet."

Bianca brushed crumbs from her lips and hair. She'd devoured one sandwich with barely a breath and started on her second. "Bianca."

"Nice to meet you. By the talons I saw, I would guess you're an avian?"

Bianca paused, waiting, but Gladus didn't continue with the obvious question of "what kind are you?" It was rude in avian culture, so she appreciated the omission. "Yes."

An unasked question lingered in the air, but it had nothing to do with her species. Suddenly, her appetite vanished. She put the second sandwich down. "Look, I'm sorry about how I acted when you were just trying to help me. It's hard to know whom to trust. I don't know who those men are or what they want."

"You've seen them before, then? This isn't just a one-time occurrence."

"No." Bianca glanced away. She didn't really want to talk about it, but she owed Gladus something for helping her. "My sister Nora and I were living together outside of Illinois. She became my guardian after our parents died. Everything was fine, but then these Hunters started following us around. I didn't know what they were until one of them tried to grab me on the streets. Nora said if anything happened, I needed to find the Purple Door District, that there would be people there I could trust and who would help me." She gripped the necklace, her thumb brushing over the feather.

"Well, she was right about that," Gladus replied. "So why'd you come all the way out here? Didn't you live in a Purple Door District?"

"No." Bianca rubbed the back of her neck. "My parents were very...selective about where we lived. I know about the District, but I never actually visited one. My sister just said it was a good place to go. Did I come to the right one?"

Gladus jerked her thumb back towards the door. "You were lucky and chose a more neutral place. Parahumans set up a motif in their establishments to indicate if they're parahuman friendly. You'll get used to it while you're here. How'd you find out about this one?"

"Heh, the purple pot and the door were kind of a dead giveaway," Bianca said with a giggle. "And you showed up on a Google search."

"I did?" Gladus asked in genuine surprise. "Well, that's lucky for you but unfortunate for me. That's only supposed to show up on the Legion Network." She made a face. "I'm sure Randal will have my head for that. 'You can create water out of nothing,' he says, 'But you can't manage to change a router password, or link a webpage to the right place.' Know-it-all werecat."

Bianca stiffened. There it was again...Legion. But if Gladus had called Legion, Bianca would have woken up in some kind of padded and barred cell, not on a plush couch. "You said you're the Marshall. What does that mean?"

Gladus picked up a cookie and dipped it in her tea. "Each district has a Violet Marshall: that's me. A parahuman leader of the area is the main contact when there are problems or certain parahumans are seeking refuge. We're the ones who get in touch with Legion... whom you don't seem to like." She tilted her head back, her dark hair and colorful scarves cushioning her head against the chair. "That complicates things for me a bit."

Bianca ducked her head at the passive reprimand. "I'm sorry. I don't have much money—"

"Don't worry about it," Gladus said, waving her hand. She munched on the cookie slowly. "This is why we're here. I get some charitable donations to help support the people who stumble in when they're in a bad spot."

"I guess I'm lucky I ran into a magus. My sister said certain parahumans aren't always friendly to us birds." She glanced at the tea in her mug and swished it around. "Wish I could use magic like that. Nora said we have a distant cousin who could set things on fire. One look, and poof, your hair goes up into flames."

Gladus choked on her drink a little. "Em…*yes*, there are a few of those, dare I say *hotheaded,* magi out there." She eyed Bianca. "Your cousin, she's not a lycan is she?"

"He, and no," Bianca said, shaking her head. "Magus married into the family. I thought lycans can't use magic anyway."

"Well no, they can't. At least, they're not supposed to. They don't have the Ether chakra."

"The what?"

Gladus smiled. "You know about chakras, right? The energies in your body?" When Biana nodded, she went on. "Magi have an extra chakra which allows us to access the natural magic on earth called Ether. We command it." She waved her hand and created a water orb out of thin air. "Bend it to our will. Create." A wiggled finger formed a living wave. "We destroy." She clenched her hand, and the water vanished. "We can sense the Ether flowing around us and through us. Witches don't have that chakra, but they still have sensitivity to the Ether and have the chance to learn it. Use it. Just not as easily as magi."

Bianca couldn't help but notice the tone of superiority in Gladus' voice. Witches didn't always get along with magi, she knew that much. Witches bonded in groups called groves, and magi formed wards. They were similar to the cloisters avians joined. What each one did, Bianca didn't know, but she *did* know that they didn't usually mingle.

She watched Gladus form a ring of water, fascinated. If she had *that* ability, she wouldn't be running from Hunters.

Gladus banished the water and leaned forward suddenly, intent. "You have no idea why those men were after you, hm? What did your sister do?"

"Worked in a pharmaceutical company. A couple weeks ago, she told me there was a breakthrough in some kind of drug, and that's when the Hunters started following us." Her hands shook around the mug until she had to set it down.

She and Nora had been eating dinner from their favorite Chinese takeout spot the night it happened. Nothing had been suspicious, and Nora had seemed completely relaxed at the time. And then the door had exploded, spraying them with shards of wood. Smoke filled the room, and the men came in, guns in hand.

"They killed her," Bianca said in a choked voice, the memories stirring in her. "There wasn't anything I could do. She was just dead."

Tears welled in her eyes. She hadn't had a chance to really mourn Nora's death yet. Being on the run made that pretty hard. And now her phone had been smashed to smithereens, the pictures lost forever. She fought back a sob and dropped her head into her hands. Her bird brushed against her mind comfortingly, but it only did so much. Nora was still dead.

Gladus touched her cheek and then pulled her into a tight hug. "Let it out, Bianca."

Bianca sobbed into the magus' shoulder and clung to her. Her heart crumbled into a million pieces. It had been bad enough when her parents had died. Now Nora was gone. She had no one left. No family. No cloister. No place to call home.

In time, she pulled herself together. She brushed the tears out of her eyes with the backs of her hands. "I don't know what to do."

"Do you have a cloister you can return to?"

Bianca shook her head. "Nora *was* my cloister. And without her, I have no one."

"That's not entirely true," Gladus said and squeezed her hands. "You have me as a friend now. And I have some friends I can talk to about finding you a safe place where you can be with other werebirds. I know I'm not going to be enough. You birds do a lot better with those of your own kind. Not to mention all the preening and pampering you do to each other. I can't keep up with it. But I know a few who might be able to lend a wing."

Bianca sniffed and looked up. "Really? And you won't call Legion?"

"I'll report the suspicious activity of Hunters in the area, but I won't tell them about you. I have to keep the rest of my District safe, though, you have to understand."

Bianca nodded. It would give her enough time to heal and

maybe flee if necessary. "Thank you."

"I'm sorry for what's happened to you," Gladus said. "But I promise, if you'll give me the time, I'll find someone to take you in. No more running for you."

Bianca heaved a quiet sigh. For a moment, the weight of the world fell away from her. "I'd like that. I'm tired of being afraid if I'm gonna wake up in the morning."

"That's something you won't have to worry about here." Gladus squeezed her shoulder. "We parahumans have to look out for each other. Rest, Bianca. You're safe."

Bianca hoped that was true.

***

Sleep eluded her. Maybe she'd slept too much during the last twenty-four hours. Or perhaps it was because birds and shadows kept dancing in her dreams.

Bianca pushed herself off of the couch around midnight. The fire burned low, and Gladus had gone to bed hours ago. Bianca headed into the kitchen and poured herself a glass of water. As she downed it, she noticed a notebook and a pen with a grocery list sitting by the fridge. She put the glass in the sink and picked up the book.

The house creaked and groaned its age as she walked through the long hallways. She hadn't explored much else except the first floor. The stairs wound as they went upwards, the walls lined with more pictures of musicians and some people who looked like Gladus. One woman even wore the same colorful cloth in her hair as the magus.

Bianca checked the rooms. They were set up like a nice hostel with clean beds, linens, and furniture. One room had an odd Victorian motif complete with a canopied bed and rustic wooden furniture. The only door she couldn't open emitted Gladus' quiet snores. Bianca hid a smile and glanced at a glass door that led out to a small patio. Moonlight stretched across the floor, landing just shy of her toes.

She settled down against the glass. Placing the pad on her knees, she used the moon to help her sketch. Images of the barn owl, the red-tailed hawk, the golden eagle, and the ring-necked dove returned to her in a flourish. She sketched every detail of them, even the individual feathers. They almost looked like they could jump off the page and soar with her across the night sky.

But then another image started to form on the pad. She furrowed her brow and sketched the dark shadow which had loomed over her in her dream. It rose, its vicious tendrils reaching out for the birds, for her.

Bianca dropped the pad onto the floor. The image of the figure filled her with the same terror she'd felt the night Nora died. The night her connection to her cloister vanished forever.

It's not fair, she thought. *I didn't ask for this, and neither did Nora. It wasn't like we went out looking for trouble.* But trouble liked to find her. Sometimes she wondered if anyone was safe around her.

As she blinked back the tears, her caracara took shape on the floor beside the drawing of the shadow figure. No one else except for Bianca would be able to see her, but at least it made her feel just a little less alone. Her bird nibbled at her fingers affectionately. Bianca stroked her head back, the warm feathers tickling her palm. The caracara was another limb, one she didn't think she could ever bear to lose.

Something flew across the moon and cast a shadow over her picture. Bianca swallowed and glanced outside.

Suddenly, Gladus' promise of protection didn't feel so comforting.

Chapter 3
The Guacamole Grill

Carlos

"Order's up!"

Carlos slid two sizzling fajita dishes across the bar to his waitress Anita. He reached for a basket of chips at the pass and spotted his chef's orange head bouncing up and down like a dancing pumpkin. The younger Latino whistled and tossed another steak on the grill. Instead of turning up the heat, he flicked his fingers together and set the meat aflame with magical fire. He flashed Carlos a wide smile, his harvest eyes sparkling.

A fae chef definitely cut down on the gas bills.

Carlos set the chips down in front of a werewolf sitting at the bar. When he noticed Anita lingering with the fajitas still in her hands, he cocked his head at his niece.

Anita sighed. "Table five is giving me problems again. They don't like being served by a *chick*."

Carlos arched a gray eyebrow and glanced at the indicated booth.

Two broad-shouldered white men roared with boisterous laughter and gulped down their beers almost in tandem. A lithe woman sitting across from them cracked a wide smile as she ran her foot along one of the men's legs. He looked her up and down hungrily. The whole scene would have seemed normal, had a third man in the booth not hunkered down as if this was the last place he wanted to be.

Newbie.

Carlos grunted and moved around the bar. "Take my spot. I'll have a word."

"Don't rough them up too much," Anita said, touching his arm affectionately. "We don't want *another* scene."

"Eh, they try to touch you, believe me, there'll be more than a scene." He cleaned his hands off on the red napkin hanging from his pants and strode over. Though not the biggest man, or the strongest, his experience outweighed both. Most werebirds didn't seek out fights, and Carlos was no exception. However, he didn't sit idly by while another avian, or *chick*, was being abused. Besides, he was the owner of the Guacamole Grill, and if he wanted to kick a few morons out, then he would.

As he drew closer, he recognized the woman. He fought back a groan.

"*Trish*, nice to see you again," he said, his voice dripping with false pleasantry.

The woman turned smoldering red eyes towards him. Her crimson lips widened and showed off pristine white fangs which were even brighter than his chef's hair. "Ah, Carlos," she purred. "So good to see you. Sorry, are we being too loud?"

Carlos' eyes darted to the man squirming at her side then to the frat-boy-like pair. A sniff told him what his eyes couldn't; werewolves. *Lovely.* Werewolf tempers. Just what he needed. "Nah, the volume isn't the issue. I hear you're giving my server a bit of grief, though."

The two werewolves snickered to one another while Trish sighed dramatically. "Carlos, they were just having a bit of fun, that's all. We didn't know the little bird was so sensitive." She smirked at the wolves. "Really, don't let us ruffle your feathers."

Carlos rolled his eyes to the ceiling, praying for patience. He jerked his thumb towards the purple door at the front of the building. "You see that? You remember what it means? It also means that this area"–he ran his finger in a circle—"is to be clear of dickish, racist comments, *especially* when they're directed at the owner's niece."

Trish pouted, her lower lip sticking out. "Oh dear, we seem to have upset him." She snapped her head towards one of the werewolves. "Jeff, say you're sorry."

The werewolf barked out a laugh. "You want me to apologize

to an avian? Peh, might as well cut my own tail off. It was a joke. Lay off, *hermano*—"

Carlos' hand snapped out and squeezed a nerve on the werewolf's neck. Two sharp talons slid through the skin on his fingers and pricked the wolf. He breathed patiently as the man froze, feeling the tight hold. The other werewolf grew still, but Trish could only smile. "I am not, nor will I ever be your *brother*. Until you can show me and my kind the proper respect, you both can leave. Don't make me call the Violet Marshall down on your asses."

Jeff swallowed, his Adam's apple bouncing nervously. "I'll tell her you threatened me."

"I'm protecting my establishment and the fine people here," Carlos said with a charming smile. "You are disturbing that peace and also trying my patience. Now, do I have to call the VM?"

He tightened his hold until the wolf flinched and shook his head.

"Jeff," Trish said. "Be a dear and run along. I fear we've outstayed our welcome."

Carlos stood back as the two wolves tossed a few wrinkled bills down on the table and left. Jeff paused long enough to give Trish a disgustingly long kiss, tongue and all, before he parted ways. Carlos didn't relax until the door swung shut behind the two dogs.

Trish leaned back. "Was that really necessary?"

"How long have you had them under your charm, Trish?" Carlos grumbled. He swiped up the money and glanced at the thin man beside her. "This one under your control, too?"

"Of course not! Ramone was *dying* to come here. See, he's heard all about the Purple Door District, but he was always too afraid, you know, being human and all."

Now *that* sparked Carlos' interest and ire. "*Human*... Trish, did you really bring one of your blood bags into *my* restaurant?" He glowered. "You know how I feel about feeding."

"It's perfectly natural," Trish said defensively. "I need blood to survive, and he has blood to give. I make sure I don't take too much, and I wipe his memories anyway, so he won't remember me or this place. It's a shame when you lose one of the cute ones." She tipped Ramone's head back with her nail on his chin. "Isn't that right, precious?"

The man's eyes widened in fear, but Ramone didn't resist.

Likely, Trish had used her charm on him already. She liked the fear; it got the blood pumping and made it taste better she often said. And she preferred to instill terror while her prey perched next to her like a bloody steak on a silver platter instead of having to chase him.

"I don't like fast food," she'd once laughed.

Carlos set his jaw and folded his arms. "Trish, let him go. I don't like having charmed folks in my restaurant, especially not when they're being fed on."

"I haven't bitten him."

Carlos motioned to two very red dots on the man's neck. "Bit and healed. I'm not stupid, Trish. Either let him go, or get out."

Trish narrowed her eyes at him. She leaned forward slowly, her brown and uninspiring irises taking on a redder tint. "Make me, bird. I'll get you for discrimination against vampires. My coven will hear about it—"

"And won't listen because they *know* how you are," Carlos retorted. "Half of the reason this bar doesn't have vampires is because they know you frequent it. *They* know my rules, and they respect them. I've been lenient with you before, Trish. Bringing in a charmed human is a step too far." He drummed his fingers on the table, the long talons emerging.

Trish snorted at him. "You avians might be faster, but I'm still stronger than you, Carlos. You attack me, I—"

A female voice interrupted her. "You'll do what, exactly?"

Trish's head snapped around, and Carlos looked up.

A dark-skinned woman wearing purple, gold, and crimson joined them. She towered over Carlos, well, almost everyone did, and she wore her natural hair back with a thick purple ribbon. Rich colored clothing acted as her calling card; people could spot her blocks away. It gave parahumans who knew not to mess with Gladus Bamore the chance to escape.

Trish's pale skin flushed with color. "You called the VM on me?" she hissed.

"Did I need to be called?" Gladus asked.

Carlos smirked to himself. In all his years working at The Guacamole Grill and living in the Purple Door District, Gladus had always been a friend to him and his family. She'd gotten rid of more than a few bad eggs from his restaurant. She'd tried throwing Trish out once before, but Carlos had taken pity on her. At that time, she'd been a weak and scared vampire, covenless and alone. Having a coven had made her bold and stupid, as well as forgetful of those who had helped her during her struggles. Carlos could only offer so many chances.

Trish growled under her breath and grabbed her purse. She reached for the man's wrist, but Gladus placed her hand on the booth next to Trish's cheek.

"No," Gladus said simply. "Take the charm off, Trish. You're not bringing this one with you."

"He's *mine*." Trish shoved Gladus' hand away and stood up, almost reaching the magus' height in her heels, but Carlos would still put his money on Gladus. Trish might have fangs and charm, but Gladus could drop Lake Michigan on Trish's head if she wanted to.

Gladus closed in on Trish, but she didn't meet her eyes. It wasn't out of fear or respect; you were an idiot if you stared directly into a vampire's gaze. That's how you got wrapped up in their web. "I'm only going to ask one more time, Trish. You know who I can call."

Trish hissed under her breath. Slowly, she uncurled her fingers around the man's bruised flesh and let him go. "Fine," she groused and tried to swing past Gladus, but the magus didn't move. Gladus gave her a look.

The vampire whirled around and grabbed the human's chin. She gazed into his eyes and spoke quietly. "I've grown tired of you. Go home."

With that, she jerked her hand away and stormed out of the restaurant. A few patrons watched her go. The moment the door shut behind her, several parahumans applauded. Carlos thought he heard a relieved, "Finally," off to the corner. They didn't have qualms with vampires, just Trish.

He glanced at the human. The poor fellow looked as dazed as if he'd been punched in the face. Carlos slid into the booth next to him and gave his shoulder a shake. "How are you feeling?"

"Wh-what happened?" the man mumbled. He put a hand to his head and made a pained face.

Sitting this close, Carlos could see that Trish had been using this one for a while. Several marks decorated his throat which she hadn't taken care to clean up. Vampire saliva had a healing component to it. What use was a reusable blood bag if he bled out once Trish fed? But she had chosen not to do much more than seal the wounds. She'd marked him, and pretty heavily. Most female vampires left what looked like a lover's mark on her prey's neck. This poor man looked rather like an animal had gnawed on him. His ashen skin suggested borderline anemia. Blood bag running on empty.

Gladus took a seat across from them and reached over the table, taking the man's frail hands in hers. Carlos didn't see the magic, but it hummed as it passed through Ramone's body. The man's eyes cleared a little, and he relaxed. Healing magic... Carlos would give anything to have that ability.

Gladus offered the human a warm smile. "What's your name?"

"Ramone," the man mumbled. He looked around, confused. "Where am I?"

Carlos held out his hand. "The Guacamole Grill. Looks like you could use a good meal. Let me get something for you. You know where you live?"

Ramone blinked a few times and seemed to come out of his trance as Gladus sent him another wave of healing magic. "Yeah...yeah. I'm not sure how I got here, though. I was coming home from work, and then everything is kind of hazy from there."

Gladus smiled. "Don't worry. I'll help you get home. But Carlos is right. You should eat something. I'll sit with you, okay?" She glanced sideways at Carlos. "I'd like a word with you later, when you have a moment."

"Shift ends at 6," he said.

Carlos slipped from the table long enough to fetch the fajita order that the werewolves had requested. No use wasting good food. The plate was still warm, so he brought it and a couple tall glasses of water over.

Once he served the man, he slipped back behind the counter as Anita poured a drink for one of the customers. She sent him a smile.

"Hopefully she won't be back again," she remarked.

"I don't think she will be," Carlos replied. He looked over at Ramone as the human dug hungrily into the fajitas. Gladus spoke with him and touched his hand every so often to help with the charm fog. He'd be fine. He was in good hands.

Not all "blood bags" were so lucky.

***

"Alright," Carlos said to Anita as he waved to his final customer. "Clock's up for me. If I'm late for dinner tonight, Haley is going to have my head."

Anita chuckled and whacked him on his rump with her cleaning rag. "Go, go. I have it here. I'll stop by later to check on the kids, eh?" She caught his shoulder before he left the bar. "Keep an eye out for Trish, okay? I don't want her causing you trouble."

Carlos leaned over to kiss her cheek. "You worry too much. I'll be fine. Besides, I have the big, bad VM here to give me a hand if Trish seeks out revenge." He stretched out his arm to Gladus as she approached him, Ramone cowering slightly behind her. "Isn't that right? You'll protect me from the mean vampire."

Gladus snorted. "I think your talons can do that well enough. Still, I'll walk you to your car." She jerked her thumb towards Ramone. "I'm going to get him home and put on a protection spell to make sure Trish stays off of him."

"You wanted to talk?" Carlos slid his arm through his leather jacket. He pulled his keys and wallet out and headed for the door, holding it open for both her and Ramone.

"In a moment." Gladus guided the men to the rows of cars outside of the restaurant. Her little gold Honda matched her attire perfectly. She helped Ramone inside and touched his head, sending him to sleep with a spell. Yet another thing Carlos wished he could do.

He leaned against the bumper of her car. "Will he remember what happened?"

Gladus shrugged. "The restaurant? Yes. Trish? No. We don't need humes running around yelling about vampires abducting them on their way home from work." She put her hands on her hips. "I was wondering if your cloister could take in another bird."

Carlos lifted an eyebrow. Well, she wasn't beating around the bush, was she? "Been a while since you brought in a stray. Explain."

"She came to me," Gladus said. "Couple nights ago, this avian showed up on my doorstep being followed by two Hunters. She's just a kid. Barely 18. I chased them off, but I've sensed some lurking around. I thought it would be better to get her deeper in the Purple Door District while I consult with some friends. Do you have room?"

Carlos smiled a little. "You know I always find room for avians around here. Family is getting big, but, we still have space. What's she like?"

"Scared," Gladus replied. "She's got a good sense of humor when you get her relaxed enough, but that's hard to do."

Carlos nodded to himself. He knew he should talk it over with his wife, but for now, the kid needed help. Turning stray birds away wasn't in his nature; of all parahumans, werebirds were most likely to perish from loneliness. And he didn't trust some of the other Fathers and Mothers of the cloisters in the area. It wasn't that they were *bad*. They just had some traditions he didn't follow. And besides, they could always find her another place later on. "Why don't you bring her by my house later tonight? I'll have an extra plate of dessert for her. Haley's making *tres leches*."

"Save me a piece," Gladus said. "Heh, that'll be a good introduction for the girl."

Carlos cocked his head. "She's not dangerous at all is she?"

"I don't think so. She got a bit defensive when she woke up at my place, but she calmed down once she realized she was safe. She's stayed huddled in one spot the past few days. She's drawing, but she doesn't have interest in anything else. I think she just wants to find a home. Her name is Bianca."

"Pretty," Carlos remarked. He patted Gladus on the arm. "Well, go get him home and bring this Bianca to me. I'll be happy to meet her."

"Are you sure Haley won't mind?"

"I'll talk with her," Carlos assured her.

"Thanks, Carlos." Gladus squeezed Carlos' shoulder and opened the driver's door.

Carlos backed off as she got inside. He stared at Ramone for a moment, but the man remained blissfully asleep. Sometimes, magic really had its perks. He could have used that sleeping spell when his kids were young.

He waved as she pulled out of the parking lot.

Something clattered near the back of the restaurant. Carlos snapped his head towards the noise and narrowed his eyes. He moved between the cars swiftly, expecting either a raccoon or someone dumpster diving. But when he got there, a large shadow disappeared around the corner of the building. Carlos sniffed the air, catching a familiar whiff.

Vampire.

Trish, he thought to himself. He clenched his teeth and grabbed his keys. Bloody vampires. Didn't know when to leave well enough alone.

As he headed towards his Subaru, he couldn't help but glance over his shoulder.

Chapter 4
Cloister

Carlos

Carlos started the car and turned the radio on. Pop music blasted through his speakers and assaulted his sensitive hearing. He scrambled to turn the volume down. Apparently, Anita had used his car on her break again. What was it with kids turning the music up so it blew out your eardrums? Muttering, he changed the channel to blissful classic rock and pulled out of the parking lot.

Traffic in Chicago moved like a funeral procession with a rush hour that could last from 3pm anywhere up to 8pm, depending on where you were. The shortcuts worked well, when not everyone knew to take them. And, Mother forbid, construction didn't cover a road with shitty material that would have to be replaced *again* the next summer.

He reached into his console and pulled out a packet of cigarettes which cost him a small fortune these days. Lighting one, he drew in a deep lungful of smoke. The smell of tobacco helped his muscles and nerves relax after the episode with Trish. Haley hated when he smoked, so he only did it on the rare occasion when he drove home from the restaurant after a hard day. It helped keep him calm, especially with so many assholes on the road.

And with vampires lurking in the shadows.

A cool breeze wafted through his car, stirring a medallion hanging from his rearview mirror. It displayed the likeness of St. Gall, the patron saint of birds. The holy man stood with a bear and a log of wood at his feet while a bird flew above his head.

Carlos wore a similar medallion around his neck, a gift from his wife. It kept him safe, he believed, and had helped him survive a car crash a few years ago. It comforted him to have something to believe in, especially when the world could be so dark and unforgiving.

Carols tapped his cigarette on the side of the window and glanced at the passengers in the car next to him. They bobbed their heads to heavy bass music that rattled his bones, both smelling of human. One kid noticed him watching and gave him the finger before the car zoomed ahead.

Carlos grunted. Humes, the few who knew about his kind anyway, rarely gave parahumans a chance. They just gave in to fear and hunted "the animals" down or ran in the other direction. Carlos preferred the runners; the others invariably turned into Hunters.

Hunters. Hunters were the worst. Carlos didn't fault people for needing a job, nor did he snub those who tried to keep a community safe. There were some *good* Hunters, those who took out the real psychopaths; some were even friends to the PDD. But there were just as many Hunters who craved murdering parahumans for the sheer thrill. Carlos had lost an innocent cloister bird to Hunters before. Said Hunter would never take another life.

Carlos didn't think of himself as a murderer. A necessary evil for justice, which was hypocritical since the Hunters thought the same thing of themselves. But really, what good person shot a daughter to death right in front of her mother?

Carlos puffed smoke again and tapped more ashes into the wind. He rubbed his temple with his index finger, his eyes drifting to a picture tucked behind the steering wheel. A young woman with skin the same shade as his and a determined smile stood beside him and a shorter brunette woman wearing glasses.

Andria...he could almost hear his little girl's laugh, though it had been silenced 10 years ago by the snarl of a gun. 10 years, but the pain stayed fresh. While Haley had drowned herself in her tears, Carlos had dealt with his grief by seeking revenge. Nothing had helped, of course, not until two new chicks came into their nest through adoption.

Most cloisters consisted just of the immediate or extended family, but Carlos had never been one for tradition. His cloister homed many adopted folks, and he wouldn't have it any other way.

Neither would Haley. She liked big families and feeding huge crowds.

Or, at least she had, up until Andria's murder. Now she unsheathed her talons at anyone who got too close to their cloister, lest they bring trouble. It made welcoming Bianca into the fold that much more difficult. Perhaps if Hunters weren't trailing the girl, his wife would be more understanding, but their family had seen enough trouble to last them a lifetime. Would he even be able to convince her to give Bianca a chance?

Someone honked, startling him from his thoughts. He glanced up and realized he'd been sitting at a green light. Carlos waved his hand in apology and continued down the road. A few more turns, and he parked on the street in front of a huge forest green townhouse he and part of his cloister inhabited. He kept searching for an apartment building with enough complexes that they could all live together. But the other part of his cloister resided only a couple streets away.

He locked the car and headed inside, the delicious scent of brisket and masa taco shells tickling his nose. Making tex-mex food at The Guacamole Grill was delicious and comforting in its blending of cultures, but it wasn't the same as the meals with his family in Mexico. Haley had decided to learn the traditional dishes so he could have a little taste of home away from, well, *home*.

He unlocked the door and started up to the second floor where his immediate family lived. Anita and her girlfriend took the downstairs. Both were still busy at work.

He opened the door and the pitter-patter of tiny feet greeted him.

"Papa!" Madison shouted as she rushed towards him. Henry ran after her, his curly red hair bouncing on his head.

"Hi, chicks!" Carlos shouted and knelt, taking both children into his arms. He hugged them tightly and showered them with kisses. Madison wrapped her arms around him and kissed him back, her white cheeks flushed from running and laughing. Her brother, his nose speckled with freckles, grinned, showing an empty spot in his mouth. "Ah! Did Mama help you get the tooth out?"

"Nope!" Henry said. "Madison hit me in the mouth with a plastic bat!"

"Henry! You weren't supposed to tell him that!" Madison grumbled.

Carlos gave his daughter a look. "A plastic bat?"

"We were playing ball," Madison said. "I tried to hit the ball, but his mouth got in the way."

Carlos snorted with laughter and ruffled his son's hair. "Better put that under your pillow for the tooth fairy."

"I will, Papa." Henry stepped back to give his father room, but Madison continued to cling.

Carlos didn't mind. He swept the seven-year-old up into his arms and walked into the kitchen with her still sitting on his hip. Henry followed behind. Carlos loved his babies. Since the first day he and Haley had adopted them, they had been the apples of his eye.

Madison had practically called the orphanage her birth-place. Kids had poked fun at her whenever she talked about the bird in her head; none of them had realized she was an avian until Carlos had found her at age 4. By then, she'd been so afraid to talk about her bird that it had taken a month for him to coax it out of her. The good thing about being an elder avian was that he'd sensed the little dove in her mind bouncing around, wanting to be let out to the world.

Henry had ended up in the foster system after his mother overdosed. His father, a sick, twisted man, took his grief out on Henry. Child Services had stepped in, a parahuman one this time. Carlos had received the call not long after Henry was brought into the system. They knew his reputation as Father and how strong he kept his cloister. Best to have birds stay with birds, they believed.

At least some foster systems weren't a total wreck.

"Mama!" Henry said, rushing in to his mother's side. He put his hands on her wheelchair arm and bared his mouth to her. "I showed Dad the hole!"

"I heard," Haley said with a laugh. She kissed his head and continued picking apart the brisket. "You're a bit late," she said and tilted her head back, her beautiful brown eyes shining behind her glasses. "Are you hungry?"

"Always *famished* for your cooking," he said. He leaned down and kissed her deeply.

"Ew," Madison complained.

"Yuck," Henry agreed.

Carlos arched an eyebrow at them. "If you don't like it," he said, setting Madison down, "then you two can set the table. Go on, get," he teased, nudging his daughter toward his son.

"But, Dad!" Madison cried.

Carlos folded his arms, looking at them with mock sternness. "Don't make me send my bird after you."

The two children feigned terror. Henry bravely stood up to his father, hands on his hips. "I'm not afraid!"

Carlos smirked. A challenge, eh? He opened his mind, reaching for the apparition of his roosting bird. The mighty golden eagle opened his eyes and stretched out his wings, his feathers glinting with hints of gold. Carlos both felt and saw a few feathers slip free from today's undue stress. Haley would need to give him a good preening tonight to get over Trish.

His golden eagle slipped out of his mind and went to Madison first, flapping playfully at her pretty ring-necked dove. Avians shared a psychic bond through their birds. Just as vampires could push charm on a human's mind, he could "push" his bird into his children and would in turn see their little avians flapping around.

Madison laughed at the same time the bird in her mind cooed and then took off, cackling. Carlos sent the bird to his son next and found Henry's puffy red-tailed hawk fluffing himself up to look larger.

Carlos' eagle screeched and nipped at the red-tailed hawk.

The two children ran, laughing, Carlos' eagle still soaring through their minds. He turned back to his wife and draped his arms around her shoulders. "How are you?" he asked and nuzzled his face into her delicate hair.

"Doing fine," she said and leaned her head back to kiss him. "Kids kept me busy today. I took them to the park and let them fly. Flew with them a bit."

Carlos frowned in concern. "How was your landing?"

She shrugged and glanced at her legs. "Rough, but I managed it. I'll have a couple of scrapes, but it was worth it to fly with them."

He nodded and stroked her hair.

The Hunters hadn't just taken their baby girl from them; they'd lamed his wife as well. Haley made the best of it and managed to get around. Adjusting to shifting became harder for her. Her bird no longer had mobility of her legs, just as the human side didn't have the ability to walk. She flew, but her landing could rival the clumsiness of a fledgling.

Haley braved her disability and learned how to make things easier for herself. They'd had an elevator installed in the house so she could get in and out. The city had plenty of transportation, and where the bus couldn't take her, one of his avians usually could.

At least the kids kept her happy.

Haley handed him a bowl of brisket and set a plate of the masa shells on her lap. "Let's eat before it gets cold."

They headed out into the dining room surrounded with pictures of his beloved family. Marks on the wall told the story of Henry and Madison's growth over the years. A mural painted with his kids' hand prints displayed all of his family's feathers with Andria's barn owl tail feather occupying the center.

To his surprise, Madison and Henry actually had the table set up for them. Carlos sat down and helped his wife serve the food. They said grace to the great Mother together then started to eat. Madison and Henry devoured the food and played with the scraps, building little models on their plates. Carlos didn't really mind; he liked when they were creative.

He glanced at his wife as she sipped hot tea. She still looked so young and beautiful, barely a stress line on her face, despite being nearly 70 years of age. Avians, like all parahumans, aged slower and kept their youthful faces and figures much longer. Carlos himself was nearing 110. He finally had grays showing in his hair and mustache, though even that would be considered early onset grays. Most parahumans could live to be about 200 years of age. Fate decided for them after that.

He drank a beer and tapped the top on the table. "Hon, Gladus came to visit me today."

"Trish show up again?" Haley guessed.

Carlos chuckled. "Yes, and you should have seen the look on her face when Gladus chased her out." He shook his head. "But that's not why she came. She found another avian that she wants to bring to us. Kid was being tracked by Hunters."

Haley paused with her mug to her lips. "You want to bring her *here*? Someone who still has Hunters on her tail?" She flushed and glanced at her children. "We have a cloister to think about, Carlos."

"I know, but she's got nowhere to go. Besides, you could use some help around the house especially with these two wild chicks pecking at your heels." He frowned. "Gladus is taking care of the Hunter issue. The kid just needs help getting back on her feet, you know, the avian way."

Haley set her mug down, eyes diverted. "I don't know if I can, Carlos. After Andria—"

"You took in two beautiful children," Carlos said, gesturing to the pair. They'd stopped playing to listen.

Haley gave him a look. "*They* weren't being hunted. We're finally stable. Happy. I don't want to risk ruining that."

Carlos sighed. "We have a duty to the avians of this town. As Father—"

"No, *you* have a duty," Haley snapped. "That doesn't mean you have to get our children involved! I won't let the Hunters come down on us again!"

Carlos heard a fork clank on the hardwood floor and glanced at Henry and Madison. They stared back, their faces twisted with surprise and worry. His eyes softened. They'd mostly finished their meals by now. "Hey, fledglings, can you bring your plates into the kitchen and then play a little in your room? Mama and I need to talk."

"I think we're done talking," Haley retorted. She put her plate on her lap and wheeled into the kitchen.

He wasn't surprised by her reaction, but he couldn't hide the disappointment. Carlos had at least gotten his revenge against Andria's murderer, but Haley and her bird were still in turmoil. The trauma from her injury made it impossible for her to have children again; adoption was the only course they could take, not that either of them minded. They loved Henry and Madison as much as Andria, but there was still a loss for both him and Haley.

A chair squeaked against the wooden floor. Henry hopped down and went to his father's side, reaching for his hand. "The new bird is in trouble?" he asked. When Carlos nodded, Henry set his jaw. "Then... Then shouldn't we help her? You and Mama are strong. And we have a big cloister. We can be her new family. Like you and Mama were my new family."

"Yeah," Madison agreed. "It'd be cool to have another sibling. Especially a sister!" She grinned and looked at Henry. "We could teach her all of our games."

Carlos smiled at his innocent little children. "She might be a bit too old for those."

"No one is too old to play," Henry said with conviction. "Maddy and I were in trouble too, but you and Mama rescued us."

Carlos bit his lip. "That was different."

Madison shook her head. "We needed a home, and we got one now. She needs a home."

Carlos sighed to himself. At least someone else agreed with him. He had to meet the girl before he decided. But he wouldn't bring her in without Haley's consent. It wouldn't be healthy for anyone.

"Thank you, chicks," Carlos said and pulled his children close. "You're both very brave."

They hugged him back then grabbed their plates, and his, and brought them to the kitchen. Carlos carried the rest of the dishes and noticed Haley wasn't there. He didn't run after her; she needed a moment.

He worked with his kids to get the dishes cleaned and put away then wrapped up the food. For the time being, he didn't grab the *tres leches* cake. Instead, he sent his children off to their room to play then headed for the balcony.

Haley's chair sat empty outside. Instead, he found a beautiful barn owl nesting in a make-shift perch made out of a flowerpot and towels that he'd built for her handicapped frame. It allowed her legs to rest but for her torso to stay upright. The towels pushed lightly against her breast feathers and held her steady. She looked out into the night, the wind ruffling her beautiful starry pattern.

He sat down in her chair and glanced at her. "I'm sorry, Haley. I wasn't trying to upset you. I just thought…"

"*I know.*" Her bird slipped smoothly into his mind, but she didn't preen him. "*You help people. It's what you do, but this is different. It feels like you're trying to replace her.*"

Carlos looked at her in alarm. "No, *never*. No one could ever replace Andria. When we adopted the kids, it wasn't to replace what we lost. It was to give them a home and to have someone to love. To hear laughter in the halls again. To see their smiling faces at the breakfast table. To *feel* their birds."

Haley closed her eyes. "*Do you still think of her?*"

"Every day. Not a day goes by where I don't think of something she said or did. The amount of time that's passed doesn't matter. She's still here." He touched his head then reached out. He ran his hand along his wife's feathered body and started to rub his fingers along her neck. She stiffened at first, then relaxed into his touch, her head feathers fluffing. "I didn't mean she had to stay with us forever. I wanted to give her a place to hide. To feel safe again. She lost family too."

"*But is it safe for our children?*"

"I can ask Gladus to put up a protective ward around our place. I'm sure she'll do it." He licked his lips and rubbed her feathers some more. "Will you at least meet her?"

Haley sighed deeply into his mind. They sat in silence for a while, but eventually, she turned her beautiful eyes to him. "*I'll meet her. I heard the kids. They're excited to possibly have a new sister, huh?*"

Carlos chuckled. "Yeah, they like the big family."

"*So did Andria.*" She fluffed her feathers up a bit then nodded towards the chair. "*You're going to have to move so I can change.*"

Carlos stood.

His wife stretched her beautiful wings and flapped, bringing her over to the chair. She settled in it awkwardly, her legs still dragging. She bowed her head and started to change. The feather patterns sucked back into her body until a thin layer blanketed her skin. Her frame grew in size, and her legs slipped over the edge of the chair. Her hair fluttered in gold, white, and brown feathers until it changed back to its usual brown color. Feathers made up her clothing then shifted to the shirt and pants she'd been wearing. Younger avians couldn't shift with their clothing, but she and Carlos were old enough that they could.

She shook her head a little and pushed her hair back as the last of the feather tattoos faded into her body.

Carlos bent down next to her chair and lifted her chin. When she looked up, he kissed her gently and smiled. "I love you."

"I love you, too."

Chapter 5
Trial

Carlos

Gladus arrived as Carlos passed out pieces of cake to his family.

"Carlos," Gladus greeted and patted his arm while a teen hid behind her.

He gestured for them to come inside and shut the door. The girl trembled at Gladus' shoulder as she followed the magus towards the table. Her clothing hung off her thin body, her hands tugging anxiously at the hem of her shirt. He yearned to reach out and comfort her, but she didn't know him, so he refrained.

Madison and Henry didn't share the same restraint. They jumped out of their chairs and ran to her.

"Ah!" Carlos grunted at them. "Manners."

The two jerked to a stop and smiled. "I'm Henry/I'm Madison," they said at the same time, giggled, and then took turns introducing themselves.

The teen offered a nervous smile. "Bianca," she said.

Henry waved good-naturedly, which Bianca returned.

"Wow! Your hair is so pretty!" Maddy exclaimed, standing on her tiptoes to get a better look. "Mama, can I get red stripes, too?"

Carlos and Gladus both fought back amused laughter as Bianca looked at the magus for help.

Haley whistled. "Kids, come on back to the table. Give her some space. And no, Madison, your hair is pretty just the way it is."

They dutifully obeyed and sat down. Haley slid two more plates across the table to their guests. "Will you both join us?"

Gladus smiled. "Have I ever said no to your baking, Haley?" She touched Bianca's shoulder and took a seat. The teen looked back and forth between Carlos and his family as she sat close to Gladus, but he also noticed her staring at the cake with longing.

He cut a hefty slice off for her and slid it over then did the same for Gladus. "Go on. My wife makes an amazing cake."

"He handles most of the other cooking, but the cake is mine," Haley said with a chuckle.

Bianca offered a nervous smile. Her fork slid through the moist dessert with ease before she brought it to her mouth. She made a noise of appreciation as she chewed. "Wow, it's delicious. My sister used to make this on special occasions. She never could make it quite like Mom, but this is as close to it as I've tasted before."

Haley nodded. "I'm glad you like it. It was Carlos' mother's recipe. Was your family from Mexico?"

"I grew up there until I was five," Bianca explained, thinking. "Then Mom and Dad moved us to the States. Said there were better opportunities here for work and health care and all that stuff. But Mom still liked to cook traditional recipes. Taste of home, I guess." She shrugged and dug in for another bite.

Carlos studied Bianca as she enjoyed her dessert. Despite her compliment, her eyes darted around as if expecting someone to pop out of the shadows and attack her. Scared little bird, wasn't she?

Gladus touched Bianca's shoulder and motioned to the family. "Bianca, this is Carlos and his wife Haley, the avians I was telling you about. Carlos is one of the better-known cloister Fathers in the area. He's the one I usually bring werebirds to, to help them adjust."

Carlos inclined his head. "Yes. We wanted to get to know you a bit, though."

Bianca swallowed her chunk of cake and glanced at Gladus. "Is it safe for them if I talk about what's happened?" Gladus nodded, and Bianca took a shaky breath. "I...well. I lived with my sister, Nora. I was set to start college this fall, but then the Hunters came, and Nora is dead. And I don't know what to do." She rubbed her neck. "I'm tired of running. That's all I've been doing, and I don't know who else to turn to. My sister mentioned the Purple Door District, so I came here, and Gladus saved me from *them*. So, yeah. Here I am."

Carlos glanced at the water magus. "She's saved more than a few parahumans who have lost their way. Without her, I don't know what the Purple Door District would really be like."

Gladus waved her hand. "Oh, stop it. You're going to make me blush. If I up and vanished, they'd find some other poor soul to replace me," she said. "I'm nothing special. This isn't about me. This is about *Bianca*," she said, touching the young woman's back.

Haley folded her hands on the table. "What do you really want, Bianca? What are you hoping for?"

"Honestly? Safety. A chance to go back to school. And mourn my sister." Her lower lip twitched before she calmed herself. "I want to know I'm not going to wake up to a gun to my head."

Haley flinched.

Carlos' heart went out to the teen. Gladus had texted him more information, letting him know that the girl had been on the run for a few weeks now. Her life couldn't have been in more shambles, and he and Haley had a way to help her; shouldn't they take that opportunity? He glanced at his wife and she at him.

Madison hopped out of her chair and went to Bianca's side. She settled her little hands on the girl's arm, gazing up at the older werebird in sympathy. "I'm sorry your sister died. It's not nice what those people did to you."

Tears pricked Bianca's eyes. "Thank you." She reached for Madison's shoulder, hesitated, and dropped her arm. "Gladus has basically done nothing but praise you guys."

Carlos beamed at the water magus. She had the knack for finding the good in people. He wished she inspired that in the Hunters, too.

Haley watched Bianca carefully beside their daughter. "What school did you get into?"

"The Chicago Institute of Art," Bianca said. "I was going there for painting. And then...well...all this happened."

Henry jumped up. "I like to draw, too!" Before Carlos could stop him, his son scampered off to his room. He returned with an art pad in hand and shoved it into Bianca's face. "See! I draw birds!"

Haley held out her hand. "Henry, honey, come here. Remember, I told you to ask people to look at your art before you get it."

Henry blushed and sheepishly walked to his mother's side. "Sorry, Mama."

Haley kissed his head.

Bianca, meanwhile, flipped through the pages of the art pad. She looked at the drawings with a critical eye, and Carlos worried about her reaction. He didn't want her to crush his son's dreams. But his worries were unfounded as she lowered the pad, a big smile covering her face. "These are awesome! You're going to be a great artist one day if you keep this up."

Henry beamed and looked like he'd just floated up to cloud nine. He hopped up and down on his heels. "Did you hear that? She likes my art! She really likes it!" He whirled back towards her. "What do you like to draw?"

"Anything, I guess. I just close my eyes and see an image in my head. It doesn't always come to me, but sometimes I get this strong feeling that I need to paint, and I create scenes. Some I don't understand. Some are just from what I expect to see in my daily life."

"Can you teach me?"

Bianca opened and shut her mouth, not knowing how to answer.

Haley rescued her. "You know, I think that would be a nice idea," she said. "Bianca, how would you like to give Henry art lessons? While Gladus is working during the day, you can come here and show Henry how to draw. We can get to know one another a bit better."

Carlos couldn't hide the pride from his face. His wife, who one moment had been so resistant to the idea of welcoming someone else into their home, actually offered to have Bianca come visit them. That was a step in the right direction.

Haley's owl brushed his mind, appearing beside his golden eagle. "*Don't get too excited. Consider it a trial run for her.*"

"*Thank you for giving her a chance.*"

Haley sighed mentally and brought her bird back into her mind.

Bianca turned a little red with embarrassment. "I'm not exactly a professional, but I'd be happy to show him."

"You got into the Chicago Institute of Art," Haley replied. "I think that says you have talent."

Carlos smiled. "I'll make some calls and see what I can do about getting you into school."

"I don't have any money," Bianca said, wincing. "With my parents and sister gone—"

He waved his hand. "I can give you a job at my restaurant. You can't serve alcohol, but you can take orders and help pass out food. It's not much, but it would help you."

Bianca stared at him in shock. "Seriously? You two don't even know me!"

Carlos jerked his thumb towards Gladus. "She vouches for you, and that means a lot. Besides, it's hard to hide much from avians."

"True," Bianca agreed. She looked around the room at everyone, her eyes lighting up. "If you'll have me, then yes. Oh my god, yes!" She laughed even as tears ran down her cheeks. "Thank you!"

Carlos gently sent his bird inside of her mind to offer comfort and security. He jolted in surprise when he found her red-throated caracara. A Mexican bird!

His eagle ruffled his feathers then stepped towards her. The caracara hesitated at the sight of his bigger frame. But she slowly edged closer and cocked her head. Once she was at his side, Carlos preened her neck feathers. She hesitated before nibbling on a new blood feather of his coming in.

Carlos opened his eyes and looked at her. Her expression softened, and he was filled with an overwhelming desire to protect her. She might not be his daughter by blood, but she could definitely be family.

"Thank you," Bianca said. "For giving me a chance."

Haley's smile didn't quite reach her eyes. "Hopefully, this will work out for all of us."

Carlos squeezed Haley's hand tightly and rubbed his thumb along her skin. He saw the flicker of doubt in her eyes. She was trying, but letting go of the demons of the past wasn't so easy. This trial would be as much for Haley as Bianca.

Chapter 6
Venom

Trish

The cool night exuded calm without a cloud in the sky to disrupt the peace. Trish felt anything *but* calm as she stormed away from The Guacamole Grill. The Purple Door Districts had been created so that parahumans could be themselves, free from the constraints of human society, able to revel in their true natures and appearances. They existed as they had for centuries, with their own laws and traditions.

Two wolves could fight for their mate without facing assault and battery charges. Fae could walk down the street with their wings on full display. A vampire could supposedly bring her prey and feed quietly in the corner of a restaurant. If Gladus hadn't been there, Trish would have made it painfully clear to Carlos why crossing vampires could be deadly.

But even she knew not to face off against a magus.

She grumbled to herself as she stalked down the street, her heeled boots clicking on the pavement. People moved out of her way quickly, sensing her ire. Trish praised herself for her intimidation tactics, though at the same time she wanted to snag one of the humes and suck him dry just to alleviate her anger. She'd already lost her blood bag for the night thanks to both Gladus and that damn avian. What she wouldn't give to bite the pair. But her venom could kill Carlos, and even if Gladus survived the transition to vampire, she didn't deserve the power that came with it.

She shoved her hands into the pockets of her trench coat and lifted her head to the moonlight. It was a relief to be out at night and not have to worry about rubbing on sunscreen a la vampire. Thank the Night Father *someone* had come up with that stuff. It made it easier for vampires to roam around without it being obvious what they were. No more hiding their skin under wrappings, scarves, shawls, hats, and the like.

Trish hopped the street and headed towards The Violet Tower: a replica of The Violet Hour, a human bar. This one more-or-less screamed vampire friendly. The single light over the front door gleamed purple and bore a black upside down triangle marked in the glass to indicate vampire safe. Trish snorted to herself, wondering just how many people thought the Illuminati governed the place instead.

She took off her long leather coat at the door, revealing a sensual black dress beneath it. She'd pulled it up since leaving her job at the bank to show off her legs and had taken off the pantyhose and her cardigan, exposing the sheer fabric over her chest. Black velvet coiled in serpentine patterns over the thin fabric, stopping just above her breasts. The dress revealed just enough to tease the eye.

She walked inside and surveyed the wooden walls of the room. They reminded her of the inside of a beer barrel with rich colored wood that breathed tangy alcohol fumes into the air. Plush seats with violet cushions sat beside tables accented with vases of fresh flowers. A fireplace warmed the room, including the two elegant vampires sitting next to it.

Trish smiled at her coven brethren. A dark-skinned man with dreads that hung down to his shoulders sat with a refined posture. His eyes gleamed chocolate brown but could turn as red as Trish's when he desired. He wore pressed pants, a white shirt, deep green tie, and a jacket that showed off his broad shoulders.

A pale-skinned German woman with golden hair that flowed in waves against her sharp cheeks sat beside him. A midnight blue dress hugged her curvaceous body and matched her icy eyes. Her perfectly manicured French tips which could easily be turned into a weapon drummed gently on her navy handbag.

"I don't know why you're expected to go and parlay with the werewolves," Fraula, the blonde vampire said. "Plenty others are going to be present for negotiations. You're needed here, with the coven."

"Joseph asked me specifically," Saul, the other vampire, remarked. "And we don't say no to Joseph. I'll be back in a week, Fraula. Don't worry yourself overly much." He lifted a crystal glass to his lips and sipped a deep red liquid from it. It stained his mouth until he licked it off, his sharp fangs standing out in bright contrast to his dark skin.

"If you're sure," Fraula remarked. She raised her glass until her sharp eyes caught sight of Trish. She paused and huffed a dramatic sigh before putting her glass down. "Trish. Well, at least you've dressed appropriately this time."

Trish colored and smoothed down her dress. The first time she'd followed them into the bar, she'd been forced out by the bouncer; not properly dressed according to the house rules. Stupid rules in her opinion, but her brethren certainly liked to put on a show. She was still learning that, though. Her human ways clung to her like a parasite. "I took note of the issue last time," Trish replied. She walked over to an empty chair and sat down. Fraula curled her lip in disdain, but Saul inclined his head welcomingly.

"Good evening," Saul said. "Are you adjusting better to your new life?"

Trish nodded and glanced at her hands. They were pale compared to the sun- and blood-kissed hands she remembered, but she was adjusting to her new appearance amongst other things. The craving for blood. The sense of power flowing through her veins. "Yes. Though I'm still figuring out where I'm welcome or not."

Fraula sighed. "It's not that difficult. The Purple Door District is marked with symbols to help you know. If you see an upside down triangle—"

"It's vampire friendly," Trish drawled. "And if there's no symbol, but the door, or something around the place is purple, then it's welcome to all parahumans."

"So what's the trouble then?" Fraula asked. "Or are you incapable of following simple rules, *bitten-born*?"

The insult made Trish's skin crawl.

"Fraula." Saul gave her a pointed look and lifted his hand to Trish. "What can we do to help?"

Trish fiddled with a marble coaster on the table next to her. "It's just this restaurant. The Guacamole Grill. The owner there is an avian, and he keeps giving me problems. And then the Violet

Marshall showed up today, and she made me leave without my blood bag. I wasn't doing anything. I was just having a bit of fun with him and the werewolves and—"

"*Werewolves*," Fraula hissed and flexed her fingers into claws. "How many times have we told you not to associate with werewolves? Your powers can't control them well, not when you're so young. And the alpha here does not take kindly to vampires toying with his property. You'll get the coven in trouble, *again*." Fraula scoffed and grabbed her glass. "Why can't you be like the other new vampires? Calm. Thoughtful. Resilient. Has there been a single night in this town that you haven't caused trouble?"

The scorn in her tone tasted like rotten fruit. Trish's stomach twisted with shame and anger. What did Fraula know? She'd been born a vampire and lived and breathed the culture. Trish had only been one for little over a year. She'd just broken free of her sire before she reached the Purple Door District. It wasn't her fault he'd done a poor job training her. She hadn't asked to be picked up off the street by a vampire.

Why he'd chosen her, she didn't know. She'd been heading home from the movies with friends when she'd been attacked. Every single one of her friends had died, but the man who had grabbed her had spared her. Instead of killing her, he'd changed her, turned her into the vampire she was today. He'd kept her caged up to control her blood lust. And for months, she'd more or less been his slave, catering to his needs, offering herself and her blood to him.

He grew tired of her once he brought home another little plaything. It had given her enough distraction to escape. She could feed without him, and she didn't feel the pull to him any longer. Her current coven had found and taken care of her, thanks to a tip from Gladus. But that was where the magus' usefulness and pleasantry ended. Trish firmly believed that if Gladus had her way, she would wipe out every vampire within a mile radius.

"Well?" Fraula hissed, breaking Trish from her thoughts. "Has there?"

Trish cleared her throat. "I don't always cause problems. I'm still learning, Fraula. I just need the right teacher."

"Saul has been your mentor," Fraula snapped. "He's wasted enough time on a novice like you. If you can't learn our ways, then maybe you aren't meant to be a vampire. And maybe you don't belong in our coven. We all have to pull our weight." She trailed her sharp nail around the rim of her glass. "What have *you* done?"

Fraula's words slapped Trish in the face. Her cheeks burned crimson as she glanced away. "I'm trying," she mumbled.

"Do speak up," Fraula said in annoyance. "Honestly, Joseph has to be more careful about the children he brings into the coven. You'll give us a bad name, *dear*, especially if you keep catching the ire of Gladus. Establishments will start barring us, and we can't have that, now can we?" She looked sharply at Saul. "What do we do about this?"

Trish bristled. "I'm sitting right here. You could talk to me or, Night Father forbid, *train* me."

Fraula tossed her hand in the air, her bracelets jingling on her thin wrist. "We've *tried*. It's not our fault if you won't listen."

Trish looked at Saul pleadingly. "Saul?"

The vampire steepled his fingers on his knee and looked Trish up and down. "I'm going away for a business meeting, so I can't be the one to help you. But I think you should go to Joseph and ask for another mentor. Fraula is right; you're bringing trouble to the coven. The avian Father has already complained, and if he does so again, we may be banned from his restaurant and side of town. I promise you, neither Joseph nor your vampire brethren will take too kindly to that development."

Trish ducked her head at the reprimand. Being scolded by Fraula was expected, but she *hated* disappointing Saul. A wise and generous man; any young vampire would be lucky to have him as a mentor. "Then what do I do?"

Fraula cut in before Saul could speak. "Do us all a favor and leave."

"Fraula. Be kind."

"I *am* being kind. If she can't cut it as a vampire, then Joseph will have no choice but to—"

"*Fraula.*" Saul didn't shout, but a dark tone echoed in his voice, warning her. Fraula wisely fell silent and sipped her drink.

Trish froze. No one had said anything about their coven Duke coming down on her if she had trouble adjusting. It wasn't her fault! The vampire instincts were overpowering and hard to ignore. "I don't want to leave."

"Then grow up, child," Fraula said. "You're no use to us the way you are now."

Trish shoved herself to her feet angrily, hitting the table that held Saul's drink. The fine crystal shattered on the marble top and spilled red liquid all over the white stone floor. Fraula snarled in displeasure while Saul sighed.

"Trish, wait," he said.

Trish ignored him and stalked towards the door, throwing her black trench coat around her shoulders with a loud *whoosh*. She heard Fraula make *some* scathing remark in the background, but Trish ignored her. She jerked the door open and stepped out into the night, the cool breeze pulling the heat from her cheeks.

Her breath came in ragged gasps as she tried to calm her pounding heart.

Contrary to most people's beliefs, and originally her own naivety, vampires did indeed have a beating heart and flowing blood. They weren't *dead*. Their bodies were predisposed to being sensitive to sunlight, some burning and blistering depending on sensitivity and the lotion they used. Their bodies craved blood as a primary food source, and what better way to feed than with their sharp fangs. A venom sack behind their left fang excreted an euphoric sedative into their prey during feeding. In high enough quantities, it could turn a human into a vampire, or kill a lycan. Vampires couldn't change lycans, only hurt them. But they could transform witches and magi, though it usually meant that the Ether-touched lost their ability to use magic.

Of course, all of this Trish had had to learn while trying to adjust to her own cravings.

She clenched her hands into fists, yearning to put one through a wall. Her eyes darted back and forth, searching for the next blood bag that she could feast on and temper her rage.

A hand caught her wrist and jerked her into an alleyway. Trish snarled, extending her sharp nails and fangs. She swung out, but the person who'd grabbed her ducked and shoved her up against the wall. Her assailant pressed an arm across her throat and the other held her wrist up near her face.

"*Easy*, Trish. You almost gave me a face full!"

Trish calmed down as the familiar face of one of her coven brothers broke through the red. He stood over her with a handsome frame and dashing good looks. His eyes flickered red like hers to show familiarity in a time of stress rather than to betray his hunger. His brown hair swept around his face, his lips pulled back in a wide smile over pearly white teeth.

Trish sighed, letting the claws and the fangs slip back beneath her skin. "Sorry, Gavin."

Gavin whistled as he released her. He hadn't hurt her, but she rubbed her throat anyway.

"You looked on a warpath, girl. Never good for that to happen when you need to hunt." He braced his hands behind his head and leaned back on his heels. "If you're looking for a bite, I can help you out."

"I don't know if that's what I need," Trish confessed. She rolled her eyes. "Besides, even if I do go hunting, I'm pretty sure Fraula will point out how I do it wrong."

"Oh, Fraula again, eh?" Gavin snorted loudly. "That bitch has a stick up her ass a mile long. I bet she was giving orders the moment she popped out of the womb." He cocked his head and reached out to cup her cheek. "What's she done this time, aside from crush the hopes and dreams of children?"

"Threatened to turn me over to Joseph if I don't shape up," Trish muttered. She sank against the wall and folded her arms over her belly. She couldn't imagine getting kicked out, not now. She'd suffered enough already, and she didn't know how to find another coven.

It had been a fluke finding this one! And even then, Joseph had been reluctant to take her in. He'd wanted to make certain she didn't have connections to neighboring covens that could bring danger to his own. She'd decided not to mention that she'd escaped her sire; no one had seen sight of him since her departure, and she hoped to keep it that way.

Gavin made a face. "Really? She's not Miss Perfect all the time either."

"Well, according to her, I'm a complete screwup," Trish shot back. She looked up at the night sky, the moon and stars partially hidden behind light pollution. "I don't know what I'm doing wrong, Gavin. I thought we were superior. I thought we were supposed to be running the city."

"Hah! What vampire have you been talking to?" He flopped against the wall next to her and bumped her with his hip. "Back in the day, vampires thought they should rule everything, once they escaped servitude to the werewolves, that is. Not sure just how much you know about our history, but we got stuck as slaves to those lycans." He made a face. "Grandma used to tell me *all* about it. She didn't live during that time, but she knew the stories, and I heard it every time a wolf did something reckless in the news. Anyway, we wanted to make something of ourselves, but we went about it slowly. Found freedom. Rose in ranks. Got ahold of businesses with a lot of money and worked well with the help of, hm, persuasion."

"Lawyers, judges, and the like," Trish remarked.

Gavin pointed a finger at her and winked. "Bingo. But, we aren't supposed to be high and mighty. Over the werewolves, sure. But we are cautious. That's why Fraula gets all pissy. She thinks we have to have all the proper decorum. She forgets how strong we really are. We're not as breakable as the lycans made us out to be."

Trish nodded, relieved to have someone willing to teach her and be on her side. Though Gavin did like to feed more than the average vampire. *And* he carelessly left dead bodies behind if he got a little too inebriated. He also enjoyed sleeping with the blood bag before feeding off of him or her.

Okay, maybe not the best teacher.

Gavin draped his arm around her shoulders suddenly and shook her lightly. "Don't let Fraula boil your blood. Come on. Let's get something to eat and unwind a bit."

How could she say no to that and to his smile?

Trish grinned back and leaned against him as he guided her out of the alleyway and onto the street. They walked in a synchronized step, Trish adoring the lights which came on overhead. Christmas wasn't for nearly two months, but Chicago decorated early. The distant ding of a bell announced storefront Santas collecting for the Salvation Army.

Trish nuzzled her cheek into Gavin's warm shoulder for comfort, the scent of his spiced cologne filling her nose. He lifted an eyebrow at her and brushed her hair delicately with his fingers.

"What's up, little bat?" he asked.

"My family and I used to walk and scope out lights at Christmas," Trish replied. "My big brother made hot chocolate, and we'd drive around town, too, try to find the most decked-out house. Nice to see that some places still have the lights."

"Yeah, I always liked it too," Gavin said. He glanced down at her, a slow smile lifting his lips. "No one says you can't do that with your coven members. I know a couple of us who even like to go caroling."

"Seriously?"

"What?" Gavin said, looking indignant. "Not like we're going to burst into flames singing about God or something. Be a pretty piss-poor way to build a flock if your people die when they say your name." He cleared his throat and started to belt out, "Away in a manger, no crib for a bed. The little lord Jes—AUGHHHH!" He flapped against her, moaning and creating a scene in front of the humans. A few sent disconcerted looks their way, but Trish waved them off and caught Gavin.

"Oh my God, stoooop," Trish complained, laughing.

"See?" Gavin chortled. "You didn't burst into flames either."

Trish punched him in the shoulder. "Okay, okay, I'd like that. But you need to stop singing."

"Come on. I'm not that bad. I did once have a BA in music. Another lifetime ago." He kissed her temple affectionately and guided them along.

Trish relaxed in his embrace. Maybe she needed to hang out with him more. At least he didn't give her shit for being herself, or how she acted. Saul sometimes said Gavin, too, walked the fine line between being in and out of the coven, but somehow, they still liked and respected him.

Most of the time.

He guided her down another alley and squeezed her hand. "Wait here."

Trish shrank back into the shadows, drawing on her natural vampire gifts to blend in. She heard Gavin speak to someone nearby and waited to pounce. But he didn't drag some hapless person into the alley. He guided her by the hand, speaking soothingly to her as she smiled like a stupid child.

"Come out, Trish. She's agreed to keep us company for the night."

Trish appeared, and the woman looked at her with a dazed expression on her face. Gavin pulled her rainbow ombre hair to the side and exposed her neck. Her heartbeat pulsed through her veins, the blood rushing like an ocean wave. Trish's gums itched, and she brought her fangs out, moving closer to the woman.

"Go easy," Gavin warned. "She's too pretty to kill."

Trish snorted but re-centered herself nonetheless. Her fangs pricked the woman's fragile flesh, causing two crimson drops to blossom through the holes. How sweet the smell…how *tempting.*

Trish sank her teeth into the woman's vein and started to suck. Gavin moved to the other side, lifted the woman's hair up, and bit her on her shoulder. The warm blood filled her mouth and tingled her senses. She moaned against the woman's flesh, reveling in the taste. She would never grow tired of this. Blood bags just weren't the same, and synthetic blood was even less desirable. No, if vampirism was her destiny, then she would—

Something small hit her in the back of the neck, but the poison inside of it struck her like a bus. It burned her skin and blood worse than a high-noon sun. Trish jerked away from the woman with a cry of pain. There were certain herb mixtures that all the lycans, magic users, and vampires were allergic to, and, apparently, someone had found out hers.

She fell back against the wall, dazed, sick to her stomach. Gavin staggered away as well, dropping the woman to the ground. His teeth had created a deep gouge in her flesh by mistake, leaving their little lamb to bleed sacrificially on the cold concrete ground. He shook his head and stumbled over towards Trish.

"Little bat," he slurred.

She tried to support him, but her legs wobbled beneath her. She wrapped her arms around him and looked over his shoulder as two men approached them.

"We only need one," a bearded man said.

Trish blinked as the second man pulled a gun with a silencer out of his holster. He pointed it. Trish barely had a second to tense before a bullet quietly entered the back of Gavin's head.

"Gavin!" Trish rasped. He collapsed in her arms, eyes still open. She slumped down with him, sobbing. "No, no!" But her grief came to an abrupt halt as a boot connected with her face.

Chapter 7
The Game Begins

Trish

Trish woke with a moan. Her entire body burned as if staked out in a desert sun, her head spinning in sympathy. She blinked through the haze in her eyes until she could make out her warehouse prison. She sat upright and pulled her arms and legs against tight restraints. Her mouth ached from being forced open with a cloth, preventing her from biting anyone, or speaking for that matter. No charming for her.

She looked around slowly and took in the door to the left, the broken wooden crates along the floor, and—

Trish sobbed into her gag as she found Gavin lying lifeless on the ground. Blood had pooled around his head, giving it a horrid crimson halo. He stared up at the sky with blank eyes, his devil-may-care smile twisted to open-mouthed shock.

She unleashed a muffled scream of sorrow and pressed her head into her shoulder. She'd never seen someone killed in front of her—blood bags didn't count. She'd been unconscious, or not present, when anyone else had perished. Gavin hadn't deserved that. Gavin… Gavin was gone.

The door to her prison swung open, and the two men walked inside. Both were dressed casually in jeans, shirts, and vests, but she could see the utility belt around their waists, and the holsters hidden in their jackets.

The bearded man brought a bag over to the table next to her

and set it down. He opened it and took out a few weapons, a syringe, a glass bottle of liquid, and a blindfold. The last he kept in his hand and walked towards Trish.

She tried to keep her head away, but he took a fistful of her red hair and jerked her until she stilled. He slid the blindfold over her eyes, stealing her ability both to see, and to charm—if she ever had her mouth freed.

The man unhooked the gag and pulled it swiftly out of her mouth, not that she would have been able to bite him anyway. She coughed and shied away from him, her head tilting so she could listen to subtle movements and know where he stood. The bearded man's shoe squeaked as he walked back to the table. His partner gave something soft a kick, and it took her a moment to realize his target was Gavin.

"What do we do with this, Chad?"

"Don't touch him!" Trish cried before she could stop herself. She heard them move, and she slumped down in her bonds to make herself look smaller.

The bearded man, Chad, snorted. "Not like he's going to feel it." More rustling. "We've been watching you. Well, actually we were watching someone else, but you became of interest to us. A bitten-born, yes? Changed recently?"

Trish frowned. "Why do you care?"

"It's part of our job," Chad replied. "We try to stop things like that from happening."

Trish fell quiet for a moment then stiffened. "Hunters…"

"Took you long enough," the other man scoffed.

"Riccardo." Chad warned. His hand touched her bare knee, sending chills through her flesh. "You were at the Grill earlier today. A woman came in, asking the owner there something about a girl. What can you tell us?"

Trish clenched her teeth and struggled in her bonds. "Why should I tell you anyth—"

Something cold pressed against her throat. Chad, or Riccardo, had moved faster than her senses could tell. Either one of them wasn't exactly human, or the drug kept her under more than she thought. The thing pressed harder until her skin split, the metallic scent of her blood filling the air. She sucked in a frightened breath and grew still.

"Answer our questions," Riccardo said, "or you're going to end up with a second smile."

"You'll kill me anyway," Trish said nervously. "Why should I tell you anything?"

Chad sighed near her. "We've been known to make deals, especially with those who had no choice in the matter. A forced change, was it?"

Trish licked her dry lips. The blade slid away from her throat. She instantly shrank back again. "Y-yes…"

"That's a real shame," Chad said sympathetically. "What about that girl you were feeding on? Were you going to do the same to her?"

"No. We were hungry. We were going to feed, charm her to forget, then let her go. We were under control but then you…" Tears welled in her eyes until the blindfold soaked them all up. "We weren't hurting anyone. Why did you kill him?"

"We have a long sheet on him," Chad said. "Your friend hurt a lot of people. And we wanted to make sure we had your full cooperation. Now, if you tell us what we need to know, we may be able to help each other."

Trish snorted. "What could I possibly want from you?"

"Your life, for one," Chad replied. "Safety. Protection. All the things you've craved but haven't found."

Trish fell silent and a chill ran down her back. Just how much did they know about her? Hunters had their sources and their spies. For all she knew, they'd gotten the information from another one of her coven members.

When she didn't respond, Chad went on. "We're willing to give you your life. To help you, you have to help us. The woman. What did she want?"

Trish almost snapped at him again, but she could hear Riccardo loading a bullet into his gun. Was he going to shoot her if she didn't answer? Her heart pounded in her chest with nervous anticipation. Did they know that she'd stayed around the parking lot to hear what Gladus and Carlos had had to say? They must, otherwise why ask her? "She asked Carlos about taking an avian in. The girl's being chased by Hunters, and Gladus thought that Carlos could protect her."

"Why?" Riccardo asked.

"He's the father of a cloister and one of the strongest in our District. And Gladus trusts him."

"The woman?"

"Yes. She's the Violet Marshall."

She heard something scribbling on paper, a pen probably. Maybe the men didn't know as much as she thought, or were they just testing her?

"What else?" Chad asked.

Trish shook her head. "I don't know what else you want to know. Carlos went home after he said she could bring the avian over."

"Do you know this Violet Marshall well? This Gladus?"

Trish swallowed a lump in her throat. "Yes. She brought me to my coven. She helps all the new people. Keeps a tight rein on everything and everyone, too."

Riccardo chuckled. "You sound a bit bitter about that."

Trish turned her head away. "She does what she thinks is right." Even if it did make her prejudice against Trish's own kind. "I don't know much about this other avian."

"But you know where Gladus would have brought her? Do you know where Gladus lives?"

The question sent off warning bells in her head. Trish didn't respond. Just like before, a blade pressed against her throat until she almost couldn't breathe. She coughed and trembled in Riccardo's hold. "Yes," she squeaked out.

"Good." Chad wrote something else down. "I'm curious about something. Did you want to be a vampire? Do you enjoy it?"

Trish didn't understand his sudden interest in her, but she dreaded the consequences of silence. "No, I didn't want to be. I like it, but sometimes I wish it never happened. My family." She grew silent. Her family had abandoned her when they'd found out about her transformation. Her father had cast her out, and her brother had called her a demon. Being changed had ruined her past life, though it didn't mean her future had to end the same.

Provided she had a future to begin with.

Chad tapped the pen against his notebook. "That little avian that was brought here. She is a key to people being forced to become something they don't want to be. She's a threat to your kind and a threat to humans as well. We're trying to collect her, but the magus protecting her put a ward around her house. We can't get in. But you can."

Trish stiffened. She didn't like where this was going.

"We need an in," Chad continued. "We need a way to get to that girl, and you are our best bet. Granted, if you betray us, we can go hunt down another vampire. There's no telling how many more of your coven brothers will end up dead at our hand. We have sheets on *a lot* of them."

Trish fought back a whimper of despair. "You want me to go in and get the girl? Gladus will never allow it. She'll kill me."

"You let us worry about Gladus," Chad said. "You just need to get her out of the house. We'll take care of her; you apprehend the girl."

They made it sound so simple. Gladus would see her coming a mile away, but they thought she could just easily walk in there and take what didn't belong to her. "Why is she so important to you?"

Riccardo started to make a snide remark, but Chad clicked his tongue. He walked towards her but stopped, she thought, just out of kicking distance, not that it would have mattered since her legs were tethered.

"Many people have been forced to change against their will, and their lives have become awful. If a monster had done something like that to my daughter, I'd want someone to help her. The avian girl has information about something that can force people to change, which we need. Her sister didn't give it up freely; neither will she. We need her; otherwise she can create a huge problem for both the human and the parahuman world."

"You don't care about us," Trish hissed.

"Believe or not, but we do. Who stops the parahumans who want to destroy their own kind, or hurt other parahumans? We do. We have very specific targets, and we eliminate them to keep all people safe."

"What about Gavin?" Trish asked, her throat tightening. "What did he do that made you choose to kill him?"

"He's been on our list for a long time," Chad said. "Killed whole families before he came here. Bloodthirsty. Cruel."

"He was not!" Trish shouted. "He was kind and caring, and you didn't know a damn thing about him!"

Riccardo sighed loudly. "Can we get this over with? If she's not going to help us—"

"*Quiet*," Chad said. "To his own kind, yes, he was kind and caring, but not to humans. He killed dozens. We have lists of several of your brethren who have killed people. You can protect them if you just do as we ask."

Trish sniffed. "You'll kill me—kill them—if I don't?" She heard a gun cock, and she stiffened, waiting for a bullet to take her through the skull next. With the drug in her system, she wouldn't have a chance of surviving the shot, just like Gavin.

"We don't want it to come to that," Chad said. "You can redeem yourself and save a lot of people by helping us. Otherwise, well, at least you'll get to see your friend again."

Trish shuddered in terror. "But you already threatened to kill other vampires."

"Only those who have committed crimes against humanity," Chad said. "Let's say, you help, we'll let them free for the greater good. This girl's ability can do more harm to *everyone* than you vampires can."

Trish swallowed. She didn't have a choice, did she? If she said no, they would kill her, or they'd murder other members of her coven. If she said yes, then she would likely get Gladus killed and turn over an avian who wanted a place to call home.

But then again, didn't Trish crave the same thing? A home? Why did she have to suffer and die because of a werebird? Why should she lose her coven members because of a magus who couldn't leave well enough alone? Maybe if the vampire target had been Fraula, Trish would have reconsidered, but she didn't want to die.

"I'll... I'll do it, but only if you swear that I'll be safe, and so will my coven, if I help you."

"I promise," Chad said. "We don't want to spill any more blood than necessary. You help us, we'll take the girl, leave, and never come back. You have our word."

Trish nodded and licked her lips. "Then I agree. What do you need me to do?"

"We'll release you, but we'll be watching. Signal us when you're ready to go after the magus, when the girl is with her, and no one is around to help. We'll know if you alert anyone of what transpired here tonight. We have more watchers out there, understand?"

Trish nodded nervously.

"Good!" Chad said with a charming tone. "Then let's get you home."

Trish wondered just how they were going to do that, when a

needle pierced the back of her neck.

Her stomach turned, and her head spun until she fell into darkness.

***

Trish jerked awake and flipped onto her back. Her hands and legs were free, and lavender incense filled her nose instead of the smell of old warehouse or dead vampire. She sat up and found herself back in her room at home. Her fingers ran over the purple satin blanket she'd been laid on. She looked around, but the door and window were both shut.

For a moment, she wondered if it had all been a nightmare.

Until she rolled over and found a small envelope near her hand. Trish opened it slowly.

A single Polaroid fell out onto her bed.

She lifted it with trembling hands and stared at herself, sitting unconscious in the chair, a knife at her throat. And at her feet lay Gavin's body, dead eyes staring back at her.

Trish dropped it with a muted sob and clapped her hands over her mouth. Two words were scrawled on the bottom of the Polaroid.

We're watching.

Chapter 8
A Vision in Portraits

Bianca

Bianca woke from a nightmare with a scream. She flailed in the darkness, cloth twisting and binding her arms and legs. Her bird flapped wildly through her head until she managed to kick free. Scrambling backwards sent her head over heels right off the bed, jarring her spine. Her bird screeched in fear and anger, adding to the confusion.

Where was she?

What was happening?

She pushed herself up and shrieked when lightning flashed through her bedroom window. Somewhere in the back of her mind she knew she was in Gladus' home, but the thought vanished quickly. The room blurred until figures crawled across the walls and floor, their claw-like nails reaching for her.

"Notebook…" she mumbled. She grabbed the desk leg she'd rolled into and pulled herself up. Her hands scrambled over the top of the desk, knocking over a cup of water, pencils, and the lamp that broke into three jagged pieces as it hit the floor. "There…no… faces…she…no…" She shook her head and finally closed her hand down around the book.

Bianca dragged it onto the floor and slapped through the pages until she found a blank one. One of the shadowy figures touched the paper just as Bianca started to draw.

She sketched the outlines of three people, two women and one man. Her eyes darted across the paper, her hand scribbling furiously and adding more detail as she focused on the dream. Colors filled in the black outlines, creating an ombre sheen to the middle woman's hair. The other woman sank teeth in the first one's neck. The man leaned back, his mouth open, fangs showing. One of the dancing shadows touched the center of his head, and she marked it with a red pencil.

Another flash of lightning jerked her to a stop.

She stared at the drawing in the glare of the streetlight from outside for a long moment then started to sketch another. This one showed Gladus in front of her house. The purple planter swung in the air, and Gladus wore a contemplative expression. The same fanged woman Bianca had drawn formed again, facing off against the magus.

Bianca picked up a gray colored pencil and made two shadows behind the woman.

The shadows…

Her heart pounded, her vision blurred, and her hand shook.

Bianca kept drawing until the images spiraling around her slowed and dissipated like smoke. She couldn't stop staring at the fanged woman. Why was she there? Why twice?

She shook her head and dropped the pencil to the floor with a soft clatter. Her caracara appeared beside her, feathers fluffed and eyes pinned. The bird snapped at the pencil with her beak and ruffled her body until Bianca brushed a soothing hand down her back.

She didn't understand what she'd just seen, but her head and heart ached. And she couldn't shake the sense that the clock ticked against her.

***

"Do you like it?" Henry asked, shoving his painting into her face.

Bianca blinked sleepily and held out a hand to block it from smacking her in the nose. A lovely barn owl soared across the page, painted with acrylics. Except for overlarge feet, and a too-big head, the drawing was impeccable.

"It's beautiful!" she praised, admiring the owl's feathers. "The color layering is great. Definitely a good replica of your mom."

"Cool! Mama, did you see? Did you!"

Haley perched in her owl form inside of the flower pot her husband had modified for her. She stretched out a wing, warming it in the sun. When she heard her son, she swiveled her head around and offered an owl smile. "*I love it!*"

Henry beamed.

Madison looked up from her nest of pillows propped against the screen door. "Whoa, that really does look like Mom," she said.

"*You* like it?" Henry asked in shock. "Then it really must be good!" He stuck out his tongue and leaned forward so he could sign his name at the bottom with a paintbrush. It looked more like a blotch to Bianca, but to Henry, he'd created a masterpiece.

Bianca smiled a little and picked up a piece of charcoal. Warm sunlight eased the bite from the late-fall breeze as it brushed through her hair. They sat together on the porch to enjoy the mild weather. Sure, it added some loose leaf fragments to their paintings, but it made Henry's lesson more interesting that way.

She returned to her sketch of a snowy forest with a black wolf and gray wolf racing through the trees. The drawing bore a lighter image than the one last night. Whatever had triggered the nightmare still lingered with her today. Her caracara paced around restlessly, and her exhaustion made curling up under the patio table for a nap sound like her idea of heaven.

Bianca started to draw another figure in the snow when Henry tugged on her sleeve.

"What do I make now?" he asked.

Bianca thought then chuckled, an old episode from Bob Ross coming to mind. "Let's do some happy little trees."

"Huh?"

"An artist I used to watch *loved* to paint trees. Usually used them to cover up mistakes. Now, I'll draw a tree, and then you copy me." She reached for one of the acrylic brushes and dipped it in brown paint. The bristles flowed across the canvas and created the puffy outline of a tree. Bianca filled it in entirely before grabbing a green brush. "He wasn't afraid to mess up. He called them happy little mistakes instead." She added splashes of green, dabbing delicately so she didn't smear the brown paint too much.

"I wanna be like that," Henry said as he watched her add branches and pine needles to the tree.

Bianca nudged him with her shoulder. "One day, you can be."

She mixed various shades of green to give the foliage more depth. Henry watched her with hungry eyes, yearning to learn. He'd be a great artist one day. A prodigy in the making, he could put some of her own drawings to shame.

"That's so pretty," Henry said as she finished up a tree.

"Thanks. Okay, you saw how I blended those colors, rights? It's just like what you did with your mom's wings." She picked up a palette filled with the same colors she'd used and offered it to him. "Now I want to see *your* happy little trees."

Henry brightened. He got to work, mixing pigments and creating a right mess of his palette, but who was she to judge? He was an *artist*. As he painted, the picture came to life. A cute little tree appeared near hers. The crooked branches and blotchy colors betrayed his lack of finesse, but that just made it special.

That just made it more Henry.

Bianca draped her arm over the back of his chair and smiled. Her caracara hunched down, wanting so badly to join Henry's red-tailed hawk. But they could both feel Haley's eyes on her, watching her carefully. The woman had warmed up to her presence over the past couple of days, but an insurmountable wall stayed up between them. Bianca had yet to feel the woman's bird in her own head, as she'd experienced with Carlos, but that wasn't entirely unusual. Some avians didn't like connecting bird-to-bird for a long time. Bianca held back mentally bonding with the children for fear of offending their mother.

Life with Carlos and his family brought peace and comfort when she'd felt neither, but a cloud of deception hung over her head. She'd had more freedom before and could come and go as she pleased. Here? Eyes watched her wherever she went. Carlos, Haley, or Gladus followed her every footstep. It was nice to have the protection, and not feel so alone, but at the same time, she felt like a prisoner. Which, ironically, *did* make her feel lonely.

She wanted to be herself, but Bianca couldn't seem to stop crushing the floor of eggshells she treaded so carefully on. Haley eyed her like a viper, Carlos kept cautioning her not to leave the house, Gladus treated her like a fallen hatchling. She could do nothing right except teach Henry how to paint.

And what's so bad about that? she reasoned. *At least the kids like me. Even Maddy's letting me read to her at night. That's a good sign, right?*

Her caracara bobbed her head in agreement.

Bianca brushed hair out of her eyes. As Henry added another tree, she did the same. He giggled and poked green paint on her tree. She gasped in return, pretending to be offended, and brushed his plant with another shade of green. They went back and forth, dotting the painting and creating a bunch of splotchy, bushy foliage. Henry squealed with laughter and suddenly poked Bianca on the nose with the tip of his paintbrush, leaving a brown mark on her face.

Bianca laughed and smeared green on his cheek.

"*Children*," Haley said mentally with a sigh.

Henry kept giggling, but Bianca put her brush down so she didn't offend the elder avian.

"Sorry, Haley," she said. She wiped her hands off and nodded to Henry. "Let's get cleaned up. Gladus is picking me up soon."

"Aww," Henry complained. But at a look from his mother, he nodded and ran inside, passing Madison. They stuck their tongues out playfully at one another before Henry disappeared down the hall.

Bianca dabbed the paint off of her nose and then gathered the supplies. "Sorry," she repeated. "It's nice to just relax and play."

"*I'm sure*," Haley said gently. "*But he still has to behave.*" She glanced at the painting. "*He's getting better with your help. You're good with him.*"

"Thanks." Bianca blushed and sat on a chair next to the barn owl. Haley swiveled her head around to get a better look at her. "I appreciate the hospitality. I'd never want anything bad to happen to your kids because of me."

"*I know. And I'm sorry for being so stiff about all of this. You have to understand, we've had bad experiences with Hunters.*"

"You're just trying to protect your children," Bianca said, her fingers caressing the beads on her necklace. "If I was a mom, I'd be doing the same." She glanced at Madison as the girl flipped the page in her chapter book. "Is it weird that I feel really protective of them, too?"

Haley chuckled in her head. "*You're not the first to say that after meeting them.*" She flexed her beautiful wings and glanced at her wheelchair. "*I'm going to shift then help you get some treats together for Gladus.*"

"Haley, I can get it. You don't have to—"

But the woman flapped past her. Bianca realized, not for the first time, that Haley's independence and stubbornness outweighed her disability.

The werebird landed with a skid in her chair. Her body changed, her wings growing into thin arms, her talons and feet shifting into two legs. Brown hair spilled down her shoulders with shadows of her feather pattern in it. She shook her head and picked up the glasses she'd placed on the table. "Better," Haley said. "I'm glad we could get out with the kids."

"Yeah, at least the weather's behaving today. I thought we'd have storms after the lightning last night," Bianca said. "It's almost unseasonably warm like the weather can't make up its mind if it wants to rain, sleet, snow, or just be sunny. It's almost as bad as Iowa." She headed to the door and reached down to ruffle Madison's hair fondly. The girl giggled. Madison grabbed her book and pillows and cleared them out of the way so her mother could come inside.

Bianca leaned against the breakfast bar while Haley wheeled into the kitchen. The sweet smell of melted chocolate in their home-made cookies filled the air. Heat ebbed from the cooling oven, providing a little warmth after being outside. Haley scooped chocolate and walnut cookies into baggies then cut two pieces of apple pie.

"Carlos loves it when you and Gladus come," Haley commented as she snapped on the lids of the Tupperware containers. "He says I bake more. I told him if he keeps gaining weight from my cooking, he's not going to be flying anywhere."

Bianca laughed and picked up a canvas bag. "I'm pretty sure he works off all the dessert when he's chasing your kids."

Haley winked. "Why do you think I let them have a cookie before he gets home?"

Bianca snickered as she came around into the kitchen. She helped Haley get the bag packed then added a few napkins. "Oh man, the churros you gave us yesterday didn't last too long. I think Gladus emptied half of the Tums bottle for heartburn."

"I told her to pace herself," Haley sighed. "I can't make those all the time."

Bianca smirked. "Since when does that magus listen to anyone?"

They shared a smile, and for a moment, Bianca bonded with

the avian mother.

She set the bag on the table and helped Haley get the rest of the food put away. Her mind wandered as she worked, drifting back to last night's episode. Shadowy figures kept wafting through her mind, trapping her in a half-dream. She'd wanted to paint a few while she worked with Henry, but teaching him had helped distract her. Besides, they weren't exactly the kind of pictures she wanted to paint around him.

The woman with the ombre hair flitted in and out of her thoughts, along with the fanged woman. She couldn't see all the details of, what she assumed was, a vampire, but the flickering image did leave a trace of bat wings fluttering behind her. Gladus popped up time and again, but Bianca didn't quite know how to connect the two.

And then the ghostly figure that seemed to wiggle his way into her dreams reared itself. The silhouette of a man holding a black staff with an orb at the tip haunted her. Any time he made an appearance, she knew it would be a bad night. He terrified her, and little could chase away his darkness, an all-consuming, suffocating sensation that left her floundering in bed.

Or on the floor.

"Bianca?" Haley said.

Bianca jolted out of her thoughts and looked over. "Huh?"

The owl avian stared back then gestured to the counter. Bianca looked down and almost jumped backwards in fright.

A portrait made of flour rested in front of her. Powdered waves coursed along the granite top, coiling around the feet of the bat-winged woman. More waves created a haloed outline of the shadow man and his scepter.

Bianca swallowed hard and stared at the flour coating her hands. "I'm...I'm sorry. I'll get that cleaned up." She started to scoop the powder in her palms, but Haley grabbed her wrist.

"This isn't the first time you've drawn images like that. Gladus said she's seen them in your notebook, too."

Bianca bristled and the caracara clacked her beak. Her notebook? She jerked her wrist free. "She's going through my stuff? Why?"

Haley pulled her hands back. "She wanted to see if you were hiding anything, and it sounds like you are. What do your drawings mean?"

Bianca flushed and clapped flour into the sink. "Nothing. They're just nightmares. Sometimes, they stay with me."

"Gladus found you curled up on a pile of drawings this morning. One showed a woman with rainbow hair and a red dress," Haley said slowly. "They found a woman who looked just like that *dead* in the streets weeks ago. Human news said it was a mugging, but the local District news channel said it was a vampire attack."

The fanged woman.

Bianca froze, hands hovering over the flour. "I must have heard about it on the news and just forgotten."

Haley gave her a suspicious look. She glanced at the portrait and wheeled her chair back. "You're lying."

"I'm not!" Bianca insisted. "I'm not trying to start something or cause problems. It was just a nightmare."

But Haley didn't look convinced. She finished wrapping up the cookies and placed them in a jar, the top slamming shut loudly. Bianca's shoulders slumped. Great, and here she thought she'd finally started to build a relationship with the avian mother.

She heard the kids come back, but Haley made her stay in the kitchen while she went and saw to Henry and Madison.

Bianca's gut twisted with worry, and she tugged at her hair. Her bird plucked a feather in kind. It wasn't her fault that she had weird dreams.

Nora said I should sketch the images out if it made me feel better, Bianca thought as she grabbed a sponge. She got it wet with soap and water and started to scrub the portrait away. *It's not like I thought people were going to go through my stuff. What the hell is that all about anyway? I'm a guest, not some criminal!*

Her scrubbing grew more urgent and her bird kept preening and plucking at feathers until one of Bianca's nails snapped. She sucked in a pained breath. "Damn." She dipped her finger in the faucet and bowed her head, sighing. *Calm down… Getting worked up isn't going to help. Just talk to Gladus. Maybe she had a reason for it.*

At least, she hoped Gladus did.

She just finished cleaning when she heard a knock at the door. She slipped out of the kitchen and answered it while Haley put the paints away with Henry.

Gladus' cheery face greeted her, her body swathed in bright yellow and purple. Golden hooped earrings framed her neck, making her look younger. The smile she wore faded as she studied

Bianca's face. "What's wrong?"

"Why did you tell her about the drawings?" Bianca hissed. So much for calm. "She's freaking out now."

Gladus made an 'o' with her lips. "We'll talk in the car. Are you ready?"

Bianca glanced over her shoulder at Haley and the kids. "I guess, hang on." She retrieved the canvas bag and paused near the door.

Haley cleaned green paint off of her son's cheek while Madison begged her mother to read to them. The perfect picturesque family.

The feathered mural on the wall reminded Bianca that she had no place in it.

She swung the bag over her shoulder and slipped out past Gladus. "Let's go."

Gladus lingered at the door for a moment. "Have a good day, Haley!" she called and started to follow.

Bianca heard little feet pounding after them.

"Bianca, wait!" Henry shouted.

She turned, and he hopped down the stairs, a book in his hand. He held it out to her, grinning.

"Here. I heard Mama say you like to draw in art pads. I haven't used this one yet. You can have it."

Bianca looked at the book and touched it. She struggled to hide her sadness. *I probably won't get the chance to use it with him anyway.* "Henry, you should keep this."

"But I want to share." Henry pulled his hands away and tucked them behind his back, forcing her to hold the book. "Can't give it back," he teased then ran up the stairs to Gladus. He launched forward and wrapped his little arms around her. "Grammy Gladus!"

"Hi, little bird," Gladus said fondly. She picked him up and ruffled his hair. "Are you being good for your mama?"

"Yep!" He glanced around then pitched his voice low. "I only stole two cookies from the tray."

Gladus gave him a stern look. "That's not very nice. We don't steal cookies." Her eyes glinted with amusement. "Unless you stole one for me, too."

Henry reached into his pocket and pulled out a very crumbly, dirty cookie. "I always get one for you, Grammy."

Gladus chuckled and opened her mouth, letting him shove it in. She chewed it right then and there, her eyes rolling back, her face taking on a look of bliss like she'd just tasted the nectar of the gods. "*Delicious*. Now, get back to your mama before she finds out about our little secret."

Henry put his finger over his lips and hopped down out of her arms. Gladus waved and shut the door behind him.

Bianca headed outside with the magus, clutching the book and the canvas to her chest. She wanted to cry. The kids were a delight to be around, and Haley sometimes exuded kindness, when she wasn't worried. But with Bianca's drawings causing a problem, the prospect of losing another cloister seemed imminent. Granted, they weren't a cloister yet. This was a trial period, but she adored the family, especially the kids. She wanted to protect them, and she didn't want to be alone.

As they stepped outside, Gladus placed a gentle hand on her shoulder. "Do you want to talk?"

Bianca shrugged her attempted comfort off. "I wish you hadn't told her. I just started to gain her trust."

"Do you draw like that often?" Gladus asked.

"I mean, yeah. I have a lot of vivid dreams. My sister encouraged it. It's nothing."

"Do any of those images ever come true?" Gladus opened the door to her car and slid into the driver's seat.

Bianca sat down and fastened her belt. "I guess sometimes. But I figured it was a coincidence. They're just dreams. What's the big deal?"

"It's nothing, I'm just curious." Gladus started up the car and pulled out. "Look, Bianca, I'm not trying to upset you. When I found you this morning, it scared me."

"Why?" Bianca asked. "Some people have the inspiration to write in the middle of the night. I draw. What's the difference?"

"The difference is, you had a broken lamp next to you, water on the floor, and you were dead asleep on a pile of really *dark* pictures." Gladus glanced sideways at her. "I'm just worried."

Bianca snorted and looked outside. "Yeah, about me, or about what I might do?"

"*You*," Gladus said with such force, Bianca turned back around. The magus did look worried, Bianca would give her that. Maybe she was reading too much into it. Gladus had done nothing else but treat her like a treasured grandchild after all.

"I... Well, I wasn't trying to scare you," Bianca said, brushing her fingers along her red tips. "It's just kinda normal for me to do that. I'm sorry I broke your stuff."

"Oh, items can be replaced. People, not so much." Gladus reached out and laid her hand across Bianca's. The physical contact startled her, but Bianca didn't pull away. If anything, she and the bird leaned into it. "Promise me, if you have a fit like that again, you'll wake me up. I'm not judging you, I just want to be there for you."

"Really?"

"Really," Gladus said.

Bianca bit her lip and blew out a breath. "I'll try."

"That's all I ask." Gladus pulled her hand back and focused on the busy streets of Chicago. "Now that that's settled, there's a District market I wanted to stop at before we go home. They have a —I guess you would call it a farmer's market for non-humes."

"Isn't it a little late to be selling vegetables?" Bianca asked.

"Eh, not for earth magi. You can still find some really good stuff. And it's not just produce. They have herbs and other things that a magus like me can use. And I figured we could get some items for you. Clothing and all that."

Bianca shifted uncomfortably. "You know I can't pay you back."

"Relax. I have a friend who said he could give you some clothing from his pack. It'll help mask your scent if the Hunters have a parahuman looking for you."

"Werewolf... you want me to wear werewolf clothing?"

Gladus arched an eyebrow. "You have a problem with werewolves?"

"Well... not exactly, I just... they... well... they scare me a bit," she mumbled, sheepishly.

Gladus chuckled and turned down the road. "All the more reason for us to go. You wanna live in the District? You need to get used to *everyone*."

Chapter 9
The Glass Caracara

Bianca

The District market encompassed a huge single-story building, larger than anything Bianca had seen before. Stalls, both open, and with colorful tarps, stood up against walls and in aisles. Parahumans filled the area, selling wares and shopping. To her amazement, artisans had crafted intricate stained-glass windows displaying lycans, magi, vampires, and fae in their full glory, unafraid of Hunters and unashamed of their animal forms and living magic.

Bianca's nose twitched, taking in all of the unusual smells. A werewolf passed her on the right, a vampire on the left. A tall woman standing next to a stall with orbs of colorful dust caught Bianca's eye the most. Beautiful iridescent purple wings opened and closed on the woman's back. Violet markings with sweeping swirls and dots covered her face and bare arms. Her black tank top had slits for her wings, but it also exposed the scars on the woman's back. Despite the marred skin, Bianca found herself drawn to the fae's beauty. When the fae met her eyes, Bianca's cheeks burst with heat. She quickly looked away.

"I've never met a fae," she whispered to Gladus, craning her head to get a better look. "Only heard about them."

Gladus followed her gaze and nodded. "They usually keep to themselves, and even in safe zones, they don't like to reveal their true appearances. Shanda there, well, she's not afraid to show she's survived the Hunter's knife. Her kind is prized amongst Hunters and some parahumans, almost as much as drakes and waterfolk."

Bianca skidded to a stop, aghast. "Drakes and waterfolk are *real* too?"

Gladus smirked. "Oh, sweet child, you're going to be making that face a lot while you live in Chicago."

"I don't get it, though," Bianca said as they walked through the rows of stalls. "How do the humans not know that this place is here?"

Gladus tapped her nose. "*Magic*. Couple of magi lend their magic to keep this place hidden. Humans walk towards it, then just kind of turn around and walk away. They get this overwhelming sense that they don't belong here. For us, it's a place of life." She touched one of the pillars holding up the building fondly. "I've left a mark on this market with my magic, too. We ask multiple magi to create the shield, just in case one of us falls."

Bianca frowned at the implication. "Does that happen a lot?"

"It's Chicago," Gladus said with a shrug.

Bianca didn't press.

Children scurried about while their parents tried to keep track of them, as well as their purchases. Most of the tables had things Bianca recognized like produce, books, clothing, even talismans. But then there were other items like herbs, spices, magical objects, grimoires and the like that she didn't know much about. She assumed they were pertinent to whatever parahuman sold them.

She shoved her hands in her pockets, feeling awkward as she walked behind Gladus. Time and again a parahuman looked up, saw Gladus, and waved cheerfully. Gladus always waved back.

They stopped at a table where a black-skinned avian sold jams and preserves alongside a bundle of feathers from different raptors. Gladus picked up one of the red preserves and smiled at the avian. "Where did you have to fly to get the fruit for this?"

"Not too far," the woman said and pointed upward. "It's more how high did I have to fly."

Gladus chuckled and pulled out her wallet. "How are your boys doing?"

"A handful. Trent shifted for the first time, and now he keeps refusing to go back to his human form. I just hope he realizes he needs to stay human while he's at school."

"Oh, I was afraid of that," Gladus laughed. "Wasn't he the one who kept trying to jump off of the swing to *fly*?"

"And broke his arm in two places? Yes." The woman sighed. "If his brother follows in his steps, I don't know who I'm going to strangle more, my son, or my husband for being on all of his business trips."

Gladus frowned. "Things still not getting better with work?" She passed the avian $6 and put the preserves in a bag.

The woman shook her head. "Busy, busy. If we weren't avians, I would be worried he was cheating on me, but I don't sense that there's been another bird in his head."

"Good. He's a good man. I hope his schedule clears up for him soon, and for your boys." Gladus squeezed the avian's shoulder. The woman touched the magus' hand and smiled.

"Thanks. Are you stopping by Rozene's stall at all? She managed to dig up some of those herbs you were asking about."

"I'm actually going to introduce her and Patyah to my friend here." She gestured to Bianca who jumped a little, startled at being brought into the conversation. She'd spent so much time hiding, being out in the open made her hands shake and her chest tighten with anxiety.

The avian looked Bianca up and down. "Another avian, huh? They seem to be flocking here lately." She laughed. "No pun intended."

"You very much meant it," Gladus teased. "But yes, we've had an influx of parahumans in general. There are worse places she could go." She shrugged the bag onto her shoulder. "Have a good day."

The avian waved. Bianca tilted her head politely to her then hurried to catch up with Gladus. She touched the woman's arm gently and drew closer. "Are you sure it's safe to introduce me to so many people? With the Hunters out there—"

"The parahumans here won't help a Hunter. I *know* them. And if they know that you're under my protection, they'll protect you as well."

Well, that's comforting, Bianca supposed. Still, she didn't like so many eyes on her. She ducked her head behind her black and red hair and moved closer to Gladus. The water magus touched her back, guiding her down the many rows.

Bianca started to recognize scents, not just of herbs, but of the holidays. Though only early November, people filled their stalls with holiday wares. Heavily-scented pinecones almost made her sneeze, but they also brought back warm memories of her family around a decorated tree and a roaring fire. She could almost taste the candied pecans Dad made by hand for them to enjoy while the winter storms raged outside.

Bianca stopped near a little tree that held glass bird ornaments in flight across the branches. She searched for one that looked like her sister, but none popped up. Why would it? Caracaras weren't exactly common birds in the U.S.A.

"Can I help you?" a voice chimed behind her.

Bianca jumped and spun. A thin, pale-faced man with blonde hair stood behind her, a smudge of dirt on his cheek. He stood at about her height and wore a simple white shirt and jeans, but a black leather apron covered most of him. A necklace rested over the apron, showing off a red stone. He held a few glass ornaments that he'd been hanging on another tree near her. "Oh, no, I'm just looking."

"Not finding the bird you want?" he asked. He hung up an ebony ornament which looked like a raven.

"No," Bianca admitted. "It's fine. I don't hav—"

"What kind of bird?" the man interrupted. "If you're not seeing the one you want, it's likely someone else is missing it, too. Or it's extra popular."

Bianca scratched the back of her neck. She looked around for Gladus, but the magus spoke quietly with another vendor. Her bird pecked at her, knowing her inner desire to see her likeness in glass. Bianca mentally swatted her away good-naturedly and fought an amused smile at her bird's vanity. "A caracara."

"Oh!" the man exclaimed, his face sparking with delight. "Well, then. Let me put on a show for you." He put the rest of the ornaments down gently and moved around into his booth.

Bianca peered over the edge of his display. He pulled a container of sand out from under the stall and placed a large pile of it on a metal table. He wiggled his fingers, and Bianca's arm hairs stood on end as magic washed over her. She took a step back, but he laughed and motioned for her to come closer.

"Relax, I'm not going to hurt you. I just put up a ward to protect you from harm. Watch." He moved his hand in a clockwise pattern over the sand. At the same time, the red stone encased in gold wire on his necklace started to glow. The sand particles spun with the motion and lifted into the air. Bianca stared in wonder as it twisted before her eyes.

The man pulled out a lighter and flicked it on. He turned his hand. Crimson flames leapt around his fingers. They should have burnt him, but the man merely laughed and bent his fingers, letting the fire jump from one knuckle to the next. Suddenly, he swung his hand, and the fire rushed up the swirling sand.

Bianca gasped in surprise, but she didn't feel the heat; the ward protected her. He spun his hands over and over again, causing the sand to melt and turn into a viscous material. His fingers danced in the air like he was playing an invisible piano or bringing life to a marionette.

He slowed his movements, and the red-hot material lengthened and bobbed to the rhythm like a serpent obeying its tamer. It bent in on itself and reformed with each new flick of his finger. As Bianca watched, a bird began to emerge in the shape of the caracara. The belly of the avian turned white while its wings remained black. A bright red, almost orange, line appeared along the cere. The man kept working until the glass caracara spun slowly in front of him, held up by his magic.

"There we go," he said and lowered the ward. He walked towards the table, the glass rotating above his palm. "It'll take a bit to cool down, but you can pick it up before you leave."

Bianca could only stare. "How did…"

"Earth magic and fire magic," the magus said and grinned. "What do you think?"

"It's beautiful." Her caracara chirped in appreciation, not that he would hear it. "But, I tried to tell you that I don't have any money with me."

The man tilted his head. She waited for him to get mad at her, but he shrugged and chuckled. "At least I have another bird to add to my collection."

Bianca blushed. "I'm sorry."

"Beautiful!" Gladus exclaimed as she came up beside Bianca. "Vic, you've gotten really good at that."

Vic tipped his head to her. "I aim to please." He continued moving his fingers so the bird wouldn't drop. "This lovely lady told me this particular bird was missing. I thought I should add it to my collection."

Gladus nodded. "How much?"

"$25," he said.

Gladus pulled out her wallet again.

Bianca quickly grabbed the woman's hand and shook her head. "It's really okay," she said quietly. "I don't have a tree to hang it on."

"I'm sure Carlos will have a spot for you, and if he doesn't, I will," Gladus said. "Besides, you said you miss the holidays with your family." She handed the money over, and Vic repeated when it would be ready. "Wonderful. We'll stop back on our way out. Thanks, Vic."

Vic offered a little bow then went back to hanging up his ornaments while the caracara floated near his head.

Gladus tugged on Bianca's sleeve before she could protest.

Bianca fell into step behind her and walked down the aisle. "You didn't have to do that," she said.

"I don't mind. Besides, I like to support Vic's craft. He's one of my ward brothers, second to me, actually." She sighed happily. "He's come a long way. He used to only wield earth magic. He's spent a long time perfecting his fire craft, and it's gotten a lot better over the years. So allow me to indulge."

Bianca tucked her hair behind her ear, thinking. "If he's a fire magus, too, why was he wearing a glowing necklace? Aren't magi supposed to be able to touch the Ether without something to help them?"

"Well, yes. But that doesn't mean we don't sometimes use things to fuel our magic. He's wearing a talisman. Magi can store magic into objects, so when we might need more Ether later for a big task, we can draw it out of the talisman instead of using our bodies to channel the Ether from the earth. It saves us energy. That's why you'll see some magi walking around with magic-imbued jewelry, or watches, or scepters."

Bianca froze and stared at Gladus' back. A scepter? That seemed like an oddly specific thing to say unless—

"My art pad," she said curtly. "You snooped again?" For a moment, she could envision the dark figure with the scepter looming between her and Gladus.

Gladus paused. "What do mean?"

"A *scepter*?" Bianca growled. "How many of my drawings did you look at?"

The magus sighed. "Bianca, you have to understand, I wasn't

trying to snoop. When I saw you passed out on the floor, I got worried. So yes, I looked to see what you'd drawn. Maybe it could give me a clue about your nightmares."

"You still didn't have the right!" Bianca snapped her mouth shut and glanced around. A few people were staring now. Great, because making a scene in the middle of a crowded market wasn't going to bring more attention to her. She lowered her eyes and clenched her fists. "You didn't have a right," she said softer.

They stood apart awkwardly for a few moments before Gladus approached her. Bianca tried not to tense when the magus gripped her shoulder. "I didn't realize how important they were to you," she said. "I won't look at them again. I promise. I only want to help and keep you safe, remember? Can you trust me?"

Bianca wanted to snarl that she couldn't trust anyone, that's why she'd been hurled into this situation to begin with, but she knew it to be a lie. She trusted Henry. And Madison. Carlos. And she trusted Gladus. "Yes."

Gladus patted her arm. "Thank you. Now, come on." She pointed towards a stall where a man and a woman, both Native American, were laying out handmade quilts, jewelry, and some jars and sacks with herbs. "Those two right there are Rozene and Paytah. They're the mated alphas of the main Chicago pack. There are a lot of packs in the area, but Paytah's is by far the largest, oldest, and the most diverse. His immediate family is all Sauk descended, but when new wolves come into the area, no matter their origin, they usually go to him for refuge. Or I point them his way. Paytah's a bit of a hard-ass, but it's just because he wants to keep the packs safe."

Bianca's heart sped up. She'd never really interacted with werewolves. Her family steered clear of them, due to bad blood in the past, not that they had ever told her what that entailed. Paytah and Rozene didn't look overly threatening at first glance.

Paytah walked around in jeans and a red plaid shirt, his black hair tied back in two braids held in place by leather straps with a starburst design stitched into them. Rozene laid out a woven blanket, her dark hair pinned up behind her and showing off a few scars on her neck. She wore jeans and a flowing green shirt with a similar starburst trim on the sleeves and collar.

She flicked back a stray strand of hair, revealing a colorful beaded earring, and said something to Paytah. When he glanced at

Bianca, she wanted to stop in her tracks. His eyes were an odd copper color, almost bordering blood red. A vampire with those eyes would have sent her running the other direction. She'd never heard of werewolves with red irises.

Gladus didn't seem to notice her discomfort. She approached the two wolves and hailed Rozene first. "I heard you found the herbs I'm looking for."

Rozene looked up, smiling. "Gladus, I wondered when you'd come by. Hang on." She reached into a cooler at her knee and pulled out a sack. "Here. Found it while I was on a run. I managed to preserve it before the frost."

Gladus opened the bag and sniffed. Her eyes rolled back in delight. "You got to it in time."

Rozene snorted and planted her hands on her hips. "Don't think I can store my own herbs?"

"Oh, put your teeth away," Gladus laughed. "I know you can. Thank you for this, my friend."

Rozene nodded and held out her hand. Gladus slipped payment into her palm. As Rozene stuck it into her pocket, Paytah came up to his wife's side and touched her hip. His eyes drifted towards Bianca.

"Is this the bird you were telling us about?"

Gladus turned towards her, only then realizing that Bianca cowered several feet away. She huffed, motioning with two fingers. "Don't be rude. Come over here."

Bianca wanted to do just the opposite, but Gladus didn't often condone rudeness. Her feet struggled to stay rooted in place, but she forced herself to join the magus. She still made sure to keep distance between herself and the wolves; her caracara puffed and made a disgruntled noise.

"*I* know," Bianca thought. "*I don't like it either.*"

"Sorry," Gladus apologized to the wolves. "Apparently Bianca here didn't spend too much time around wolves where she came from."

"Ah," Rozene said. She flashed a smile that both calmed and unnerved Bianca. "We don't typically bite, unless you anger one of us. You don't intend to anger us, do you?"

"N-no."

"Then there's nothing to worry about." She turned back to the crates she'd brought with her. "Give me a second. I brought a few things for you. I think you're about Kaitlyn's size."

While she fished around for the clothing, Paytah came closer. His eyes burrowed into her very soul, breaking through mental walls and peering into the eyes of her bird. The caracara made a trilling noise of warning. Bianca drew another step back. Unlike Rozene, he didn't wear the friendliest smile. He gazed upon her with cool, calculating eyes which looked her up and down, not in a lascivious way, just to take her in. "You sure this is a wise idea, Gladus? Do you know why they're after her in the first place?"

"Not sure," Gladus confessed. "She thinks it has to do with her sister's past profession. The Hunters haven't been around my home since I took Bianca in. No one has even tapped at my shield. My guess is if they'd wanted to kill her, they would have done it by now. Or else they're regrouping to come back at us a different way." She shook her head. "She's staying with Carlos when I'm out and about."

Paytah made a noise in his throat. "How has Haley taken to that?"

"Better than I expected," Gladus admitted. "They were doing mostly well today."

"Mostly?"

"Well…" Gladus glanced at Bianca.

Bianca looked away nervously when Paytah zeroed in on her again. "We're still getting used to each other," she said.

"Hm." Paytah shook his head. "It's unfortunate that you've come to us under these circumstances. Several of my own wolves have been chased to Chicago. I fear that the Hunter threat is growing. I understand the purpose for some of them, but marks are being placed on parahuman's heads." He chuckled dryly under his breath. "I suppose once we stop hating each other because of color and origin, we start finding other ways to despise one another." He unrolled another blanket and smoothed it out on the table. Two wolves howled across its surface while an eagle soared high above their heads. "If I hear anything, I'll let you know."

"Much appreciated, Paytah."

Rozene reappeared with the clothing in her arms. "These should do well. I'm sorry it still smells like wolf. I hope that doesn't unsettle you too much." She held out the bundle.

Bianca swallowed and slowly took it. "It's fine. Thank you."

Gladus gave her thanks. She headed away from the table with

Bianca trailing behind her. Bianca couldn't help but glance back at the wolves. Rozene returned to her supplies, but Paytah kept watching Bianca, even as she walked away. It took Rozene's sharp tug on his sleeve to divert his attention.

They made their way through the market with Bianca clutching the clothing and lingering a step or two behind Gladus. Gladus picked up purchases, mostly herbs and items from magus or witch tables. Bianca wanted to enjoy this. She wished she could be more open to the people interacting with her and Gladus, but each time she thought to, the ghostly pang of henbane gnawed at her leg. She missed painting with Henry and baking with Madison. For a moment, she'd been part of a family again. For a moment, there weren't people after her and Haley didn't look at her like she was some kind of pariah.

She missed being *normal*.

Eventually, the magus brought them back around to Vic's station. The display tree had fewer birds than Bianca remembered; someone was doing well with his sales.

Vic smiled in greeting to them, the glass caracara resting in his palm. "There you are. The caracara was a good choice, kid. A lot of people like how it looks." He held it out to her. "Here you go."

Bianca reached for it. "Thank you. It's really—"

Her skin brushed his, and suddenly, the world slowed to a crawl.

Shadowy images flashed in front of Bianca's eyes and danced around her. She turned in place, watching them, and the urge to paint—draw—do *something* hit her like a hammer to the stomach. Her hands fumbled with the caracara and it fell.

Bianca looked down at the pile of sand that Vic had at his workstation. She ran her hands through it, drawing the images again. The dark man with the stick, no, the scepter. The woman with the bat wings. And now a wave crashing into another figure.

Color! She needed color.

Her caracara came to the rescue and forced a talon through her flesh. She cut the tip of her other finger, causing blood to drip in the drawing. She smeared it across the workstation until the wave turned crimson.

Wave of blood. A warning.

Glass shattered; the world moved again.

Bianca stood over the work table, panting, her chest aching as if she'd flown for miles. Vic fell backwards to the floor, clutching his hand and looking horrified. The glass caracara lay in pieces on the ground.

Bianca blinked stupidly and looked around. The area nearest to her had fallen deathly silent and people stopped to stare at her like she'd grown horns. She turned slowly in a circle, her panic rising, her head still spinning. Her shoe crushed the fragile glass ornament even more and she looked down at it in regret.

"Vic, I—"

"What *are* you?" he hissed.

She looked up to find him on the floor as far away from her as possible.

Bianca opened her mouth, but only managed a weary sigh as her mind spun, and she crashed to the ground, unconscious.

Chapter 10
Crimson Waves

Gladus

Gladus had seen a lot of strange things in her long life, but nothing like what happened the moment Bianca touched Vic's hand. A wave of magic passed over everyone within a twenty-foot radius, though where it originated from, Gladus didn't know. She didn't sense it from Bianca herself, but she didn't feel it from Vic either—she *knew* Vic's magic. The Ether had just appeared out of thin air, and now Bianca lay unconscious on top of glass shards and blood, and Vic cowered in his vendor stall, clutching his hand.

Gladus knelt beside Bianca and placed a hand on the werebird's forehead. The avian's brow burned with fever, her face glistening with sweat. Gladus glanced at a drawing she'd made in the sand. Three people stood together, one holding a scepter, one bearing bat wings, and one getting devoured in crimson waves. She couldn't fathom what they meant, but she recognized a couple of the drawings from Bianca's art pad.

Gladus' stomach twisted with dread and fear as she started to piece things together. She placed her hand against the teen's cheek. "Oh, little bird, I'm so sorry."

"What *is* she?" Vic asked again. Her ward brother stood up slowly, staying well behind his glass ornaments, as if they might protect him from Bianca.

"I'll take care of her," Gladus told him as she slid her arms beneath the young woman. She held the girl close, and before anyone could question her, she tapped into the Ether. It filled her with the warmth of an old friend's hug. Her veins and body hummed to the melody of earth's magical field. With a whispered sound, she teleported from sight with Bianca in her arms.

She appeared in her home and dropped an inch to the ground. Faint waves of magic rippled off of her in a wide circle. The curtains fluttered, and the old chandelier above her trembled. Gladus leaned over Bianca, panting.

Few magi had the ability to teleport. It took age, experience, and a hell of a lot of Ether. But Gladus' age and status as priestess of her ward afforded her a touch more magic. Bonding with her members also meant she could pull snippets of Ether from them when absolutely necessary—like now. Vic, as close as he'd been, would feel the effect of her pull the most. She tasted the mingled fire and earth in his magic as it dissipated from her grasp.

Teleportation still drained her, but she gladly paid the price to get Bianca away from the other parahumans. She didn't think that they would hurt her charge, but she couldn't be certain, especially if they figured out what Bianca *was*.

"Oh, child," she sighed. Gladus placed Bianca gently on the red satin couch in the receiving room, the same one she'd carried Bianca to when she'd arrived, half dead, weeks ago. She draped a warm midnight blue quilt over the young woman's body and touched her cheek.

The heat in her skin had fled and left her flesh icy and clammy.

Gladus started the fireplace and went into her kitchen. She placed a kettle on the stove and grabbed a bowl of water and a rag. She'd tried hot and cold packs, but when it came to soothing someone after magical shock, cloths were far more comforting.

Gladus returned to the room and knelt down. She grimaced, her old bones protesting against the movement. She felt her age and hated it.

She dipped her hand into the water and concentrated. Magic swirled into the bowl and made the water heat up around her fingers. Her power would hold the temperature steady. She pressed the cloth in, wrung it out, then placed it on Bianca's head. The teen moaned, but she still didn't stir.

Gladus sighed to herself. *Idiot. I should have been more careful.*

She'd suspected an anomaly about the girl, and yet she'd still pushed Bianca to be around stressors. What sort of mentor put her pupil in danger? Yet another reason she didn't often take care of avians. Fellow werebirds were better equipped to help another bird. Carlos and Haley would have known something was amiss with Bianca well before Gladus had the girl been with them from the start. They might have been able to avoid the whole situation.

And yet, was it really Bianca's avian side which had caused the problem in the market?

Gladus glanced at the stairs and bit her lip. She left the cloth in place and started up the steps. Wood creaked beneath her weight, betraying its wear and the many feet that had passed through Gladus' home over the decades.

Portraits dotted the walls around her, each one displaying a magus in her family. Her parents, siblings, grandparents, even her great-great-grandfather. All were gone now save for Gladus, some ravished by age, others caught in human games. Her great-grandmother had fallen victim to the Salem Witch Trials, and she'd only been passing through! Had it not been for Gladus' Oakfield Ward, and the Purple Door District of Chicago, she would have been truly alone.

Maybe that's why I keep taking people in, she thought. *They're not the only ones who need companionship.*

She paused near a picture of a young woman wearing golden hoops around her throat that matched the ones in her ears. The woman smiled out from the photo, her hair tied up in green cloths; a healer magus. Gladus could heal as well, but not like her great-great-great-grandmother who had once healed an entire village of a plague, for which she was praised.

Until religious zealots found out, labeled her a witch, quite the curse to call a magus, and burned her for her transgressions.

It wasn't an unfamiliar story. Many magi had died over the years, hunted by those who didn't understand them and feared their magic.

That prejudice made Gladus terrified to think that Bianca possessed any gift other than her avian wings. Lycans who did somehow have the ability to tap into the Ether were dangerous and a threat to humans and parahumans alike. If Bianca had somehow been crossbred with magic, Gladus would have to—.

She shook her head, unable to finish the thought.

She walked through Bianca's room and picked up the art pad.

She'd promised never to look in it again, but she'd break her word to potentially save Bianca's life.

She sat down on the bed and flipped through the pictures. A dark man and his scepter, as well as the woman with the bat wings made a constant appearance. She turned to the picture of two people with an ombre-haired woman. The woman greeted death's door, killed by vampires, and here Bianca had drawn a picture of vampires drinking from her.

She looked through a few more pages and paused on one of a tree. It stood in an open field with no other trees around it. Golden light poured from it like magic. Long willow branches reached out to people with symbols above their heads and pricked their fingers. Light wrapped around the chosen, showering them with magic. As Gladus stared at the symbols, she could pick out a wolf, a vampire, a werecat, a magus, and a witch. The bark of the tree had been etched to form a single "E."

Gladus closed the pad and walked downstairs, a sick feeling rising in the pit of her stomach. The kettle whistled in the kitchen. She made a detour to fill two mugs with hot water and soothing tea, chamomile for Bianca, and Lady Grey for Gladus. With the art pad tucked under her arm, she brought the cups into the other room.

The glass almost tumbled from her hands as Bianca jerked up on the couch. The avian gasped and grabbed her head, her eyes darting left and right wildly.

I wish she'd stop doing that.

"Bianca," Gladus said and set the mugs and art pad down. She rushed to the werebird and touched her shoulder. "Shh, easy. Breathe."

"Wh-wh-what happened?" Bianca stammered. She turned to look up at Gladus, tears brimming in her eyes. Her pupils shifted shapes and feather patterns formed on her cheeks and faded. Her bird's distress mirrored Bianca's own. "What did I do? Wh-what happened to me? What am I!"

Gladus sat down on the edge of the couch and pulled Bianca to her. She ran her hand through the girl's hair and pressed her cheek to Bianca's temple. Bianca clung to her, trembling like a leaf. "Just breathe. You're safe with me right now. It's okay."

"It's *not* okay," Bianca said, tears rolling down her cheeks. "First the Hunters, then Haley hates me because I drew images in flour, and now this? Gladus, I don't know what's wrong with me."

Gladus sighed deeply and leaned her head more against the girl's. "I know you don't understand. But, I think I do."

"You do?" Bianca lifted her head. "Then tell me! How do I stop this?"

"You can't." Gladus saw the horror in Bianca's eyes. She wanted to take away all of the werebird's fears, to free her of this burden, but while she could call on rivers and oceans, she couldn't heal Bianca of her plight. "Bianca, tell me about your dreams."

"What?"

"How do you feel when you wake up and draw them?"

Bianca shook her head. "What does that have to do with anything?"

"Please, tell me." Gladus waited patiently while Bianca wrestled with the request.

"I...don't know," Bianca finally said. "I just wake up and I see the images around me. Spinning, like ghosts. They spin and spin and tell a story that I don't know how to tell. I tried to ignore them for a long time, but if I didn't draw the pictures, they wouldn't leave my head, and then I couldn't sleep. They're just images. They're nothing special."

Gladus lifted an eyebrow. "Are you sure? You got pretty defensive when I looked through your pad." She slid the book onto Bianca's lap. Bianca's fingers curled tightly over the spine. "Think of all of the drawings you have made. When did they start?"

Bianca tightened her hold on the book like a lifeline. "I was about 14. That's when I knew I wanted to be an artist. One day, I woke up, and I just had this passion to draw, and so I did. But the drawings were strange. I almost stopped making them, but Nora encouraged me to keep going. To tell her everything."

"Have any of the images seemed familiar to you?" Gladus asked "Have you ever drawn something and had it come true?"

Bianca shuddered, and Gladus knew her answer. "Gladus, don't make me say it."

"Bianca, please. It's important. I can't help you unless I know the truth."

Bianca barked out a laughing sob. She jerked the art pad to her chest in a crushing hold, the feathery pattern accenting her face once more. "I had a dream of a caracara holding a red poppy. She looked like my sister. She had this unique pattern. She put the poppy against her breast feathers and looked me in the eye. Then, without a word, she turned and flew away and vanished into a forest. I remember being sad when I woke up. It seemed so final." She sniffed and hid her face against her folded arms. "Two days later, the Hunters came, and they shot her in the chest, right where the caracara had put the poppy. Blood splattered all over the tv. There was a movie on with a forest in it." She whimpered and trembled. "I tried to forget the dream. I tried."

Gladus' heart ached for Bianca but this also confirmed her suspicions. And there was no easy answer to her suffering. "Bianca, have you ever heard of a seer?"

"Like, seeing into the future type of thing?" Bianca asked through her tears.

"Yes." She settled her hand on top of the art pad cover. "You're seeing things before they happen, or as they happen. What may seem like dreams to you are actually visions. In the magic world, there are seers and oracles. Seers get inklings of the future, but they don't always come true. Oracles..."

Gladus fell quiet. Oracles were dangerous, because their visions *always* came true. They *forced* a future to happen. Magi donned death's robe and eliminated oracles, to save others from predestined fates, but Gladus couldn't imagine doing something to Bianca. She'd grown far too fond of the girl.

"Seers don't have to be magi or witches, they can be anyone who is sensitive to magic," she went on. "And you, my dear, seem very sensitive to it. More than anyone else I have ever known."

Bianca stared at the art pad. Suddenly, she cried out and threw it onto the floor. "No! I don't want this! I don't want to be this *thing*! You-you're telling me I saw my sister's death. You're telling me I could have stopped it!"

"No!" Gladus shook her head and grasped Bianca's hand. "Not all visions come true, Bianca. They can mean so many different things. It's up to how we interpret them. Think of tarot cards. They hold different meanings for people, but they can be right for everyone. That picture could have meant something else."

"She's dead!" Bianca screamed. "What else could it have meant? She's dead, and it's all my fault!"

Gladus shook her head and wrapped her arms around the avian. She pulled Bianca close until the young woman pressed her head into Gladus' chest and sobbed brokenly. Gladus didn't try to stop her. She stroked Bianca's hair and held her fiercely, protecting her against the truth and the world. What she wouldn't give to take all the pain away.

They sat like that for a while as Bianca cried out her tears. Gladus didn't say a word. She held the young woman and listened to the fire crackle behind her. At long last, Bianca's tears subsided, and she leaned heavily against Gladus for support.

"I don't want this," Bianca said quietly.

"I know. I don't want it for you either," Gladus whispered. She looked down at the art pad. It had fallen open to the picture of the tree. "I wish I could train you how to use your seer abilities, but that's not my talent. All I can do is sit with you and talk you through your visions. Do they come every day?"

"No, but they've been more frequent this past year. Nora said it was better if I jotted the images down and showed them to her. She wanted to see them, but I couldn't show her the one of her death. I was scared."

"Why was your sister so interested?" Gladus asked.

Bianca shrugged. "Probably because she wanted to see how crazy I got. Once the dreams started, she gave me shots of medication that were supposed to help, but I think the meds just made it worse."

"Shots?" Odd. Unless they were tranquilizers to numb the mind, she doubted anything would influence or calm a seer's ability.

"Yeah. I had trouble sleeping because of the dreams, so she gave me the shots to make me tired. I haven't slept well, honestly, for years. Not since the bad batch of flu shot came through." Gladus gave her a look, and Bianca frowned. "Nora brought the flu shot home from work to give to me. It hurt more than usual. And then like, right after that, I got sick and started having problems sleeping. She said that the company gave her a bad round."

Gladus narrowed her eyes. "How old were you?"

"14," Bianca replied without hesitation.

Gladus set her jaw and glanced down at the tree in the picture. Thorns on the branches pricked people. Could that be... Goodness, just how precise were Bianca's dreams? Was she an oracle rather than a seer? "Tell me about the tree."

"The tree?" Bianca looked down when Gladus pointed. She stared at the picture for a moment. "I keep seeing a tree that pricks people. And then suddenly, they're covered in magic. I don't

recognize any of the people or anything, but I know *what* they are."
She pointed at the symbols. "The tree appears in a lot of my
dreams, like the guy with the scepter. It's weird."

"Indeed," Gladus said. She looked at Bianca and saw the
exhaustion creeping into the young woman's face. Her visions had
strained her enough, and Gladus hated pushing her. They had time;
they could talk about it later.

So she leaned down and closed the art pad. "I think that's
enough for today." She thought of the image that Bianca had drawn
at the market. The dark man, the woman with bat wings, and the
crimson wave. What was more important? Discovering the
meaning behind the images, or ensuring Bianca didn't dash away
into the night because of fear?

Gladus rubbed the werebird's back and tilted her head. "I think
we could use a little pick-me-up."

"What do you mean?"

Gladus smiled and hugged her gently. "Just sit right here. Do
you like chocolate and peppermint?" Bianca looked at her in
confusion but still managed a nod. "Good." Gladus picked up the
mugs and went back into the kitchen. She dumped the water and
poured milk into a saucepan on the stove.

It had been a bad day for Bianca, and Gladus didn't want her
running off because of guilt. Gladus wasn't blind. The girl perched
like a bird ready to take flight, and she had a feeling that if Bianca
thought herself a danger to anyone, she would fly away to save
them. An idiot thing to do, but Gladus couldn't fault her. So she
needed to find a way to make her stay.

She'd seen the joy that lit up Bianca's eyes at the market when
she looked at the holiday decor. The way she talked about her
family and their traditions reminded Gladus very much of what she
used to do with her own family when they'd still been alive.

She pulled a jar of powdered chocolate out of the cabinet and
some sugar and crushed peppermint. As she waited for the milk to
bubble, she looked outside.

Snow fell beyond the glass, dotting the ground in a white
shroud. Gladus leaned forward and smiled to herself. She loved the
snow, and it had nothing to do with her being a water magus. As
she stared, she saw the ghostly images of herself and her siblings
building snowmen and chasing each other in ivory fields. The
snowball fights they used to have, oh how she missed those. She

and her sister waved their hands, creating hundreds of perfectly formed snowballs, and rained them down on their younger brother. He hid behind his snow fort and used a small, homemade trebuchet to chase his sisters away with snow boulders.

A passing car sprayed slush into her memory, making the image vanish.

Gladus fixed the mugs of hot chocolate, a sad smile on her face. She fished around in her cabinet and found a container of mixed cookies leftover from one of Haley's baking extravaganzas. She put them all on a plate and brought them into the receiving room. She handed a mug to Bianca then went over to the radio and started to fiddle with the dials. It didn't take her long to find Christmas music. They always started it so early, it was a wonder they didn't hear it in October. "There, I think this might lighten the mood."

She sat down on the couch next to Bianca, the cookies between them, and propped her feet up on a padded stool. "I know this is difficult for you, Bianca, but I promise I'll do everything I can to guide you through it. You're not alone."

Bianca lifted the mug to her lips and took a slow drink. She breathed out heavily and leaned her head against Gladus' shoulder. "Thank you."

Gladus pulled Bianca's quilt over their legs and sipped on her hot chocolate. The young avian played with her purple necklace. Music filled the room. Neither one of them spoke; they just listened and enjoyed each other's company.

What a delightful change of pace.

Gladus had grown accustomed to being alone at her house. To finally have a companion made her happy, though she knew Bianca would be staying with Carlos more often before long.

Gladus glanced down at Bianca as the teen dipped a cookie in the hot chocolate. The avian's tension eased, her skin exuding warmth and not as deathly cold as when Gladus had brought her back to the house. "I think I'll introduce you to the rest of my ward tomorrow. One of my members dabbles in studies about seer abilities. I think he can help you, too."

"You mean it?" Bianca asked. "Do you think he can teach me how to stop the visions?"

"I don't know about that," Gladus said. "But he might be able to teach you meditation exercises that will allow you to fight the visions, so they don't tempt you so much. We'll find a way to make this right. For now, we need to keep the visions between us." She quieted. "You know it's not your fault, right?"

"What isn't?"

"Your sister's death."

Bianca held the mug closer. "I could have stopped it."

"No," Gladus said with a shake of her head. "Even if you'd figured it out in time, you had no way to stop it. Visions just show what *could* happen. One path. It's not your fault that those men killed your sister. You have nothing to blame yourself for."

Bianca looked ready to argue, but a knock at the door stopped her. She looked over at it with a start.

Gladus smiled and set the mug of hot chocolate down. "Keep drinking that. It'll make you feel better." She headed for the door. She wasn't expecting anyone, but her magical ward held firm, so no Hunters lurked about. Maybe Vic had come to check on her. She opened it and grunted when she saw the person huddled outside.

"Trish, how can I help you?"

The vampire swallowed and tucked her hair behind her ear. Her red lips stood out in sharp contrast to her pale skin. "I just wanted to apologize for what happened at the restaurant a few weeks ago. I didn't mean to cause a scene." She shifted anxiously on her feet. "I'm still trying to find my place in the District. Sometimes I think *force* works better than *reason*. Saul and Fraula reminded me that that's not the way of the District."

Gladus slowly lowered her hand from the door and offered a sad smile. "I've been trying to teach you that for a while now, Trish. You can find a comfortable place here if you just respect all the different kinds of folk."

"I know, I know," Trish said. She rubbed the back of her neck. "I'll try to be better, Gladus. I had a talking to from Fraula. She made it *very* clear that I've been a disappointment, and I don't want to risk getting kicked out."

Gladus softened a little. For a moment, she saw the same scared vampire who had fallen at her doorstep over a year ago. Gladus still pitied her, but the more Trish fought her help, the less sympathy she held. "For what it's worth, if you change for the better, and your coven still gives you trouble, let me know. I can help."

Trish looked at her in surprise. Something glimmered in her

eyes, but Gladus didn't recognize it. The vampire just smiled timidly and nodded. "Thank you. It's a comfort to know that." She glanced over her shoulder. "I should go. It's getting late, and it's cold." She held out her hand. "Thank you, Gladus."

Gladus took Trish's hand and was promptly yanked forward.

Something hard pressed against her stomach, and a sharp sound rang out, followed by Bianca's scream. Gladus didn't feel anything at first. She looked down and stared at the barrel of a gun against her abdomen.

Blood stained the front of her brightly colored clothing, branching out into a spider web pattern around her stomach. Gladus slowly looked up at Trish. "Why?" she whispered.

Trish, eyes crimson, grabbed her throat and threw her.

Gladus toppled, falling down the length of her porch stairs. She cried out, the pain suddenly striking her as she huddled in the fetal position at the bottom step. Trish looked back at her then vanished into the house.

"No…" Gladus whispered weakly. She heard Bianca yell, and Trish swear. "Bianca!"

The snow crunched near her head. She painfully turned and saw the two Hunters she'd banned from her home standing over her wearing smug expressions. The non-bearded one crouched down at her side and pressed the barrel of a gun to her temple. "Not so mighty now, are you, *witch*?"

Gladus heard a commotion at the door. Trish dragged Bianca out of the house by her hair. The vampire dug sharp claws against Bianca's throat, pricking the skin. Bianca already had a black eye and a bloody lip. She looked at Gladus in terror and struggled, but another jerk from Trish's hand forced her to stand still.

Gladus knew she had to choose.

Her magic fizzled and popped, too depleted from teleporting them earlier to do much more than that. She closed her eyes, the pain stealing her breath, her vision blurring and twisting.

"I told you to drug her," the non-bearded man snapped at Trish. "You're going to cause a scene and bring someone down on us."

Gladus opened her eyes.

"Fine," Trish growled and shoved something into the back of Bianca's neck. Bianca moaned, wavered, and then collapsed against the vampire. The light in her eyes faded until she fell unconscious. "What are you going to do with her?" Trish asked, nodding to Gladus.

The bearded Hunter looked down at Gladus without feeling. "Make sure she doesn't cause any more problems for us."

Gladus heard the gun cock. She stretched out her fingers and wrapped her magic around Bianca's unconscious body.

"*It's not your fault,*" she said mentally, though she knew the girl couldn't hear her. With a final burst of magic, she teleported Bianca away from Trish.

The vampire fell.

The gun fired.

Chapter 11
Werewolves of Chicago

Paytah

Paytah drove his green Toyota Tacoma through Chicago rush hour traffic, grumbling to himself about not leaving the market earlier. It had already taken an extra hour to get home; the first snowflake of the season meant everyone forgot how to drive.

He leaned his head against his hand, shifting his right black braid over his shoulder and down his back. Country music hissed and popped through the speakers, reminding him that he needed to get the electrical circuits checked in the truck before it got too cold outside. Snow floated down from the sky, dusting the streets; at least he knew his battery purchase from a month ago would last.

Rozene crocheted a blanket on her lap next to him, which Paytah would rather be doing than driving in the weather. Age frosted her hair, but her complexion remained youthful and beautiful. The fire blazing in her eyes had drawn him to her years ago, and nothing could make it simmer. A perfect match. The perfect—

"Watch the road," she teased. "I know I'm beautiful, but we don't need to wrap around a light pole."

Paytah chuckled and stared ahead. "We did well at the market today. How many quilts did you sell?"

"Almost 10. Lots of birthdays and holidays." Rozene rocked her head left to right and rolled her shoulders; he heard the pops. "Supposed to be a cold winter. Helps that some of the other local packs were around and wanted to support ours."

"Heh, get in good with the alpha, hm?" Paytah smirked. "They'll have to do more than buy blankets to stay out from under my nose."

"I think they know it, too. That's why they bought the preserves." Rozene pulled on the yarn. "What did you think of the girl that Gladus brought to us?"

"Trouble."

"That's what you say about *every* new person." Rozene sighed. "Gladus typically brings in good people, excluding that one vampire who keeps trying to charm our wolves. Ugh, if Gladus wouldn't come down on our heads, I'd teach her a lesson myself."

Paytah smiled fondly at his wife. "I know you would. And I would love to be a fly on the wall when you did." More vampires were coming into the area, and he didn't like it. While vampires and werewolves could mostly get along in the District, that didn't mean there weren't the occasional disputes. Joseph, the local coven leader, parlayed decently with Paytah, but the vampire knew that if he sent his people anywhere near Paytah's territory, he'd be several vampires short.

Gladus helped keep the peace on all fronts.

The avian she'd brought with her; what a curious little bird. He hadn't liked the smell about her, though he couldn't put a finger on why. Perhaps he was just unfamiliar with the scent of her bird— though he found that hard to believe—or maybe she held secrets. Paytah despised secrets. Her little fainting spell at the market had drawn a lot of suspicion, and Vic had been taken aback by her antics. Gladus vanishing with the kid hadn't helped.

No, this Bianca was not a regular avian by any means.

"Brooding?" his wife interrupted his thoughts.

"Just want to keep the pack safe."

She reached out and placed a warm hand on his thigh. She squeezed it and leaned over to rest her head on his shoulder. He wrapped his arm around her, comforted by her scent. She was his, and he was hers, their bond unbreakable, and woe to the man, or woman, who tried to ruin it.

"I had a thought," she said. "Once we unpack, let's go for a run. You're tense. The pups will sense it and think something's wrong. Especially Kat."

Paytah sighed.

Yes, the *pups*. Not their children, no, theirs were grown and either living in their own houses or off with a pack of their own. When new wolves came to Chicago and needed a place to stay, Paytah opened his home first. He had two pups with him now, one a very stubborn 16-year-old who had lost his father to a drive-by shooting—a wrong place, wrong time, situation—and a 21-year-old woman who had just escaped an abusive boyfriend. They were good kids who pulled their weight, but they were overly sensitive to his moods. One growl directed at someone else could send them both running, the boy into danger, and the girl away from it.

Rozene scolded him for his temper more times than he cared to count.

"I think a run would be nice," he said. "Want to shake off some nervous energy."

Rozene squeezed his leg again then returned to her work.

They lived on the outskirts of the city. Paytah had bought the two-story house specifically for the acres of wooded space around it. Thanks to his pack mates, and a friendly witch, buying the surrounding houses, they didn't have to worry about humans sticking their noses where they didn't belong. The territory was open enough for wolves to run and enjoy themselves, especially in the cooler weather.

It helped him the way beer or a cigarette couldn't.

He pulled up the driveway, the tires creating grooves in the snow. It fell heavier now. Paytah turned off the engine and climbed out. Their wares were hidden under a tarp in the back. He went to reach for it, considered, then whistled sharply.

The door opened and Kaitlyn slipped out into the snow, holding a shawl to her thin shoulders. A frail little thing, she hardly wore the healthy weight of a werewolf her age. Her blonde hair looked dull, but with more weight on her, it had started to take on a golden tint. She glanced at him with hazel eyes then looked over her shoulder. "Nick," she called.

Nick came barreling out, a teenager with the same fire that Paytah had had at his age. He hopped down the steps and jogged towards the truck without a jacket. "How'd we do?" he asked.

"Pretty well. I need you and Kaitlyn to get things inside. Rozene and I are going on a run."

"Ah, come on, man, why can't we go?" Nick protested.

"Alpha business," Paytah replied with a little growl. "Can you do this, please?"

Nick curled his lip but hopped into the truck and started to pull the tarp off. Muscles rippled beneath his dark skin. "Hey, Kat, come on over. I won't give you the heavy stuff." Much to Paytah's surprise Nick had taken quite a shining to the young woman. He claimed himself as her protector, which wouldn't have been a problem, had it not caused Nick and Paytah to bump heads.

"Got it," Kaitlyn said. She came to the side of the truck and reached up, taking a couple quilts in her arms.

Nick scooped up boxes of preserves and hopped down with a grunt.

Paytah watched his pups fondly before turning to his mate. "Shall we?"

She gave him a flirtatious smile and headed for the trees.

Young parahumans, like Nick, couldn't change into a four-footed wolf. They were typically stuck in their biped form, looking more like the traditional werewolves you saw in movies. Both over 100, Paytah and Rozene learned long ago how to shift into wolf forms, which made things less awkward when you were out hunting and trying to avoid detection. Kaitlyn defied the odds of lycans her age who could actually shift all the way to a four-footed form, though her past had a lot to do with the forced change.

Paytah stretched his arms over his head and shifted in the snow beside his wife. His arms shortened but his hands grew larger. His face contorted, his mouth elongating and turning into a vicious muzzle filled with sharp teeth. He transformed almost seamlessly and painlessly. The older and more practiced you were, the easier the change. He went down to all fours, his tail forming and wagging behind him. A black pelt with white wisps rippled over his body. His hands, which had started to chill from the snow, quickly grew pads and fur, warming them.

Rozene changed beside him, turning into a much smaller but faster wolf. Her pelt took on a red tint to match the meaning of her name; rose. She stretched out her beautiful frame, patches of white and black fur interspersed amongst the red. A goddess amongst all wolves, Rozene put any female to shame, and he remembered each time she changed one of the reasons he married her.

He trotted to her side and leaned down, nuzzling her face and ears affectionately, his warm breath creating white plumes around them. She licked his cheek and brow and stood up on her hind legs to get better purchase to nuzzle deeply into his neck. Suddenly, her teeth closed around his ear. He yipped, and she took off running through the snow.

Paytah released a playful growl and ran after her, kicking up snow behind him. He rushed through the trees and open space, leaping over a fallen branch that he had yet to clean up after a bad storm. The wind coursed along his body, though the chill scarcely penetrated his thick fur. He breathed in, letting go of his human instincts and allowing his more animalistic side to take hold. There were no wolves to lead here, or humans to protect them against, just Rozene, his beautiful, fierce mate.

Rozene dodged him and ducked around a tree. The moment he reached her, she zoomed past him, causing him to stumble. He whirled and chased her, nipping at her taunting tail.

Rozene laughed in his head. *"You're getting old, my love. That trick never used to work on you!"*

"I'm just wearing you down," Paytah warned. *"False sense of security."*

"Right. It has nothing to do with those extra servings you're taking at dinner."

Paytah growled and launched himself at her. Rozene threw herself to the side and rolled, sending him tumbling head over tail through the snow. Paytah landed in a heap. He rolled over, shaking snow from his head, and looked at his mate as she quaked with laughter.

Paytah's tongue lolled, and he scrambled to his paws. He darted after her as she took off running again. She made it several yards before she suddenly pitched forward and went into a roll herself. Only, this didn't look intentional. She flipped and skidded on her side, panting. He winced in sympathy and ran to her side.

"Rozene?" He licked her ears worriedly.

"I tripped over something. I didn't even see it." She wiggled herself back up to her feet and padded back towards the spot where she'd tripped. Paytah followed.

They both froze as they came across a body lying face down in the dirt and snow. Paytah jumped in front of his mate and forced her back, growling. Who had come into their territory? And what were they still doing there for that matter? He walked forward warily, snarling a warning, but the person didn't move. As he got closer, he smelled blood and something else unpleasantly familiar.

Paytah walked around the body. By the layer of snow on it, it must have been there for a while. He nudged it with his nose then scrambled back when he recognized the smell. "*Bianca*?" he asked, though she couldn't hear him unconscious as she was.

The avian, who had been his whole point of contention, lay on her side in the snow. Her bruised eye swelled, and blood froze on her chin from a split lip. Pinprick marks lined her blue-tinted neck, like someone had scratched her. But what in the world was she doing here? She was supposed to be with Gladus!

Rozene reached his side and gasped in his head when he saw the avian. She started to shift back, and Paytah shot her a look. "*We have to warm* her up," she said, her voice switching from mind to verbal speech as she changed. She shook herself and shrugged off her jacket, placing it around the girl.

Paytah knew not to argue, and besides, if this had happened to Bianca, what of Gladus? The Marshall would never abandon her charge, not unless Bianca had hurt her. He shifted back and reached for the girl. "Let me take her. You might have to fend off the pups."

He tucked Bianca's face protectively against his chest then started to jog back towards the house with Rozene beside him.

Above, the snow spiraled down, and Paytah had a sickening sense that a storm brewed above the Purple Door District, threatening to destroy them all.

***

"Whoa, who's that?" Nick asked unhelpfully as he blocked Paytah's way into the house. The alpha brushed past him and carried Bianca into the living room. Kaitlyn sprang off the couch and scurried back, her eyes turning golden and more wolfish.

Paytah's hard features softened. "Easy, Kat. We know her. Go get blankets and heat up some tea. Make it with the herbs in Rozene's violet container. Nick, turn up the temperature and get the fire going. She's not a threat, son." At least, he hoped she wasn't.

Nick prowled close to Kaitlyn and eyed the newcomer warily, but when Paytah growled a warning, the teen went to work.

Paytah laid Bianca down and checked her pulse. It drummed weakly against his finger, likely due to the cold. He reached for her shirt and hesitated before glancing at his wife. "Her clothing's wet from the snow. Can you?"

Rozene motioned him away, and he turned around as she took off the young woman's shirt. Avians weren't shy about exposing themselves, not because they were crude, but because avians were, generally, intimate and easy going around one another. Paytah's intimacy extended to his wife alone. He glanced at the stairs as Kaitlyn came down with a bundle of blankets. He gestured behind him with a quick jerk of his thumb.

Rozene wrapped a blanket around Bianca's body and shifted the girl against her chest. When Kaitlyn returned with the tea, Rozene tilted Bianca's head up. "Help her drink. We need to warm her up from the inside. Paytah? You should give Brighton a call and have Tess stop over." She sniffed. "I can smell henbane in her blood, and traces of magic. Nothing about this was an accident."

Kaitlyn helped Bianca drink a few sips of tea and took hold of her while Rozene shifted into her four-legged werewolf form and settled down next to the frozen girl.

The heat kicked on a notch higher before Nick returned. The teen stopped next to him and stared at Bianca. He sniffed and sneezed.

"She's an avian. Why are we helping her?"

"She's one of Gladus' people," Paytah said.

"Oh." Nick headed over to the landline. "Want me to give her a call?"

Paytah turned away from the women and walked towards the phone. "I want you to get some warm food going for when she wakes up. And mind yourself. She's not an intruder; she's a guest."

"I know, I know. I just want to make sure Kat's okay."

Paytah gave Nick a look. "Do you think me incapable of protecting my pack?"

Nick narrowed his eyes but kept his opinion to himself. Instead, he tilted his head, baring his neck, and went off to the kitchen to do as Paytah asked.

Paytah hid a slight smile. At least Nick acknowledged the hierarchy.

He grabbed the phone and dialed Gladus but, no surprise, no one responded. He ground his teeth then took Rozene's advice to heart and dialed the number of a local officer, who happened to be one of his wolves. "Brighton, it's Paytah. Can you send your daughter to my house? I have a wounded avian who needs some warming up. Get some of your people over to Gladus' place. I have

99

a suspicion something happened to our Violet Marshall."

"Right, Boss. Tess is in the area, so she should be there shortly," Brighton replied, and that was that. He didn't ask questions, a trait Paytah admired about the wolf. Stupid questions led to stupid tragedies.

He sat down on a recliner with a grunt and waited.

And waited.

Another fifteen minutes passed before Paytah heard a knock. Nick rose but Paytah motioned him back and headed to the door, just in case. To his relief, though, Brighton's adopted daughter, Tess, stood just outside.

Her raven hair barely reached his shoulders. Dressed in a black-laced gown with beige leggings and a leather jacket, she hardly looked a threat, but Paytah knew better. Snow melted half-an-inch above her jacket and hair; Paytah shied away from the magical heat pulsing off of her body. His discomfort made her red-painted lips pull up in a wide smile.

"You rang?" she asked.

Paytah gave a jerk of his head and brought her inside. Though a magus, Tess belonged to Paytah's pack. Her mother, a magus also, had married ones of his wolves, so that made both of them pack as well, even if Tess could be contrary to his rules. She liked pushing the limits and seeing how much she could get away with. Fortunately, when trouble came calling, he knew he could rely on her.

He brought her to Bianca, Kaitlyn, and Rozene. Tess cocked her head and flicked an ebony nail towards the unconscious avian. "Who's the icicle?"

"Her name's Bianca," Paytah explained. "She's Gladus' ward."

"Huh, so why isn't Gladus the one healing her?" Tess knelt down and rubbed her hands together. Crimson magic danced around her fingers and many rings. Older magi could hide the magic while using it, but Tess was younger; she didn't quite have as much control yet so her power blazed within her eyes.

Paytah sat down on the couch nearby. "That's what we'd like to know."

Tess, fortunately, didn't ask any more questions, taking after her father. She placed a hand on Bianca's head then on her belly. As Paytah watched, magic seeped into the young werebird's body. Bianca took a shaky breath and shuddered, prompting Rozene to move closer.

Color returned to Bianca's pale cheeks as she started to thaw. Paytah watched her face and noticed the split on her lip seal. Her natural healing power kicked in and broke through the remaining traces of henbane. Thank goodness for a parahuman's supernatural ability to heal faster than humans. With her body already responding, he knew she would be okay.

Tess rocked back on her heels and glanced up at Paytah. "Dad wanted me to stick around until we heard news. I figured that way I can make sure she doesn't have a heart attack or something. I should have warmed her up enough from the inside, so she won't have issues."

"Thank you, Tess."

The magus tossed a small salute then headed over to Paytah's previously occupied recliner. She plopped in it and picked up a book to read, but Paytah noticed the way her foot started tapping, anxious as the rest of them to get news.

Another hour passed.

Rozene slept, and Kaitlyn nodded off against Nick, who remained ever vigilant. Paytah watched the boy's posture and could tell by his tense muscles that he was on high alert. He'd likely make a good scout one day, maybe even an alpha if he calmed that temper of his—Paytah was one to talk.

Bianca moaned and started to shift against Rozene. Her eyes fluttered open, and in a flash, she scrambled to get away from both Rozene and Paytah. "No, no!" she screamed, kicking blankets aside. She realized, belatedly, she was naked, and she quickly wrapped herself in a discarded quilt.

Rozene jerked with a start, and Nick put himself in front of Kaitlyn who stared with wide eyes at the avian. Paytah reached for Bianca's arm. He caught her before she squirmed too far away.

"Bianca. I—"

She hit him.

Talons grew on her fingers, and she hit him full in the face, leaving deep, bloody gouges in the skin. His head swung, and he let her go to touch his bloody cheek, shocked.

Nick took action. With a snarl, he lurched forward, his body shifting as he moved. He grew in size, rising to nearly 7 feet, gray fur rushing over his body and his elongating muzzle. He stood on hind legs and spread out the sharp claws on his front paws.

He was almost on top of Bianca when Rozene pounced and knocked Nick to the side. He rolled into a nearby end table, smashing it under his girth, and tried to stand, but Tess flicked her finger and pressed red magic down on him.

"Cool it, pup," she ordered.

Rozene, her red fur bristling, stood in front of Bianca and snarled.

"*Back down! Can't you see she's scared?*" She glared at Nick until he whimpered and slumped down. When Tess freed him, he lumbered back over to Kaitlyn's side, still in his biped form.

Rozene's alpha strength filled the room. Paytah backed off a little, more for Bianca's sake than because he feared his mate. When it came down to it, Paytah's strength surpassed hers, making him the top leader of the pack. Still, he exposed his neck a little to her and scooted back out of respect.

Rozene huffed and looked over her shoulder. Bianca had pushed herself against the wall by that point. "*Bianca, you know me. I'm Rozene, the werewolf you met today at the market. We're not going to hurt you.*"

Bianca stared at Rozene with frightened eyes. She tried to focus on her breathing, but her gaze kept darting around, looking for something or *someone*. Rozene padded back to the avian's side. She settled down on her belly and dropped her chin against Bianca's feet. "*We aren't going to hurt you. Can you tell us what happened? We found you in the snow outside.*"

"You found me?" Bianca asked, sounding drunk. "Gladus? Where's Gladus?"

Paytah and Rozene exchanged looks. He stayed quiet; at least the girl responded to his mate. "*We were hoping you could tell us. You were unconscious and near frozen in the snow.*"

Bianca put her hands to her mouth and made a strangled sound that could only be described as a keen. "It was a vampire. A vampire came to the door and pulled Gladus outside. She-she attacked me, and then the Hunters, they." She released a broken sob. "The vampire shot Gladus. Then she pricked me with something. I passed out; I don't know where she is. But the Hunters!"

"*Hunters,*" Nick hissed mentally. "*Of course it has to be those fuc—*"

"Nick!" Rozene barked. She gave him a look then nuzzled

Bianca's leg. "*My husband sent a cop, one of our wolves, to find Gladus. We'll hear soon what happened. Until then, you need to rest. Just stay with us. We'll keep you safe.*"

Bianca gave her a look that said sleeping was the last thing on her mind.

Kaitlyn got up off of the floor and grabbed a blanket despite Nick's look of warning.

"Here," Kaitlyn said. "You need to stay warm. My name's Kaitlyn, but you can call me Kat."

Bianca took the blanket and nestled into it. She quaked with fear, but at least she wasn't hyperventilating. Kaitlyn offered a smile and sat down next to her. She touched Bianca's knee. The avian shuddered then relaxed a little. "Why am I naked?" she asked after a moment.

"Because you were a popsicle," Tess explained nonchalantly. She plopped back in her chair and folded her legs. "Had to get you warmed up, and your wet clothes weren't helping with that."

"I'll get you some of mine," Kaitlyn offered. "I left your necklace on, though. It's okay." She smiled, glancing at Nick. "He looks scary, but he's a big softy. And so is Paytah."

Nick snorted and slowly started to change back into his human form.

Paytah smiled to himself. Despite her cruel beginnings, Kaitlyn's heart remained pure and open to the suffering of others. She probably saw another person like herself in need who had endured far too much for her young age.

He stood up and brought more blankets over for the girls while Rozene cuddled up close to them. Bianca shut her eyes, and the stress and warmth sent her back to sleep.

Paytah settled near his wife and reached out to stroke her furry head. "Vampire. Why does Trish immediately come to mind?"

Rozene growled under her breath. "*I was thinking the same. Should we contact her duke?*"

"Not just yet. We don't know if this was an isolated attack or if the coven has decided to turn against the District."

"*They'd be stupid to do that. Their forces can't defeat ours alone, never mind all of the other parahumans in the area.*"

"I know, but we should still wait." He hated waiting. He didn't like thinking that Joseph aimed to upset the peace. For all he knew, Trish had been caught up with the Hunters, and she alone caused the trouble. Maybe they had something on her. Or maybe Gladus had finally picked the wrong sort of pupil to trust.

Paytah's stomach twisted at the thought of Gladus.

Two Hunters *and* a vampire.

She could stand against a lot as a magus, but even Paytah dreaded those odds. It sounded like these Hunters were well trained. And Trish—the foolish child—had the speed and veracity that even werewolves envied. Wolves had complained about her speed and prowess before she caught them in her charm. It did not help his nerves.

He glanced at Kaitlyn and Bianca. The avian had fallen asleep, but Kaitlyn stroked the girl's hair, wide awake. Her expression softened a little, and she gave him a sad smile that spoke of her own worries. Gladus had found Kaitlyn and brought her to the pack. The magus was one of the best Violet Marshalls the District had ever had. To think something horrible had happened to her left his gut in knots.

Rozene brushed his leg with her nose. "*Rest, Paytah. I'll wake you if they make the call.*"

Paytah touched Rozene's cheek. Instead of moving to the couch, he settled down on the rug and rested his head on top of one of his mate's paws. She licked his forehead, and he closed his eyes. If Gladus was gone, the District would be in turmoil, and Paytah would have to be at his strongest.

All the leaders would.

Chapter 12
Crime Scene

Paytah

Paytah'd just drifted off when the phone shattered the quiet. Bianca jerked awake, and Kaitlyn touched her arm to steady her as he answered the call. Tess scurried to his side so she could listen. Paytah didn't stop her only because her father spoke on the other end.

"Paytah."

"Alpha." Brighton's frustrated voice filled his ear. "I'm sorry it took so long. We got to her place, and the *wiggle fingers* were casting their magic on her."

Tess pouted. "*Wiggle fingers,* I heard that, Dad!"

Paytah prayed for patience as he pushed Tess lightly behind him. "How is she? Did she say anything?"

The line went quiet.

"Brighton?"

"Boss, she's dead."

Paytah pulled the phone away for a moment, wishing he'd heard wrong. Dead. It didn't seem possible. Gladus had always been a force to be reckoned with. He slowly brought the phone back to his ear. "Then why were they casting magic on her if she's… *how?*"

"Someone shot her in the head and the stomach. There's so much blood. I'm trying to get the coroner to inspect the body, but Vic is being an ass. The ward almost ruined the crime scene with all their spells and wailing. She's been out in the cold for a while."

"Why wouldn't the ward call it in?" Paytah asked.

"Something about needing the magic sight clear, or some shit. Hang on, let me give you over to one of hers."

Shuffling noises assailed the phone until a familiar man spoke on the other end.

"Alpha," Vic said, his voice laced with exhaustion, his nose stuffy, but Paytah doubted it had anything to do with the cold. "Can you tell your wolf to back off while we finish?"

"What are you doing, Vic?"

"Trying to figure out who murdered our priestess!" Vic shouted in the phone.

Paytah normally would have taken offense at the disrespect, but he could forgive the magus for his grief. "And have you had any success?"

"There were four entities here when she died. Her bond with us broke over two hours ago, and we rushed to her home and found her like this. We've tried to ask if anyone saw anything, but we can't get answers."

Paytah looked over at Bianca. "I have one witness here. She said she saw the attack. But not…" He grew quiet. "I'll tell my pack. Vic, I have to ask you not to do anything rash."

"They killed our priestess and a Violet Marshall. We can't just let them go!"

"We won't," Paytah promised. "But you need to let Brighton do his job. And you need to help your ward mourn."

Vic fell quiet for a long moment. "Who saw it? Who was here? Was it the *bird*?"

The warning in Vic's tone made Paytah's neck hair bristle. "You're not going to put a hand on her, Vic."

"I didn't make a threat. The girl had a vision earlier today at the market. She saw what was going to happen. How do we know she wasn't involved?"

"Believe me, she wasn't," Paytah said and glanced at the small avian huddled against Kaitlyn. "I'm sorry for your loss, Vic. Truly. Can you put Brighton back on?"

"She is not going to die in vain," Vic growled, the only warning Paytah knew he'd get.

After another shuffle, Brighton took back the line. "Been a long time since we lost a Marshall like this." He cursed quietly.

"She was one of the good ones, Boss. What sick twisted bastard did this? She didn't deserve it."

"I know, Brighton. Get the information you need. If you want to interview the witness for information, let me know. Also, make sure the ward doesn't go on a rampage to avenge their priestess. We can't have more bloodshed."

"Will do. Thanks. Can you send my kid home?"

"Of course. Stay safe, Brighton." Paytah hung up the phone and leaned over it with a heavy sigh.

Gladus. It all seemed like a bad dream, like he'd wake up and she'd be there scolding him for worrying about her. Or insulting his cooking. Or helping him deal with a colicky pup.

His arms shook and he took a steadying breath. He might not have been the biggest fan of magi, but Gladus had been one of the good ones.

"*Paytah?*" Rozene inquired gently in his mind.

He looked back at her then at Nick as he knelt close to Kaitlyn. Bianca met his eyes, and he saw the color drain from her face. "Gladus is dead," he said bluntly. "Murdered."

His wife drew in a sharp breath, and both Kaitlyn and Nick jerked back in shock. Even Tess' brusque nature vanished for a moment as she fell back into a chair.

Bianca just stared, her mouth hanging open. Her cheeks turned ashen as she put her hand over her lips. "Was there...was there blood? A lot of it?" she asked behind her palm.

Paytah thought it an odd question, but he nodded. "Yes."

Bianca pressed the palms of her hands to her face. "Give me paper and a pen," she demanded.

Nick and Paytah looked at her in confusion. But Kaitlyn stood and picked up a pad near the phone. She handed it and a pen to Bianca. The avian started scribbling, head bowed, red-tipped hair brushing the yellow page. Paytah stepped towards her and tried to watch, but her hand moved so fast. Bianca pulled her legs in, anger and tears filling her eyes before showering on the page. She kept drawing.

Rozene gave Paytah a look, but he could only shrug. It looked similar to what others had said she'd done at the market. So he let her be.

Bianca didn't work for long. The pen tumbled out of her hand as she stopped and stared down at the picture. "The man and the scepter," she whispered, tapping the middle picture. "The vampire," she said touching a woman with bat wings behind her. "Crimson waves," she mumbled. She'd drawn the likeness of Gladus on the page getting covered by a wave. Bianca bit her finger and touched the bloody tip to the page. "Crimson waves," she repeated. She shut her eyes.

Suddenly, she hurled the book with a grief-pained scream. Nick jumped back, and even Rozene looked startled. Bianca grabbed her head then scrambled to her feet with a sob. "I saw it! I saw it! I knew it was going to happen! She's dead because of me. She's dead because of me! Just like Nora!"

Paytah lifted his chin and took a step back. She'd seen it? Seer? Had Gladus been hiding that from him? Did that explain why he didn't like the smell of the bird?

Tess must have come to the same conclusion. She stood and called a ball of fire to her hand, her eyes narrowing. The flames snarled and coiled through her fingers, hungry for a target. "Seer. She's a *seer*? How the hell is that possible? She—"

"*Tess*," Paytah said in a low growl. "Go home."

"But—"

"*Go. Home.*"

The magus glared at him, but even she wouldn't ignore the order of her alpha.

Tess shook the flames out and made a wide berth around Bianca before heading for the door. But the look she sent the bird made Paytah's throat tighten with worry. Even in the magical community, seers weren't well liked. There were those who thought seers stole someone's free will. Paytah didn't know enough about it, but he didn't think Bianca had done it on purpose.

Nick kept his distance, but Kaitlyn stood up and went to Bianca, placing both pale hands on the avian's arm.

"It's not your fault," she said quietly.

"Yes it is!" Bianca scrubbed angry tears out of her eyes. "She told me I was a seer. She was going to teach me! And instead, she's dead because I didn't know what the visions meant. She's dead because of me. They wanted *me* not her." She looked at Paytah, her eyelids red. "The two Hunters that attacked her are the same ones who came after me. She protected me from them, and now she's dead. Dead! She must have done something to save me from them and the vampire. That's how I ended up here. She saved me instead of herself!"

Paytah cocked his head. "Wait. This vampire. What did it look like?"

"Bright red hair. Crimson lips. Red eyes."

"*Trish*," Rozene said in Paytah's mind. He nodded in agreement. That seemed to be Trish's calling card: red.

Kaitlyn tried to pull Bianca close. "There's nothing you could have done. If those Hunters wanted you, they were going to go through anyone who got in their way. It's their fault. You're the victim, not the killer. You just wanted to be free, to be away from the pain."

Paytah eyed Kaitlyn and frowned inwardly. How many times had he tried to convince her of that very same thing after she escaped her abusive boyfriend? Other people had gotten hurt because of him—*she'd* gotten hurt—and she'd blamed herself, not his assholery or his actions. Males were the dominant ones in werewolf culture, but some could get truly out of line. Paytah had promised himself that if he *ever* discovered the one who'd hurt Kaitlyn, he'd take care of the bastard himself.

But for now, he stood quietly in support as his pup lent strength to the avian. Bianca breathed heavily, nearing a panic attack. Kaitlyn pulled her into a hug and let Bianca settle her chin on her shoulder. The unspoken kinship between the two women made Paytah's heart swell despite the pain of losing Gladus.

"It's not your fault," she said again. "It's not my fault," she added in a near whisper.

Bianca shut her eyes and let the sobs unleash. She cried so hard, Kaitlyn had to take her back to the ground. Rozene settled next to her and placed her chin on Bianca's knee this time. Bianca showed no fear of the wolves as she hid against Kaitlyn and let Rozene comfort her. It was touching, but for the worst reasons.

Paytah glanced at the window as the snow continued to fall. He couldn't take Bianca anywhere tonight. He'd bring her to Carlos in the morning and let him know what had happened. Tonight, he'd protect his pack, including the little lost bird.

109

Chapter 13
Blame

Paytah

Paytah shifted into his four-footed wolf form. He'd be more formidable this way if someone tried to charge through the door. He walked over and settled on the floor with his mate, pup, and the bird. Kat touched his fur with light fingertips. He licked her hand affectionately and glanced at Nick. The young man had yet to get close after the news about Gladus. By his tense shoulders and posture, Paytah could guess where his mind lingered.

"I know you might not understand or like it, but until we get her to Carlos, she's pack tonight. Gladus believed in her and risked her life to save her. So... We keep her safe."

Nick opened his mouth to speak, but Paytah could see the doubt in his eyes. And the last thing Bianca needed was a wolf giving her grief.

"If you have something to say, then shift into your wolf form. We should let the girls rest."

Nick grunted in frustration. But he knew better than to argue. Once more, he shifted into his biped form, with a little less ease this time. Shifting drained the body, especially during times of stress. He plopped down next to the fire, tail thumping agitatedly on the ground.

"She's right. She did get Gladus killed. We shouldn't have her here. It's not safe for us. I don't need any more of my family getting shot." His gaze drifted to Kaitlyn pointedly.

"*It's not safe going out there either. They won't know where she was sent. I don't like it either, but I will* not *let Gladus' death be in vain, understand?*"

Nick flicked his ears back. He warred with his thoughts for a moment then grumbled and settled down on his belly. "*Fine, but I'm not cuddling with her.*" He flopped over on his side and spread out his legs a bit so the fire could warm his stomach.

Paytah almost let the conversation die, but Nick's tension had yet to vanish. The young wolf's ears flicked back, and his tail partially curled between his legs; hiding one's emotions in wolf form was a near impossible task. "*Nick?*" he said more gently.

Nick heaved a sigh and rolled back over. "*Yes, Alpha?*"

Paytah considered his next words carefully. "*I'm proud of you for trying to protect the pack when Bianca struck me. You saw your Alpha get injured, and your instinct was to eliminate the threat. That's the sign of a loyal wolf and someone with the makings of an alpha.*"

Nick lifted his head a little, his ears perking forward. "*Really?*"

"*I know I'm hard on you, son. I tend to show Kat more favoritism because of everything she's been through, but you're struggling too. Losing your father... It can't be easy.*"

"*Paytah, look—*"

"*Don't worry, I'm not going to talk about him. I just need you to know that I'm proud of you, and I push you because I see myself in you. And I know I needed more guidance when I was a pup. You're a good wolf, Nick. And a strong, kind, young man.*"

Nick wrestled with his emotions, his ears twitching along with his tail. Paytah didn't expect a big speech. Nick's soft and humble, "*Thank you,*" said what he couldn't.

Paytah left him to rest and listened to Bianca cry. In time, she grew quiet and fell asleep from her grief. He almost suggested they bring her to a room, but when he glanced back, he saw Kaitlyn asleep as well, still holding Bianca. Rozene leaned over to nuzzle his cheek, which he lovingly returned. As they all settled down to rest, Paytah watched as his mate, and then Nick, drifted off, leaving him awake.

In the quiet, Paytah gazed into the fire as his entire body trembled with grief. Gladus had been a dear friend to him and the District. No one else had led it with such fairness and kindness. No one else had turned their home into a protective sanctuary for those

111

they didn't even know. He'd saved dozens of pups with her help. Part of his pack consisted of wolves she'd brought to him. Gladus had had a knack for finding lost souls and trying to save them. Her kind heart had made her a great friend, but it had made her a target as well.

Trish.

He suddenly hated the vampire more than he hated the Hunters who had finished the job. She'd betrayed Gladus and the District. She'd brought this all upon them. His teeth itched, wanting something, or someone rather, to sink into. Damn telling Joseph about what his vampire had done; Paytah would take care of her himself.

But his anger ebbed as the pang of loss filled his heart. No more visits. No more stories of the past. No more making special preserves just for her. No more pups rescued by her.

He snuffled, trying to mute the grief, but he just couldn't. He appreciated that his wolf form couldn't cry. But that didn't stop the whimper from escaping his muzzle as he shut his eyes and tried to sleep.

***

Paytah woke before everyone the next day and got changed into fresh clothing. He prepared a light breakfast, but even when everyone rose, no one seemed interested in eating. He couldn't blame them. Gladus' loss weighed heavily on them all.

He went outside and cleared off the few inches of snow from his truck. The beautiful sunny day mocked the injustice that had occurred the night before. After getting the heat going, he stepped back into the house and stomped his boots on the entrance mat. "Kaitlyn, go get Bianca some fresh clothes. I'm going to take her over to Carlos."

"What? Why?" Kaitlyn asked, glancing at Bianca. The bird leaned over her plate, appearing half dead. Only her fingers moved, toying with her purple necklace. "We should let her rest here."

"Gladus wanted her to be with Carlos' family. She'll mourn better with other birds. Besides, Carlos needs to know what happened."

Kaitlyn opened and shut her mouth, torn with a response. Paytah didn't know why she struggled so hard to obey his orders until she spoke. "I'll go with you."

"Kat," Paytah started to say at the same time as Nick. "You can't."

Kaitlyn lifted her chin. "You talk with Carlos, and I'll take care of her. She needs a friend."

"You don't even know her!" Nick argued.

"Yes, I do," Kaitlyn replied. "I know how this feels."

Paytah held out his hand before Nick could keep arguing. He didn't want to put Kaitlyn in danger, but Bianca wasn't in any mental shape to move or do much of anything, and he didn't have the same bed-side manner that Kat did. So he nodded.

Kat helped the werebird up, and they went into Kat's room to get changed.

Nick put his drink down, hard. "This is stupid. Pack comes first. You know those Hunters are out there. Kat can't protect herself yet!"

"Do you doubt *my* ability to protect her?" Paytah asked in a low tone.

"No," Nick said, shaking his head. "There was a vampire involved. How many more are mixed up in this? It might not just be three assholes out there trying to kill you."

Rozene shot him a look. "*Language.*" She drummed her nails on a cup. "He has a point. But two wolves are better than one." She sighed. "Paytah, I'll speak with the pack while you take care of the girl. Word's going to get around fast, and we don't need any wolves doing something foolish like attacking a vampire to avenge Gladus."

Paytah nodded in agreement. "Thank you. We'll have enough trouble with the ward. I'll return as soon as I can. It shouldn't take long." He turned to go wait outside for the girls, but something stopped him. In a swift motion, he went to his mate and pulled her into a hug. He kissed her soundly on the lips and pressed his head to hers. "Be safe."

"You, too." She put her head to his chest and touched his braids. "I don't want to lose you."

Nick made a sound of annoyance and stormed from the room. Paytah watched him go, but Rozene just tapped his chest. "I'll talk to him. Go. Take care of Kat."

By the time Paytah and Rozene parted, the girls were ready to go. Both were dressed in warm pants and shirts. Kat had let Bianca borrow one of her older coats, a puffy green thing that made Bianca look like a moldy marshmallow. She probably wouldn't approve of the comparison.

Paytah motioned to them and headed out to the truck. They climbed in, him in the driver's seat, the girls in the back of the cab. Kaitlyn wrapped her arm around Bianca who settled easily against her. He looked back in the mirror at Kat. They all knew avians needed touch and attention to feel whole. He never expected skittish Kaitlyn to offer physical touch to someone else, not after her experiences.

He pulled out, tires crunching over snow, ice, and rocks. The main roads would be plowed, but the back ones were still messy. He turned on four-wheel drive and headed off towards the interstate.

The sun warmed Paytah as he drove, and he breathed a sigh of relief to see that the traffic flowed better than the night before. Saturday mornings were always better. He turned on the music quietly to help fill the silence. Bianca closed her eyes, but Kaitlyn watched the road, always alert. She didn't leave the house very often; she feared her ex would find her, or someone would grab her. So to have her go with him to Carlos' spoke volumes of her dedication to help Bianca.

"Bianca," he said after a little while. He saw her open her eyes in his rearview mirror. "Is there anything else about these visions that you can tell us?"

"Paytah," Kaitlyn warned.

Bianca sighed. "I don't know. Gladus said that a woman was murdered by vampires. I drew a picture that looked exactly like her and had vampires in it as well. At least, I'm guessing they were vampires. She was asking me about a drawing I made of a tree, too."

"A tree?" Paytah pressed.

"It poked parahumans with thorns and gave them magic. She said it concerned her, but that she'd help me learn how to read the visions."

Paytah pressed his lips together. A tree giving magical powers to parahumans. A dystopian novel waiting to happen. Lycans were strong enough without magic, and magic users could be frightening in and of themselves. They didn't need *more* power. Hopefully, it meant nothing or was a bad dream, but based on her other drawings, maybe not. "Are you sensing anything now?"

Bianca shook her head. Her face started to redden as she fought back tears. "Every time I close my eyes, all I see is Gladus bleeding."

Kaitlyn shifted, pulling Bianca closer. "Enough," she said in a low growl. "You don't need to upset her more."

Paytah almost corrected her, but he liked this new, fiery side of her. So he shut his mouth.

The drive on the interstate went by smoothly, and the roads were either plowed or the heat from the asphalt had melted the snow by the time he pulled up in front of Carlos' house. He found a spot a block down and climbed out of the truck. Kaitlyn and Bianca got out after him and walked with him down the street.

Paytah tucked his hands in his jacket and kept his head down, but his eyes darted left and right, looking for trouble. A man walked towards them, but one look from Paytah caused him to pause, tromp through the snow, and make a wide berth around the two werewolves and the avian.

Paytah reached the door and climbed up the steps, avoiding the ramp that Haley used. He rang the doorbell and waited. It took a little longer than he expected, but he eventually heard the *thunk* of Carlos running down the stairs. The man opened the door and looked at him, then at Bianca.

"Bianca?" he said in surprise.

"Can we come in?" Paytah asked. "I'd rather talk to you in private."

Carlos frowned but stood aside. "Come in." He turned as the downstairs door opened and a sleepy woman in PJs stepped out. "Go on back to bed, Anita. I got this."

The woman leaned against the doorframe, arms crossed. "Wolves usually don't show up at our door first thing in the morning for no reason." She yawned deeply. Two dark arms suddenly slid around her waist and another woman appeared behind her. She dropped her chin on Anita's shoulder.

"Come back to bed," the other woman cooed.

Paytah reddened slightly as they exchanged a deep kiss in the middle of the hall. He had the urge to cover Kat's eyes, but she'd swat him away. Why did avians have to be so *public* about their affections?

"Anita, go on," Carlos urged.

The woman rolled her eyes and ducked back inside with her girlfriend.

Carlos offered a sheepish smile. "Sorry about that." He headed up the stairs first, likely to warn his mate that two wolves were about to enter her home.

Paytah motioned for the girls to go ahead of him then followed. He looked around once more then locked the door behind him. The stairs squeaked under his heavier frame as he walked up. He heard Carlos and Haley speaking in heated whispers, and he had to wonder if they already knew about Gladus.

He shut the upper door behind him and lifted an eyebrow.

Henry sprang out of his breakfast chair and ran over to Bianca. "Bianca! I drew something for you!" He slowed, and his smile faded however when he saw Bianca's exhausted face. He reached for her hand. "Bianca? Are you okay?"

Madison lowered her buttered toast at the change in Henry's tone. She slid out of her chair, only to have her mother hold out an arm to block her from moving forward. Haley glanced sharply over at the werewolves *and* Bianca, surprising Paytah. Gladus wanted to leave Bianca with *her*?

Carlos sighed and motioned to the living room. "Please, come sit. Henry, let's let Bianca have some space."

Paytah nodded his thanks. He nudged the two towards a couch, Kaitlyn sticking close to Bianca. Henry, heedless of his father's warning, held fast to Bianca's free hand and sat near Kaitlyn. The young didn't know any better about fearing other parahumans until their parents taught them. The innocence of children never ceased to amaze him.

Paytah sat on the arm of the couch next to Kaitlyn and watched Madison plop in her mother's lap and Carlos sit in a recliner. Carlos nodded for him to speak. Paytah wasn't sure how to break the news, but he hadn't exactly ever been good with tact. In retrospect, his wife could charm a snake out of a basket. Maybe she should have been the one to come.

"Gladus is dead."

Carlos breathed in sharply while Haley jerked forward as if she'd been shot again. She clutched Madison to her a little tightly, causing the girl to fuss. "What did you say?" Haley gasped.

Bianca sucked down a sob. "It's my fault. The Hunters—"

"Shh," Kaitlyn said, rubbing her arm.

Haley's expression changed in an instant, and not for the better. Shock turned to rage and she rounded on her husband. "I told you it wasn't safe to have her here. If the Hunters went after Gladus, then they'll come after us, too!"

Carlos held up his hand at his wife and looked at Paytah. "What happened?"

Paytah decided Bianca had been through enough already. "Bianca said that she and Gladus were attacked. A vampire, I'm guessing, Trish, pulled Gladus out and shot her. She attacked Bianca, and Gladus sent Bianca to me and my wife. Brighton found Gladus, and her ward, in front of her house. Shot in the head."

Haley put her head in her hands. "Nooo," she moaned.

"Mommy?" Madison whimpered, reaching for her mother's arm. Paytah wondered just how much the little girl understood.

Bianca held Henry close, his eyes growing wide and filling with tears. "Grammy Gladus? She's...she's gone?"

Bianca swallowed hard. "Yes."

Henry started to cry, his small body shaking with grief. He ran to his father, while his mother cradled Madison. Carlos scooped him into his arms. Bianca still had her arms outstretched for a hug, but she slowly let them fall down to her legs.

Carlos held his son and rubbed his back. "With the Violet Marshall dead, the District—who's going to take over? Gladus never named a successor."

"It might be in her will," Paytah suggested. "Otherwise, we're going to have to have a vote."

Carlos snorted and looked down at his son. "Yeah, who's going to run? Joseph who can't keep hold of his vampires? You? The felines will probably revolt. And you'd rebel if the felines stepped in."

"Stop it!" Haley shouted. "We need to deal with the real problem in the room first."

Paytah nodded his agreement. "She's right. We need to be on the lookout for the Hunters."

Haley snorted. "No. We know what to do with them." She pointed at Bianca. "We give *her* to them. She's the one they want, not us. Gladus is *dead* because of her. Because of her *visions*." She glowered at Bianca. "I don't know what kind of freak of nature you are, but our little District was *fine* until you brought those bastards to our door."

"Mama," Madison interrupted. "Bad word."

Haley flushed. "Gladus brought you in out of the goodness of her heart, and you killed her."

Carlos shot his wife a look. "That's enough, Haley. She didn't pull the trigger."

"She might as well have!"

Henry cried harder and suddenly jerked back. "Stop it! Stop it! Stop it! Stop yelling! She's my friend and you're being a big meanie!" He flung himself out of his father's arms and ran to his room.

Paytah winced as he heard the door slam behind him. Poor kid.

Bianca stood up and shook Kaitlyn off. "She's right," she said. "Haley's right. It's my fault. You all would be better off without me."

Carlos held out his hand again. "Bianca—"

"No, she gets it," Haley said. "She knows what she did. She's an abomination. She doesn't belong with us. If she never came, Gladus wouldn't be dead!" She clutched Madison to her chest. "I won't let my children be taken from me again because of *you*. Gladus should have ended you the moment she realized you were a seer. All you do is hurt people."

Paytah didn't move fast enough. Bianca gave a soul-crushing sob and fled from the room. She ripped the door open and ran down the stairs. Kaitlyn jumped to her feet and dashed after her, but Paytah heard the downstairs door open before Kaitlyn even got to the first step.

Carlos sighed heavily. "Kaitlyn won't catch her."

Paytah knew it. Avians were *fast*. Faster than wolves and vampires. That didn't mean Kaitlyn would stop her hunt, though. He rose to go after his little wolf, but he stopped and looked at Haley first.

"I know what happened to your daughter, and I know you mourn her every day, but that girl out there is a *child* compared to us. She deserves a chance. It's not her fault these people are after her. You're an *avian*. You should understand the importance of finding family and a place to call home more than anyone."

"I *understand*," Haley spat. "I understand loss. I understand pain. I understand staying up at night crying over your dead child. I understand going past her room and thinking you see her standing there when you know she's in the ground. I understand being afraid whenever my children leave the house because they might not come home. You have no right to lecture me, Paytah. Until you lose a child, you can't comprehend what I'm going through."

Paytah pressed his lips together. "And what will your children learn from their mother who turned away a child like them? I hope they don't grow up so cold-hearted."

And before Haley could say another word, Paytah walked downstairs and met Kaitlyn at the door. She ran up to him, panting, shaking her head. "I can't find her. I followed her scent, and then it vanished. I didn't see any clothes, so I don't know if she took off flying in bird form or... or..." She flushed. "I was too scared to follow further."

Paytah squeezed her shoulder. "I know, pup. We'll find her." He rubbed her back and looked over his shoulder. Carlos stood at the top of the stairs while Haley wheeled past him towards Henry's room. Carlos bowed his head, and Paytah knew that he didn't intend to follow.

Coward.

Apparently Paytah'd be rescuing the avian then.

He took a step down the stairs.

A shrill scream froze him, and his heart, in place. "HENRY!"

Chapter 14
Birds of a Feather

Bianca

Bianca ran. Through the pain. Through the tears. She ran until her heart pounded in her chest and ears. Ran until her tears blurred her vision and the world around her; until her feet ached and she faltered. Ran until her bird's broken keens turned into her own verbal sobs.

And still she couldn't escape her pain.

Haley's cruel words, blaming her for her mentor's death echoed in her ears. And to have someone curse her and call her an abomination because of something she couldn't control; it broke her. She had come to the Purple Door District to find safety and companionship.

Now Gladus lay dead and broken, her intended avian family hated her, and the only *friends* she had were werewolves, whom her parents always warned her against. She'd heard Kaitlyn coming after her, calling her name, but even her newfound friend had stopped and let her run into the busy streets of Chicago.

Sunlight warmed her damp face, but the early winter winds threatened to freeze the tears. She scrubbed them away and ran across the street. Horns blared and people shouted at her, but she didn't care. She just kept running. Maybe she'd run far away enough that no one would know her name. The Hunters who wanted her life wouldn't ever find her, and no one else had to suffer or die.

An abomination. It wasn't her fault she was a seer. It wasn't her fault she drew visions that came true. And yet, Gladus' death fell heavily on her conscience.

Bianca sucked in a shaky breath and stumbled. The concrete caught her toe and sent her tumbling to the ground near a bench. Bianca flopped backwards into the snow, a clump of white bracing her head like a pillow.

She heaved in and out, her breath wheezing from the run. She stared up at the sun and wanted to curse the day for being so bright and cheerful while her heart shattered into a thousand pieces. She wanted to go back to yesterday, to eating cookies and listening to Christmas music on the couch with Gladus. She wanted to go back to when Nora was still alive. To staying up late watching movies and throwing popcorn at one another.

Most of all, she wanted to go back to when her parents were alive, before the accident. To the dinners they shared and the feeling of wholeness. Back to when she lived in Mexico and listened to the caracaras sing outside her window.

Avians needed family.

Without it, she was hardly an avian at all! Carlos' kin and Gladus had started to heal some of the damage to her heart, but now the wound gaped open, and Bianca bled out her grief. She rolled onto her side and cried quietly on the ground, next to a green bench, in the middle of a park. Her bird wept in her mind, tucking her head back into her wing miserably. They were together, but still so alone.

Cars drove past, but no one stopped or cared for her wellbeing. It seemed fitting. No one wanted her except for the very people who wanted to kill her. Maybe Haley was right. She should give herself over to the Hunters so that no one else would get hurt. No one deserved to die because someone had a vendetta against her. Gladus had paid the price of knowing her. Who was next?

I won't let anyone else die because of us, she thought to her bird. The caracara brushed her mind with her wing. Bianca longed to hold her, or any bird for that matter, in her arms, but she couldn't let her avian out. *You're all I have left.*

Bianca sat up slowly and braced her back against the bench. Icy snow bit through her borrowed jeans, but she didn't care. The cold brought some pain, distracting her from the agony in her chest. She pulled out her necklace and wrapped her hand tightly around the silver bird feather, forcing an imprint into her flesh.

I wish you were here, she thought to Nora. *You'd know what to do, and you could explain everything to me. Why couldn't they have taken me instead of you? The Great Mother is supposed to protect us. Where is she now? What do I do, Nora? I don't know how to stop this.*

She heard footsteps nearby, but she didn't look up. If the Hunters were there, they could just finish her for all she cared.

The steps stopped near her. Someone patted her arm.

A young woman stood over her with a kindly expression on her face. She wore her dark hair bunched around her warm golden-brown cheeks.

"Fallen on hard times?" she asked in a voice that was feather light. She withdrew a five from her wallet and held it out. "Go get yourself something to eat."

Bianca almost didn't take it. She didn't want pity money. But if it meant getting out of Chicago… She accepted it and tucked it in her pocket. "Thank you."

"You know," the woman said and sat down on the bench uninvited next to her. She looked around, a calm, happy smile on her face. "I used to hide away from people because I didn't think anyone liked me. It was cold and lonely, and all I wanted was a friend. It took me a long time to open up my heart and trust someone, to tell them my story." She looked down. "Do you have a story to tell?"

"No," Bianca mumbled. "Just a stupid girl with stupid dreams."

"I hear stupid dreams are some of the best ones if you know how to follow them." She shuffled around on the bench and held out a small notebook and a pen. "Here, maybe this will help."

Bianca looked at it then up at the woman in confusion. "Why are you giving this to me?"

"Need a place to keep your dreams, right?" She winked, her bright eyes opening a window into an old soul in such a young body. How that was possible, Bianca didn't know. Another sensation flowed off the woman, a little dark, but also comforting at the same time. Bianca didn't know what to make of it, but she liked it. Her bird pressed forward, sensing it too.

Bianca slowly took the notepad and pen and settled back against the bench. "Thanks."

"You're very welcome. I hope you find what you're looking for like I did." The woman rose. "Good luck. Just remember, not all who wander are alone." She gestured to the book.

Bianca opened the first page to a scribbled note. "Not all who wander are lost." She looked up, but the woman had vanished. All that remained was a black and white swan feather floating in the air. Bianca caught it in her hand and a sudden wave of comfort filled her and her bird. The caracara breathed out a contented sigh. She held the feather close.

Some said that, in avian culture, there existed a Mother or a Father, depending on your beliefs, who looked out for their little birds. They came to those who needed them most, and Bianca needed the guidance.

She hugged the feather and stuck it gently into the notebook.

When the cold grew to be too much, Bianca pulled herself up onto the bench and sat in the sunshine to thaw. Her heart beat a little calmer, though the pain of losing Gladus remained fresh.

She closed her eyes, but when she opened them, the park didn't look the same. A violet fog curled in and out of the trees, turning everything a dark hue. A roaring silence made the hairs on the back of her neck stand on end. Her caracara puffed her feathers to twice her size in a defensive posture. She no longer existed in the regular world; she watched it pass in front of her from the realm of her nightmares.

Shadowy figures walked through the fog, purple tendrils caressing their obscure bodies. The man with the scepter stood in the center, waving the item back and forth, clearing the fog, but remaining just as elusive.

A pool of golden light started to swirl around one of the trees. It crawled up the bark and through the branches, filling it with Ether magic and making it glitter in her purple world. The branches turned willowy and reached out to the other shadows, pricking them with thorns. Crimson blood dripped down the shadows' injured arms, but now a golden light throbbed at the pinpoint wound.

The tree swayed in the wind. Like magic, a plaque materialized at its base. One by one, a letter appeared on it until the word Eden burned across the surface.

Something coiled around her wrist. She lifted her arm and stared at a golden root holding her captive to the tree. Her caracara perched on her other arm, another root keeping hold of her leg. She and Bianca exchanged haunted looks then watched as magic poured out of them through the tether and distributed it to the other shadows. Their veins started to glow with the newly-given magic, linking them all together.

Bianca blinked again, and the real world and sounds returned. There were no shadows or roots. She looked over her arms, freed of the tree's bonds. The book laid open on her lap, filled with sketches of what she'd just seen. She stared at the portrait of her own face and swallowed a lump in her throat. And then, blissful silence.

For a moment, she could think straight.

She slid the swan feather between the pages to bookmark them before closing the cover.

Bianca pushed herself up and started walking. She made her way deeper into the park along a trail. The trees were beautiful with their branches dripping water onto the stone path. She tucked her hands into her pockets. Kaitlyn hadn't given her gloves, and her fingers ached with cold.

She wished for the wolf's warmth and her soft, comforting hands. Something about Kaitlyn called to her. Made her feel safe. She almost regretted running from the werewolf.

"*Then go back,*" her bird and mind whispered to her.

Bianca bit her lip. *But it's not safe,* she said. *Not for them. I'm better off on my own.*

"*Nora thought the same thing, and so did your parents.*" The caracara preened her wing and shook herself, shedding a few loose feathers. "*They didn't join a District, and now they're all gone. You have a chance. They* want *to help.*"

But I—

"*Gladus told you Nora's death wasn't your fault. So then neither is Gladus'. You know she would say that. And we're not supposed to be alone.*"

No, they weren't, but how could she justify putting other people in danger?

She shook her head sadly and glanced up at the sky.

A young red-tailed hawk flew above her, a dark shadow blotching out the sun. She watched it fly, and she expected it to land in a nearby tree.

But the bird just circled overhead, following her further into the woods. She stopped and eyed it suspiciously.

Suddenly, the hawk dove towards her, its wings flapping furiously to try to keep it aloft, not from injury, but inexperience. It couldn't be older than a fledgling!

Bianca backed up, knowing how sharp those talons could be. Did it have its eyes on a mouse or something else she couldn't see?

But then a voice broke into her mind.

"*Bianca!*" little Henry shouted.

Bianca gasped and sent her bird up to him. "*Henry! What are you doing?*"

"*I can't stop!*" he wailed.

He descended too quickly. Were he a peregrine falcon, he might have made it, but not with his size and inexperience. Bianca raced towards him and held out her arms with little regard for her own safety. He tried once more to slow, but too late. She took him into her chest, wings and all. The force of the blow knocked her backwards. She fell but kept her arms around him so he wouldn't smash his head or beak on the ground.

Bianca rolled onto her side and held the small red-tailed hawk gently in her arms. A few downy feathers floated near her face as he squirmed to right himself.

"Henry? Henry! What are you doing here?" she asked and sat up, setting him lightly on his feet. She looked down at her arms and saw gouges where his talons had cut her. Thank the Mother for his small stature otherwise he could have ripped an artery. Well, he still could.

Henry danced around a little, wings spread, until he got balanced on his feet. He tucked them against his sides, flicking them with nervous agitation. "*You can't leave!*" he shouted a bit too loudly in her head.

Bianca winced. "*Softer, Henry. I can hear you just fine.*" When she realized she was still speaking mentally to him, she quickly made her bird retreat. She'd never gone into his head before for fear of Haley's reaction. The brief mental connection left her feeling a little less alone. She looked around for signs of his family or the Hunters, but the park seemed deserted. She wiggled out of her coat and set it on the ground, motioning to it. "Step up on that so your feet don't get cold."

Henry climbed onto the soft fabric and shifted anxiously from one foot to the next. "*You can't just leave. Mom was really mean to you. I... I don't think she meant what she said."*

Bianca's shoulders slumped. "I think she did, Henry. And she has every reason to be afraid. I get people hurt because of whatever it is I am. Your Grammy Gladus died because of me."

"No!" the young bird shouted. *"You didn't kill her. Bad men killed her. She liked you. She wouldn't have brought you to us if she thought you were mean."* Henry ruffled his wings and stepped forward. He leaned his feathered head against her arm. *"Why is everybody so mad at you? You didn't do anything wrong."*

"But I did." Bianca reached into the pocket of the coat and pulled out the book. She opened it to the page with her visions. "I see things, Henry. Bad things. I know when bad things are going to happen to good people, but I don't know how to stop them or how to warn them. If I had understood that one of the pictures I drew showed Gladus in danger, then maybe I could have helped her."

"So?" Henry said. He pecked at the drawing. *"Bad men hurt her. She wouldn't want you to leave or give up."* He looked up at her with pale amber eyes, *"I don't want you to give up or leave me. You're so nice to me, and I like painting with you. Please, Bianca, just come home."*

"Home." Bianca laughed bitterly. "I don't have a home anymore, Henry. It disappeared when my parents and my sister died. I thought I could find one with your family, but your mother hates me, and she has every reason to. I ruined everything for her and—"

Henry nipped hard at her arm. He didn't break skin, but he definitely bruised it.

"Ow!" Bianca yelped. The caracara jerked her foot into her chest, just as startled. "Why'd you do that?"

"You're being mean to yourself, and that's...that's not okay! Mama's just scared. That doesn't mean she hates you. I can make her not hate you! You're my friend, and I wanna have another sister." He brushed his head against her hand again. *"Please, come home?"*

Bianca stared down at Henry's cute little face and her heart melted. She might have anticipated Carlos coming after her, but she'd never expected this sweet boy to come track her down. He must have really grown into his eyes and wings to have been able to find her like this. Mother, did his parents even know where he'd gone? She couldn't imagine that Haley would let him leave without her at his side.

Which meant Haley haunted the skies on a warpath to find him.

Bianca sighed and gave Henry a look. "Your mom doesn't know you're out here, does she?"

The red-tailed hawk looked away. "*Um, no?*"

Bianca could only shake her head. Honestly. Well if he'd wanted her to go back, he'd found a way to force her hand. She couldn't leave him out here by himself.

She reached for her jacket and tugged on it until he stepped off. "Well, I guess that means I should get you home."

Henry brightened. "*You mean, you'll come back?*"

"Just to make sure your mom finds you," Bianca said, holding up a finger. Then she curled it and lowered her hand. "And maybe, I'll try talking to your mom again." She pulled the coat on and held out her arm to him. "Hop on."

Henry carefully closed his talons around the coat so he wouldn't hurt her. She silently thanked him for not abusing her arm further. She ran her hand down his feathered head, smiling.

"You really are a handsome bird, but you need to work on those landings."

"*Do you think you can help me? Mama can't land well, and Dad is really busy.*"

Bianca swallowed. "I can try. We'll see what your mom says."

Henry nodded and nestled against her chest. His physical connection warmed her heart, though it made walking through the busy city more challenging. People stared. People asked questions. And Bianca didn't have a phone, otherwise—

Something slammed into Bianca's back and sent her falling forward. Henry jumped off of her coat seconds before Bianca hit the ground. She skidded and swore in pain as her head hit pavement. The blow dazed her, and she lay still for a moment, trying to breathe and get the pain to ebb.

"H-H-Henry?" she slurred. "Are you okay?"

"He's not the one you need to worry about," a voice hissed near her.

Bianca rolled over too quickly and saw the world spin and double. When it came into focus, her heart skipped a beat.

The same vampire who had attacked Gladus, as if conjured by her thoughts, stood across from her. Trish's hand wrapped tightly around Henry's legs, leaving him flailing upside down. He flapped his wings and screeched in protest, but he couldn't get enough leverage to reach up and bite her.

Bianca struggled to her feet. "Let him go!" she barked.

"*Bianca! Help!*" Henry shouted mentally, causing her to wince. Her head already pounded like someone had dropped an anvil on it.

The vampire sneered and shook the young bird. "You already cost me once. It's not going to happen again."

Bianca narrowed her eyes, not understanding what she meant. But as she stared, she noticed bruising around the vampire's neck and face. It almost looked like a rope soaked in mistletoe had been wrapped around her throat and left an angry red necklace behind. The vampire winced as the sun broke through the shifting clouds, and Bianca realized she might not have the sun-resistant lotion on, or at least, not enough. She didn't have a lot of time.

Bianca held up her hands. "What do you want? Look, I know you came after me before. He doesn't need to be involved."

"Oh, I think he does," the vampire growled. She shook Henry. "You're not escaping again. Get down on your knees."

Bianca swallowed hard. She stared at Henry as he trembled, upside down, in the woman's hand.

Slowly, she knelt down on the ground and held up her hands.

"Take your coat off," the vampire barked. "And toss it to the side."

Bianca did so and threw it towards some bushes. When it fell, her little art book tumbled into view. Trish glanced at it briefly before she reached into her pocket with her free hand and threw something. Handcuffs skittered across the concrete to Bianca's side.

"Put those on, hands in front. I'll know if the cuffs don't click shut."

Bianca swore inwardly. Damnit, the vampire had come prepared. She glanced briefly left and right, but she didn't spot her Hunter henchmen. That didn't mean they weren't far behind. Haley and the others had to know about Henry's disappearance by now. Could she stall long enough for them to get here and save him?

"Put them on!" the vampire shouted and shook Henry again.

The caracara hissed in protest at Henry's rough treatment. Bianca shared her rage, but her hands were tied.

Bianca grabbed the cuffs and locked her left wrist. She put the right cuff on and started to shut it. She left it just a little loose, but a glare from the vampire told her she wouldn't get away with that. She finished the lock and settled her hands in her lap. "Please, just let him go. He doesn't need to be part of this."

"I can't have you running away again," the vampire said. She carried Henry like some broken toy and curled her finger. "Get up and come to me. Slowly."

Bianca stood and kept her hands up to show her submission. She walked towards the vampire and glanced briefly at Henry. She wanted to speak to him, to comfort him, and to tell him her plan. But she couldn't risk him messing it up. Still, she touched her caracara and sent the bird into his mind to ease his fears. She found his little red-tailed hawk huddled, looking more like a puffed-up cotton ball than a fierce predator. The caracara preened the hawk's feathers. "*It's going to be okay.*"

Bianca made it to the vampire's side and took a shaky breath. "See? No one has to get hurt. He's—"

Bianca struck, faster than the vampire could move. She pushed her talons through her fingers and brought them down on the vampire's arm with full force. At the same time, her caracara bolted from Henry's mind and flew into Trish's, clawing, attacking her mentally.

The woman shrieked in pain as blood wept from her wounds. Henry fell, but Bianca caught him so he didn't hit his head on the ground. She turned and flung him into the air. "Fly! Fly home!" she shouted to him.

"Bitch!" the vampire hissed.

Bianca fisted her hands and brought them around, cracking the vampire in the face. Trish staggered to the side, but Bianca didn't let her go. For a moment, her vision went red as she thought of Gladus and the gun the vampire had shoved into her stomach. Gladus' death stained the vampire's hands crimson. It was Trish's fault that Bianca could never go back to her new home.

She screeched in rage and pounced on Trish, taking her to the ground under her weight. She could hear Henry flying in the air behind her as she brought her fists down again, her caracara screaming her own outrage into Trish's head.

"*Bianca! We have to run!*"

"Henry, go!" Bianca shouted. "I'll follow!" She didn't know if that would be true, but she could distract the vampire long enough for him to get away. Her caracara dug her talons into Trish's mind, causing mental damage like no other lycan could.

Henry hovered a moment longer then flew off, leaving Bianca to pin the vampire on the ground.

Bianca panted, her hands aching from striking the other woman. The vampire cowered beneath her, hands up to protect her head. Bianca looked at her in disdain. She flipped the vampire over and pressed the chain of the cuffs against her throat. "*Why*?" Bianca growled. "Why did you betray Gladus like that?"

"You don't understand," the vampire whispered. "They'll kill my coven if I don't obey. They want you, and they wanted Gladus gone. I had to do what they said."

Bianca leaned back slowly and frowned. Was it true? Was this woman as much a victim of these Hunters as Bianca? She glanced over her shoulder to make sure that Henry had made it far away enough that Trish wouldn't be able to get him. When she looked back, the vampire smashed a rock against Bianca's face.

Stars exploded in her eyes. She collapsed backwards with a cry of pain and grabbed her face. Her bird fell out of the vampire's mind and returned to her. Warm, sticky blood flowed onto her fingers. Bianca tried to staunch it, but the vampire thwarted even that. The woman grabbed Bianca and jerked her cuffed wrists above her head. Trish straddled her, keeping her pinned, and grasped her throat with her free hand.

"I'm not letting my coven die because of *you*," the vampire growled. Her pupils dilated, the red irises growing a deeper crimson and swirling with power. "Sleep. It'll all be over soon."

"No, no!" Bianca shouted. She refused to die like this! She shoved her caracara against Trish's attack, but the bird found herself snatched up in Trish's magic.

Bianca blinked furiously, trying to ignore the charm settling over her. She bit her lip until it bled, struggling to fight through the exhaustion creeping through her and fogging her mind. The vampire leaned down, repeating her command, and though Bianca wanted nothing more than to smash her face into the vampire's, her eyes glazed, and she fell asleep.

Chapter 15
Remembrance

Haley

"Henry!" Haley shrieked, her cry turning into her barn owl's screech. She stared at the empty bed covered in her son's recently discarded clothing. Blue and yellow polka-dotted curtains flapped around the open window, and she knew, she knew in her heart that her son, her sweet baby, had flown away. He had to have gone after Bianca. Again… *again* that girl disrupted Haley's household.

Haley yanked her cardigan off and tossed it on the bed. She would not leave her son to roam the skies alone. She closed her eyes and started to shift in her chair. A pretty brown and star-lit pattern started to appear on her skin before feathers protruded through the flesh. Her head shrunk, her eyes grew wider. Her mouth twisted until it turned into a sharp beak. She shrank down in her chair as she heard footsteps pounding into the room.

"Haley?" Carlos asked. He moved around the chair as she finished her transformation. "What are you doing?"

Haley breathed heavily as her lower limbs turned into barn owl legs and feet. But they were just as broken and limp as her human body. She flopped down onto her belly, barely able to hold herself up. "*He went after Bianca,*" she told her mate mentally. "*I'm going to find my son.*"

"Dios mio," Carlos whispered and looked at the window. "It would be better if we went together. Paytah and Kaitlyn can help us."

"*We don't need the help of werewolves. They can't smell our child from the sky.*"

"No, but they may be able to pick up Bianca's scent, and where she is, we're sure to find Henry."

"*I'm not waiting that long. You go with the wolves. I'm going to find our son.*" Haley swiveled her head around to look at her husband fiercely. "*Now are you going to help me outside or not?*" She could take off from her chair, but it would be awkward, and a threat loomed of her hitting the side of her son's bed before she built up enough air to lift her up.

Carlos' shoulders slumped, but he didn't argue. Instead, he gently cupped her under her belly and brought her to the window. "Be careful, mi amor. Keep your mind open to me. Let me know if you find him."

"*I will.*" Haley shifted and prepared herself. Carlos pulled her close, kissed the back of her feathered neck, then flung her out the window.

Haley spread her mighty owl wings. She blinked wildly in the sunlight, trying to adjust to it. She flew better at night, but that didn't mean she couldn't fly during the day. She banked right and curved around her family's two-story house, spotting Paytah and Kaitlyn outside, then flew off into the distance, searching for the familiar red tint of her son's tail.

She couldn't believe she might lose another child. Hunters were murderous, hateful people who didn't care if they destroyed a family with their actions. They'd ruined hers, and Haley couldn't let it go. She remembered what they did every time she woke in the morning. Every time she looked at the picture of her daughter.

Her mind drifted, going back to that terrible day when those monsters had destroyed her world.

***

Haley knelt in the family garden, pulling up carrots and beans. The sun made sweat bead on the back of her neck, but the big flower hat that her granddaughter had gotten for her on Mother's Day protected her head. She smiled at the small girl beside her as the child pulled at weeds by accident instead of the vegetables they'd been working so hard to grow.

Haley grasped her granddaughter's hand gently. "Here, Willow.

Pick this one." She placed the girl's hand over a bean.

Willow laughed and pulled it off of the vine. "It smells good, Grammy," she chirped.

Haley smiled, her eyes softening. Willow had just turned three, and she bore the beautiful golden hair of her father. Her skin tone was slightly darker than her mother's, her eyes a deep riveting brown. No other child could hold a torch to Willow's beauty, but Haley admitted her bias. It was her granddaughter after all.

"Is she pulling up the weeds again?" Andria asked.

Haley looked over her shoulder as her daughter hung up damp sheets. Their dryer took terrible care of sheets and blankets and forced the family to hang them in the warm summer sun to dry. Andria shook the purple fabric out, Willow's favorite, and tucked black hair behind her ear. Her darker complexion made her look more like her father than Haley, but Haley could see herself in her daughter's brown eyes and thicker lips.

"Oh, they need to come up anyway," Haley said and turned back to her granddaughter. "What if Grammy makes a bean casserole tonight. Would you like that, my egg?"

"Yeah!" Willow put the bean in the basket and started to grab more in her chubby hands. She scuffed dirt on her yellow sandals, but she didn't seem to mind.

Andria sighed and put her hand on her hip, next to an empty holster. She would be on duty in a couple of hours, and though Andria wore her officer attire, Haley didn't allow guns in the house, especially not around Willow. She had nightmares of Willow grabbing the gun and shooting herself or someone else. Haley refused to lend life to her nightmares.

Watching Andria go off to work each night left Haley in a shaky, stomach-twisted state until her daughter arrived home in one piece. Legion had offered training sessions to help her become a parahuman police-force member. She scouted the Chicagoland area and kept parahumans in line, and Hunters off their back. Firefights left Haley in near hysteria whenever she got the call, but Andria was a tough bird, and though she didn't always come back without a scratch, she did always come home.

Haley stroked Willow's golden tresses and leaned forward. "Keep picking beans, sweetie. I'm going to help your Mama."

"Okay!" Willow made herself at home in the middle of the garden and continued picking.

Haley dusted the dirt off her pants as she headed for her daughter. "That bust is tonight, isn't it?" she asked quietly.

Andria paused, her hands reaching towards the sheet. Her shoulders slumped before she went back to straightening it out. "You were listening on the other line again, weren't you?"

"You were getting quiet. That usually only happens when something big goes down. And you asked me to watch Willow." She hesitated. "Mitchel is going with you, isn't he?"

"Yes," Andria replied. "It's a big one, Mom. We heard about parahuman trafficking in the area. Hunters are buying them and selling them for parts or making them fight one another to the death. We finally have it narrowed down. We have to strike tonight before they figure out we have a spy in there."

"Andria—"

"I know what you're going to say," Andria said, turning towards her. The purple sheet waved in front of them for a moment before Andria pushed it to the side. "I know you're scared. I am too. It's going to be a big, *big*, bust, but we're sending in a force, and it has to be done, Mom. People in the District are getting afraid. Loved ones are going missing, turning up dead. This is supposed to be a safe haven, not one filled with fear and distrust. I have Gladus' blessing." She picked up another sheet. "Werewolves are having disputes with vampires, avians with felines. Everyone is uptight, thinking that one of the other groups is killing their people. It's easier to think that than to believe there are Hunters milling about, snatching up parahumans on the street or from their beds."

Haley moved around the sheet and touched her daughter's elbow. "But does it have to be *you*?" she asked. "You're a mother. You have a daughter who needs you. If you and Mitchel both go... If you both...." She couldn't bring herself to say it.

Andria leaned forward and kissed her mother on the forehead. "Willow will have *you*. Besides, if it's not me, then it'll be some other mom, or dad, or someone's child. I've been trained for this, Mom. This is what I *want* to do. And I'm proud to defend the community." She picked up the basket and brought it to another line. She draped a new sheet over, smoothing it down with her hands.

"You and Dad always taught me to do what I thought was right. Well, that's defending our community. I want to make it safe for Willow so she doesn't have to grow up walking the streets in fear. She's an avian. People pick on us because they think we're weaker, but we're not. We're strong. We're united. We are a people who know how to love and respect our families better than anyone else does, because we have the bond." She touched her head, and Haley closed her eyes, feeling her daughter's beautiful barn owl flap into her head.

Oh, Carlos had been jealous when he'd found out his daughter's bird had taken after Haley. Haley sent her own barn owl to her daughter and preened her head feathers gently.

Behind her, Willow, and someone else laughed. She looked over her shoulder as her niece, Anita, ran outside with a ball. She put it next to Willow and pushed it to her. The girls tossed the ball back and forth, giggling.

Haley smiled to herself and turned to her daughter who wore the same grin. Andria's eyes softened as she nodded to the two girls.

"I'm doing this for *them*, so they have a chance to live happy, safe lives. This community is always going to need people to come together and do the right thing, even if they're afraid. I'm afraid, I won't deny that, and so is Mitchel, but that's not going to stop us."

Haley reached out and touched her daughter's cheek. "I know, baby. And I'm so proud of you. I just worry."

"Heh, you wouldn't be my mom if you didn't worry," Andria said. She leaned her cheek into her mother's hand affectionately. Her owl snuggled close to Haley's. "It'll be okay, Mom. We've got —"

Five explosive pops broke the peaceful summer air. Haley jumped and looked out across the street where a car had pulled up. Two men sat inside, a gun held in each of their hands.

Andria's owl jerked back in pain and collapsed in Haley's mind at the same time Andria cried out and staggered, clutching her side. "Mom! The kids!" she shouted, her voice laced in pain.

Haley didn't hesitate. She rounded on the girls and ran towards them while Andria reached for the gun that wasn't there. Willow sobbed, and Anita clapped her hands over her ears. Haley dove at them and grabbed them both, shoving them inside the house. "Stay in there!" she shouted. "Get Carlos!" She slammed the door and turned back at the same time a bullet slammed into her daughter's chest.

Andria pitched backwards, blood splattering across the clean hanging linen. She fell to the ground, the shots still ringing out. Haley screamed in grief and terror as she ran towards her daughter, heedless of the bullets. Andria held out her hand towards her as if to tell her to stop, but Haley didn't. She flung herself to the ground and covered her daughter with her body, blocking her from the bullets.

"M-M-Mama," Andria's voice trembled.

"I got you, baby girl, I got you," Haley wept, holding her close. She wiped blood and sweat off of her daughter's pale face. "Hold on. Papa will get help. He'll—"

Pain shot through her spine, her legs, her entire body. Haley screamed and bowed her head over her daughter's, trying to fight through the blinding agony

"Mama..." Andria said again, her voice fading.

Haley looked down at her daughter, her first born, her *only* born. Andria forced a faint smile and touched her mother's cheek. The sound of gunshots had ceased until all Haley heard was her daughter's rasping breath. "It's okay. It's going to be...okay."

Haley grabbed her hand and held it tightly. "I know. Just keep breathing. Papa's going to be here soon." But even as she spoke, she could feel Andria's owl flickering in and out of her head. Her own bird wrapped her wings around the injured owl and held her close. "Andria, baby, please..."

"See?" Andria whispered. "Gotta come together... Gotta help each other. Tell Willow, I love her. Tell... Tell...."

"Andria," Haley said in a choked sob. She held her daughter's limp hand and looked into her wavering eyes. "Look at me. You tell Willow yourself. You're not leaving me. You're not leaving *us*."

Andria just smiled, a smile that froze on her lips as her eyes rolled back into her head. The owl twitched in Haley's mind. It flickered, once, twice, then vanished as her daughter exhaled a final time.

Haley pressed her ear against Andria's heart and listened. Silence. No beat, no sign of life.

"Andria..." She shook her daughter. "Andria!" she screamed until her cry turned into an agonized screech.

***

Haley's wings faltered as the ghostly sounds of gunshots rang through her mind. How many times had the Hunters shot at her daughter before they left her for dead?

The whole operation fell apart after that. The Hunters had gotten word that forces were closing in on them, and they'd decided to take care of some of the District police force before they could act. Mitchel had been targeted too, but he had been in the wrong place, stuck at the bank instead of at the cafe where he'd arranged to meet a contact.

His contact had died gruesomely.

The officers had still carried out the operation, but by then, the Hunters had created enough of a distraction that they'd taken their *property* with them, leaving little evidence behind of what they'd actually been doing beneath the surface of Chicago's streets.

The Purple Door District had mourned the deaths of the parahumans who had perished at the hands of the Hunters. Gladus had been there to officiate the funeral and lay the dead to rest. Still healing from the bullet wound in her back, Haley had been unable to attend the funeral and say a final farewell to her daughter. Even after all these years, she'd never visited Andria's grave.

Mitchel had gone mad after that. Losing his wife and several of his closest friends shattered him.

He packed up his bags a week later, said goodbye to Carlos and Haley, and left with Willow crying in his arms.

They'd had little communication with Mitchel since then, though Haley did manage to get the rare e-mail or two from her granddaughter, now a beautiful, though sassy teen. Mitchel, Haley believed, blamed her for not allowing Andria to wear her gun around the house. Maybe if she'd had it, she could have fought back. Maybe she would have survived.

Mitchel could blame her all he wanted; no one could beat Haley down more than she could. She *hated* herself for failing to save her daughter. And to feel Andria's bird die in her mind...she'd never recover from that. So, she focused on *her* family and *her* family alone.

To have the sanctity of her home threatened by bringing Bianca in had almost been too much for her. Maybe if Bianca hadn't been hunted, Haley would have considered it, but not now. Not when the Hunters had murdered Gladus and might grab hold of her son. She would *not* lose another child.

Haley headed towards a park she frequented with her children.

She looked around and reached out with her mind, her mental voice carrying only so far.

"*Henry! Henry, it's Mama! Answer me!*"

No reply. Haley panted as she flew. She hadn't flown this far or long in quite some time. Normally she rested between flight spurts, but landing proved a challenge, and it could injure her. Then what could she do for her son? He needed her.

"*Henry!*" she shouted again and banked to the left, circling the city. She didn't see anything unusual and flew off to another one. The city blurred beneath her as she flew, though she managed to catch sight of Paytah and Kaitlyn headed towards the park. A flash of sunlight suddenly stung her eyes and she struggled to focus. She reached out for her son again and again.

"*Mama!*"

Haley jerked around and looked back and forth, trying to spot her son's familiar form. "*Henry, I'm here! Come to me, Baby.*"

"*Mama!*" his mental voice called, a little louder now.

Haley turned back towards the new park and spotted movement ahead of her. She flapped towards it, her wings aching. She swooped and caught a thermal, helping to lift her up a bit. And there, several yards from her, flew Henry. He flapped along, his feathers mussed and his head whipping back and forth as if searching for something. She assumed he was looking for her, but the moment he met her eyes, he looked away again.

"*Henry!*" she called and flew to him. She circled around him, checking him over. "*Are you hurt? What were you thinking?*"

"*Bianca! They took Bianca!*" He panted and started to lose altitude. They were avians, yes, but he needed to build up his endurance, and Haley didn't have much of her own. He circled and headed towards the closest tree. "*I have to land, Mama.*" He stretched out his mighty-taloned feet and grasped a branch. His talons cracked off bark, sending it clacking through the empty branches to the melting snow below.

Haley swallowed and searched for a section of the tree where she might be able to land without severely hurting herself. She spotted an old nest and went towards it. It wouldn't quite fit her body, but it might still fulfill her purpose. She tried to bend herself, to swing her legs forward. But a branch caught her wing and sent her spinning into the tree. She hit the nest hard and started to slide backwards.

She fell out and crashed down between three of the branches before she came to rest in a nest of fine twisted branches beneath her. Haley flopped onto her stomach and spread out her wings, panting. She *hated* landing.

Henry flapped awkwardly as he landed in a branch near her. He appeared ruffled and exhausted, but otherwise she could see no obvious injuries on him. "*Mama!*"

"*Oh, thank the Mother,*" Haley sighed. She tried to get closer, but Henry quickly moved to her instead. She preened his feathers and clacked her beak lightly against his, inspecting him over. "*Are you okay? What happened?*"

Henry fluffed up and looked down. "*I found Bianca. She caught me when I fell, and then I tried to make her come back with me. She was gonna, Mama. She was gonna.*"

Haley glanced below, but there was no sign of the avian. Maybe she'd done the wise thing and flown off, leaving Haley and her family alone. "*She left?*"

"*No!*" Henry shook his head and puffed again, dancing a little on the branch. "*A vampire, that one Dad doesn't like. Trish? She attacked us! She grabbed me and shook me and made Bianca cuff herself. She said she'd hurt me if Bianca didn't listen.*"

Haley hissed in rage as only a barn owl could. Trish dared do that to her child? To *her* little baby? The vampire would not live to breathe another day once Haley got a hold of her. But then she realized that, though Trish had threatened Henry, he remained free and in one piece. "*Go on.*"

"*Bianca fought her! She saved me, and she told me to fly home! Trish hurt her, Mama. She took her away. I landed in the tree over there and watched Trish run off with Bianca on her back.*" He flexed his wing towards a nearby tree. "*We have to help her.*"

Haley could only stare at her son. She knew Bianca and Henry had bonded, but she never expected the other avian to put her life at risk for Henry. Especially not after Haley's outburst. And for that, shame engulfed her. Here Haley had been afraid that Bianca would bring the Hunters down on her family. And while Henry had indeed been caught, it had only been because he'd followed Bianca after Haley's hateful words.

She closed her eyes and swallowed hard. Andria would be so ashamed of her. Her daughter had insisted they shared the responsibility to take care of each parahuman, and what had Haley done but turn the needy away? She'd betrayed her daughter and betrayed her own heart.

"*Mama?*"

Haley opened her eyes and looked at her son. She sighed and preened him again. "*We'll tell your father. Paytah and Kaitlyn are following. They'll find us.*" She opened up her mind and reached out, sending a thought towards Paytah and Kaitlyn. They wouldn't be able to respond in their human forms, but they could at least hear her directions.

"*I found Henry. We're in the trees in the park.*" She sent them a mental image of what the park looked like, unsure if Paytah would know the name of it or not. "*Tread carefully. Trish was here and kidnapped Bianca.*"

"*I hear you,*" Kaitlyn's soft voice spoke in her head. "*We're on our way. Paytah's human. I'm werewolf.*"

Haley sighed in surprised relief. It meant she didn't have to keep reaching out to them over and over again. She settled in the trees with her son and searched the ground. Some people ran through the park, oblivious to what had happened there not even an hour ago.

She almost reached out for Kaitlyn again until she spotted Paytah jogging towards them with a pretty golden dog at his side. She could have easily been mistaken for a husky instead of a wolf. Kaitlyn sniffed the air then trotted over to the tree where Haley and Henry hid.

Paytah looked up at them. He held out his arm and clicked his tongue to Henry.

Haley nudged him. "*Fly down to Paytah. I'll follow in a moment.*"

Henry shifted along the branch, tail bobbing. He eyed Paytah's arm, his flesh protected by a leather jacket. He flexed his wings and tail then flew down. He wouldn't win the award for most graceful landing, but he managed to get to Paytah. The werewolf patted Henry's feathers down gently and looked up.

"Are you all right?"

"*Yes. Once I get out of the tree I can fly back home. We need to talk to Carlos. I think this is a lot bigger than we thought.*"

Paytah nodded. "Let's go back. We'll—"

"*Wait!*" Henry shouted in their heads. Paytah grimaced, Kaitlyn whined, and Haley hissed at the force of his thoughts. Yes, teaching Henry how to project his voice moved to the top of their lesson chart.

Henry looked around then fluttered down to the grass. He waddled, rather than strutted, through the snow and searched around until he stopped next to something in the dirt. He tapped it with his beak. *"Bianca drew in this. We have to bring it. Maybe it'll help us."*

Paytah and Kaitlyn followed him. The man swept up the small notebook, a feather fluttering out of it and to the ground. Haley leaned forward sharply at the sight of it. A black *and* white swan feather? With Bianca? But Bianca was a caracara. Why would she have a swan feather? What if the Mother of Avians had visited her?

Haley's guilt rose as Paytah looked through the book.

"Anything?" she asked.

Paytah nodded. "She drew something. Come on, let's get back. Henry, you stay on my arm. Kaitlyn, beside me. Haley?"

"I'll meet you there. Take care of my son." Haley angled herself in the tree and took a breath. She used her wings to push herself out, and she folded them as she fell through the branches. Two feet from the ground, she snapped her wings out and caught the wind. It carried her up and back into the air. She circled long enough to watch Paytah help Henry back up on his arm. She didn't want to leave her baby behind, but with two werewolves to guard him, she knew he'd be okay.

Haley flew back towards her home, staying high above the city and trying to remain well out of sight. She couldn't shake the guilt twisting in her stomach. If the Mother of Avians had visited Bianca, then the girl was more special than she'd even thought. She needed protection, and Haley had failed her, and thus failed the Mother.

Her mind went to Trish, and she growled inwardly. The vampire had betrayed them, betrayed Gladus. She'd helped kill the Violet Marshall, she'd attacked Henry, and now she had an avian in her clutches likely for those damnable Hunters. Why? Did Joseph have no control over his vampires? She sincerely considered calling upon the coven leader then and there, but that would waste more time than they had. Hunters moved quickly, except for those who had trading and fighting pits. Normally their targets ended up dead within a day of being found.

She headed for Henry's open window once she spotted her

home. She flew through it and into a cloud of vampire stench. Haley's heart skipped a beat in fear and rage. Had Trish come back to take care of the rest of her family? Where were Carlos and Madison?

She flew into the living room. She spotted her husband and daughter sitting on the couch while two people towered over them. They reeked of vampire. She flew at them, knowing that her talons would do little damage. She could still try to crash into them and give her mate and daughter a chance to escape.

Carlos saw and heard her first. He sprang to his feet, catching her in his arms before she hit the black man with dreadlocks standing beside a pale, blonde-haired woman.

"Haley! Don't!" he shouted. He held her gently in his arms and straightened out her wings, pressing them to her sides. "Stop, they came here to find Trish, not to hurt us."

Haley panted and glared at the two vampires. The man inclined his head politely to her while the woman glared down her nose at her with icy blue eyes. Her golden hair strained in a tight bun that made her face and cheekbones look that much more severe.

Carlos rubbed the feathers along Haley's neck, easing some of her anger and tension. "Haley? Did you find him?"

Haley flicked her tail feathers. "*Yes. He was in the park. Paytah is coming back with him and Kaitlyn.*"

"What about Bianca?"

Haley stared pointedly at the two vampires. "*Your coven sister kidnapped her for Hunters. She helped murder Gladus.*"

The male vampire nodded. "We know. News of Gladus' death traveled quickly to our coven, especially when we determined that Trish might be at fault. Joseph sent us to look for her. Fraula and I were in the area when your mate called Joseph to tell him of what had transpired. Carlos feared your child might have been swept up by Trish as well. Joseph asked us to come here to see if we could work together to solve this Hunter problem."

"*And vampire problem,*" Haley snapped back. "*Does your leader have no control over his minions?*"

Fraula bared sharp fangs. "*Careful*, bird. You risk a snapped neck for insulting our duke."

The other vampire held out his arm. "Calm yourself, Fraula." He gave her a look then touched his chest. "My name is Saul, and this is Fraula. We wish to help, not cause problems. If you have a vampire working against you, it is best to have a vampire helping you as well. Our duke would like her returned to him, *alive*."

Haley snorted. "*And why should we agree to that? She threatened to kill my son in order to kidnap one of our avians.*"

Saul touched his forehead with two fingers as if to draw in patience then sighed. "And again, for this, we're sorry. But I must insist. You can be assured that Trish will be punished for her transgressions, but this is a vampire issue."

Haley jerked her head up in anger. "*Avians were attacked, therefore, it is also an avian issue.*"

"Haley," Carlos said. He brought her over to her chair and settled her into it gently. "Let's wait for Paytah and talk. I think you'll want to hear what they have to say. Anita's keeping an eye on things down below." He looked at the vampires. "I'll make tea. Madison, come help, Daddy."

***

They waited some time for Paytah to make it back to the house with Henry and Kaitlyn. But they didn't arrive alone. As Carlos let the werewolf in, Haley jerked in surprise at the sight of the dark-haired magus behind him.

"Tess?" she asked.

"I thought she could be of some help, too," Paytah explained. "The ward is going to be out for blood right now, and if we need help locating Bianca, Tess may be able to provide that service."

Tess snorted. "You do realize I'm not an upper-class magus, right? Gladus might have been able to pick a needle out of a haystack, but I still see straw." When Haley gave her a tired look, Tess held up her hands. "I still have tricks up my sleeves, though. Let me see what you've got to give me."

While the others got settled, Carlos took Henry into his room to help him change back to human and get into his clothing. Her son looked exhausted when he came out. Haley held out her hand to him, and he went to her eagerly and crawled into her lap. Haley held him close and kissed his ears and shoulder, breathing in his scent. "I have you, baby," she said quietly.

"I'm sorry I couldn't help Bianca, Mama."

"You were really brave," Haley assured him. "We'll find her and bring her home."

Carlos got tea made for everyone, and they sat around the room, looking warily at one another. Paytah sat close to Kaitlyn who remained in her werewolf form.

Saul and Fraula sat on a stool and in a chair respectively. Saul's broad frame dwarfed the stool humorously, but he didn't complain. Carlos perched on the couch with Madison at his side and Haley to the left of him. Tess lounged on the floor, cross-legged. She pulled a black bag around in front of her and started to take out a few items, mostly herbs and vials of some kind of substance. Bianca's book lay open on the table with the image of the tree sketched in the center.

Carlos took a breath. "So, Trish has been acting against coven interests for a while and has somehow gotten caught up with Hunters," he summarized.

Saul nodded. "I don't believe she did it of her own free will. We found the body of one of our vampires, Gavin, floating in the river a day ago. He'd been shot in the head. Gavin spent much time with Trish, so if Trish landed herself in trouble, Gavin was likely the only one privy to it." He sighed. "Gavin was a good man. He tried to help Trish adapt to being a vampire, but she's always had trouble. She can be easily swayed."

Carlos lifted his mug of tea and curled his lip. "There was no love lost between her and Gladus."

"We know," Saul agreed. "But unless the Hunters forced her, I do not think she'd kill Gladus. She might not have liked the Marshall, but she knew the benefit of having Gladus lead the District." He glanced at Fraula then back to the others. "The District is already in chaos. We've heard word of her death. Some people are vying to be the next Violet Marshall. Others are taking this opportunity to act out. A few werewolves already robbed a feline establishment." He held up his hand to Paytah upon the werewolf's sharp look and Kaitlyn's growl. "Not of your pack. Other parahumans are threatening to leave without Gladus here."

Carlos frowned. "I need to check on my Cloister. If any avians cause problems, I'll have words with them. But for now, we need to focus on finding Bianca. We find her, we find the Hunters and Trish. We need to end this and rescue Bianca."

Paytah nodded in agreement. "If Bianca is a seer, then her visions could help our enemies, and we can't have that. It makes her dangerous." He sighed. "My family will take her in if need be once we've freed her. We—"

"No," Haley said, shaking her head. "She's an avian. She should stay with us."

Carlos, Kaitlyn, Paytah, Madison, and Henry all looked at her in disbelief.

Haley hugged Henry against her chest and settled her chin on his shoulder. "What I said to her, what I did, was wrong. I spoke out of turn. I was afraid for my family especially after what happened to Andria." She gave Paytah a look. "I may not agree with what you said about me and my daughter, but you were right to call me out. I was too harsh on Bianca. It's not her fault the Hunters are after her, and it is our duty to protect those like us. We have enough problems with humans. We don't need to be fighting amongst ourselves." She looked at the group. "How do we find her?"

Fraula gestured to the art book. "Her drawing is the key. Carlos said this is different from ones she made before, yes? That this has more detail? Provides a name?"

Carlos nodded. "Madison noticed the differences." He smiled proudly at his daughter. She blushed and ducked her head against his shoulder. "So we have a tree named Eden, and we have parahumans getting touched with magic. What does it mean? Where are they?" He looked at Tess. "Can you work any magic to help us out?"

Tess rocked forward onto her knees, looking at the art pad. She ran her finger over the word and pressed her lips together. "*Maybe.* I have an age-old device that could probably help."

Haley tensed, clutching Henry a little harder. "It's not dangerous to the children is it?"

"Only if you let them stare at it too long, and it rots their brains," Tess said offhandedly. She reached into her back pocket and pulled out a cellphone. Haley frowned while the magus typed into it and clicked through pages. "Ah," Tess said at last and set the phone down on top of the drawing. She wiggled her fingers. "Abracadabra. Eden Florist Shop."

Haley leaned forward with the others. Sure enough, the logo on the screen nearly mirrored the Eden plaque on the tree.

Fraula scoffed. "I hardly think Hunters would be hiding in a florist shop."

"Maybe they would when it's been closed for four months,"

Tess replied. "Last information they have on it is it's meant to be demolished. And maybe if it's not the actual florist shop, it could be the warehouse where they used to keep all of the flowers that were being prepared for delivery. Out of sight. Out of mind. And gonna guess there's a basement there."

Haley glanced at her mate. "That might be our best bet at this point. We don't have Gladus to perform a spell to try to find them. And I don't know a magus who is strong enough to do that."

"Well, thanks for that," Tess said with a roll of her eyes. "I still managed to put us in the right direction with, *oooo weeee oooo*, the magic of the internet." She waved her hands over her cell like a cauldron despite Haley's deadpan expression.

"Tess, thank you, but that's enough," Paytah admonished. He touched Kaitlyn's back gently and ran his hand through her golden fur. "Then we should go. Between the four of us, I think we can help free Bianca."

"Four?" Carlos, Haley, and Tess asked together.

Kaitlyn sat up on her haunches and glared at Paytah. He stared back at her. "Well, it would be better for Haley to stay behind. With all due respect, you are a powerful flyer, Haley, but we're going to be on the ground. Tess, your father would kill me if I let you go."

"I can defend myself, thank you," she retorted.

Paytah grunted at her and looked at the golden wolf. "And Kaitlyn, you're not trained for battle."

"*I can defend myself, too,*" Kaitlyn argued. "*You, Rozene, and Nick have all been training me to fight. Besides, if you, Fraula, Saul, and Carlos are busy taking care of the Hunters and Trish, someone needs to help drag Bianca out of there. I can do that. You need my help.*"

"I—"

"*I* want *to help.*" Kaitlyn stared hard into Paytah's eyes, making Haley suspect they were having a private conversation together. The alpha sighed heavily after a long moment and placed a hand on her head.

"Very well. Five of us."

Tess cleared her throat. "Um, no, I'm not sitting this out. You have at least two Hunters *and* a vampire out there, plus a captive. If they hurt her, you're going to need someone who can heal her." She waved her hand. "Fire magus and healer, right here. Besides, if we run into worse trouble, I can get my dad there pronto."

Paytah considered then breathed out deeply. "You pups are trying my patience," he grumbled, but when he posed no other argument, Tess gave a silent fist pump.

Kaitlyn licked her muzzle and looked around. "*Forgive me for stating the obvious, but shouldn't we bring this to Legion?*"

Fraula snorted. "Legion's policy is to shoot first, ask questions later. They take too long to get where they need to go. And if they think Trish is behind this, they'll kill her instead of giving her a fair trial. No, Duke Joseph explicitly said to keep Legion out of this."

"If you want to keep Bianca alive, the vamp's probably right," Tess added. "Seers go in; they don't come out."

Paytah squinted at her suspiciously. "You seemed dead set on taking her out when she was at my house."

Tess shrugged. "The pack's rubbing off on me. Let's just say I didn't want her spouting a vision of someone's death."

Haley held Henry tighter and looked at Madison as she clung to her father. Normally Haley would have insisted that Carlos stay there too, but she had to learn to let go. Andria would have been at the head of the group; Carlos could do that now.

Carlos rose. "Then we should go. We'll take Bianca's book with us in case it provides more information that we didn't have before."

Madison reached for his hand. "Daddy, don't go."

Carlos picked her up and hugged her tightly. "I have to, little bird. I need to bring your new sister home."

Haley reached out an arm to her daughter. "Come here, Maddy. It'll be okay."

Madison tucked her head under her father's chin. She hugged him back tightly then went to her mother when he put her down. Carlos walked over to Haley's side and leaned down, pressing his lips warmly against hers.

"I love you," he whispered.

"I love you, too. Just come back. Both you and Bianca."

Carlos pressed his head against hers and held her and their children tightly. "I'll send Anita and her girlfriend up to keep you all company."

And to offer them extra protection, Haley knew.

"Can we stop wasting time?" Fraula sighed loudly. "Your bird could already be dead."

Haley reluctantly released her mate. She smiled at Carlos then watched as he and the other parahumans headed out the door. Haley held Henry close then glanced at the knife block in the kitchen.

Her smile turned into a grim line.

If anyone came after her family, she'd protect them. No one would take them away from her.

Chapter 16
Ether

Bianca

Bianca woke slowly, her neck and head aching like she'd been thrown into a brick wall. Her head bowed over her body. She rolled it back until it thudded against wood. She sat upright, but she couldn't move and couldn't see. Something covered her eyes. Her wrists and ankles were bound down by rope. When she struggled, it burned and caused her to hiss in pain.

Henbane-soaked ropes.

The vampire must have taken her to the Hunters already. She moaned and shook her head to clear it. Dear Mother, she hoped that Henry had escaped. Trish had seemed more interested in her than Henry anyway.

"Boss, she's waking up," a familiar male voice called.

"Good," came a silky, deep reply. "Riccardo, you can take the blindfold off. We don't need it."

Bianca listened as someone approached her. Hands grabbed at the knot of her blindfold, tearing at delicate hairs tied into the cloth, before they yanked it free. Bianca blinked a few times to adjust to the light of the room. There wasn't much to see. She looked around slowly, finding herself in a cold, stone area held up by a couple beams. A sniff brought the scent of mold, water, and earth to her nose. Yes, probably a basement, though the earthy smell made it a bit hard to place.

She looked down at the wooden chair she'd been tethered to.

Her wrists were secured firmly to the arms. More ropes wound around her waist and chest, so she couldn't try to yank herself free. The chair had also been bolted to the floor making tipping out of the question. When she glanced at her right arm, she noticed a needle sticking in it. The other Hunter sat drawing blood out of her arm. He glanced up at her, his bushy mustache twitching above his lips as he smiled.

"Good morning, sunshine," he said.

Bianca tried to struggle, but they'd taken extra precaution to make sure that she couldn't move her right arm either. The needle and syringe looked strange. Magic pulsed dully around it as it sucked her blood through a clouded tube. Even her blood looked odd. It appeared red, of course, but she swore she saw dark flecks in it. But maybe Trish had hit her head harder than she thought.

Riccardo lit a cigarette and leaned against a pillar, smirking at her. Bianca glared back. She didn't see the other man who had spoken, but she did spot Trish in a corner of the room. To Bianca's surprise, the vampire sat chained by her wrists and throat. A muzzle tied her mouth shut, preventing her from using her fangs. Her face bore bloody, fresh bruises, and Bianca couldn't tell if they were from the fight, or the Hunters. The vampire glanced at her then turned away and leaned against the wall, holding herself.

"It's good to finally meet you," the odd voice said again.

Bianca searched the shadows. "Who are you? What do you want from me?"

"Such *tired* questions," the man sighed. The shadows near Trish seemed to shift and a figure stepped forward.

Bianca could make out some of the veins in his arms through his pale skin. He hardly looked a threat, but his eyes suggested otherwise. They burned and glimmered with purple magic. Ebony hair spilled down his head, held in place by a single purple cord. His black and violet robes caressed the stone floor as he walked towards her. "Who I am is of no consequence, not right now. And what I want, I'm already getting." He nodded to the Hunter at her arm.

The Hunter pulled the needle out and pressed a cotton ball over the wound, staunching the blood. He wrapped the wound and brought the blood over to the strange man. "This should be enough."

"Thank you, Chad." The man took the syringe carefully into

his hands as if coddling a babe. "You really have no idea why you're here, do you?"

Bianca frowned in confusion. "No. All I know is that these two killed my sister."

"What about your parents?"

"They...they died in a car accident."

The man chuckled and shook his head slowly. "And you believed that. Did your sister? Nora was deep into conspiracy theories, wasn't she?"

Bianca's stomach flip-flopped at the implication. Nora hadn't said much about their parents' deaths, just that they'd gotten into an accident on the bridge and their car ended up in the water. Was there more to the story?

"Aww," Riccardo laughed. "I think you got the girl all riled up, Lanzel."

"Pity." The man—Lanzel—walked towards her, magic rippling off his body, though far less than Gladus' power. He bent down in front of her and grasped her chin. Bianca tried to wiggle away, but he kept a firm grip on her.

"Did you ever wonder how, as a simple werebird, you were able to see visions of the future? Lycans don't typically demonstrate elements of magic. It's not in your design. But you, you're special, but you were *made* that way." He moved closer, his warm breath brushing her cheeks. "Tell me, what was your sister doing at her pharmaceutical company before my men put a bullet in her? Do you know?"

Bianca swallowed hard as his hand tightened. "N-No, she didn't talk about her job. She said she was making something to help parahumans."

"Hmm, partially correct. You see," he flicked his finger and a chair skittered across the floor towards him. He released her as he sat down on the edge. "She initially was trying to aid parahumans. She and her team, including your parents, were busy putting together medicine that could help others open themselves up to the Ether. Earth magic." He steepled his fingers, bracing his chin on his knuckles. "That would mean that lycans like you could call upon the Ether and, more or less, make magi obsolete." He pouted. "You can see how that might make magi rather uncomfortable. *We* still have human bodies. Fragile. Imperfect. Our benefit, our *gift*, is that we can access magic and use it to protect ourselves from your kind.

But if you were able to wield both your genetic abilities, and Ether, what hope did we have?" He flexed his hand.

Purple magic sparkled on his fingers and danced around the tips. "Your family had to be stopped to an extent. I mean, magi can only use so much magic. To open ourselves completely to the Ether? Do you have any idea how powerful we can become?"

Bianca clenched her teeth, tears stinging her eyes. "You killed them then? My parents? My *sister*?"

"Your parents, yes. Your sister? No, my men did that for me. I had resources who gave me the components for the medication, but I couldn't have someone like your sister running off to tell others. It was bad enough that she tested the drug out on you."

"*What*?"

"Oh? You didn't know?" Lanzel laughed. He shook his head and ran his hand along his long ebony hair. "My, such secrets your family kept. You started having visions about four or five years ago, didn't you? Around the time your sister gave you a special flu shot?"

The color drained from her face and her hands turned to ice. Her caracara tensed, her feathers rising with her growing stress. The henbane dulled her connection with her bird, but she could still feel her. "But… she said…she—"

"B-b-but," Lanzel mocked then laughed. "I guess she didn't want to tell her little sister that she was a guinea pig." He tapped Bianca on her bandaged arm, causing her to flinch. "She gave you the medicine to see if you could touch the Ether. And look at you now? Full of visions. Unfortunately, your visions are far too close to exposing the truth of the medicine. The tree? The parahumans being touched by magic? No, no, we can't have this getting out now can we? We don't want other parahumans getting the information or stealing your blood. And magi... Well, we don't need them to be any stronger."

Bianca frowned in confusion. "But, aren't you a magus?"

Lanzel smirked. "I can use magic, but I'm not just a magus. I'm a senka."

Bianca's heart skipped a beat. A senka, a dark magic user. Oh dear Mother! She'd heard horror stories about them. They used forbidden magic and made sacrifices to help tap into the Ether, to draw more power to themselves. Sometimes they even used death to their magical advantage. *Necromancy*. The thought that a senka might be able to access even more magic made the hairs stand up on the back of her neck.

She heard a gun cock and glanced over to Chad. The Hunter aimed his weapon at Lanzel, his eyes wide.

"You never told us you were a *senka*." He said the word like a curse. "You said you'd eliminate the medicine once you had the girl's blood."

"Oh? Didn't I?" Lanzel asked. He put the needle to his arm and pressed it into a vein. In quick motion, her blood disappeared inside of him.

Riccardo trained his gun on Lanzel next, the cigarette still sticking out of his mouth. He sneered at Lanzel. "You really think we were working with you to help *you*? All you filthy magi and parahumans don't belong here. You're demons, spawns of the devil —" He suddenly choked and reached for his throat with his free hand. His cigarette tumbled to the concrete floor.

Lanzel sighed, holding out one hand towards Riccardo and another towards Chad. "You really talk too much. Both of you." He curled his fingers and the two men cried out in pain and turned towards one another, guns pointed. "You served me well, but I don't need you any longer."

"Wait," Riccardo pleaded, his finger shaking on the trigger. "Don't—"

Bianca looked away with a cry as the two men shot one another. She heard their bodies strike the ground hard, the guns clattering out of their hands. She wanted to be glad that they were gone after what they'd done to her sister, but not like this. Not while bound to a chair and being threatened by a senka.

Worse still, he'd learned to use blood magic, actual blood magic. He must have spilled their blood at some point to get control of them like that. They never would have killed each other if they hadn't been commanded!

Trish's muffled cries of fear made her look up.

Lanzel walked towards the vampire and looked her over, an amused smile on his face.

"Stop," he said and flicked his fingers. The vampire froze in place, trembling in her chains. "I need blood sacrifices from time to time. You'll be a perfect candidate. Don't worry. You'll be kept alive for a while longer."

"Stop it," Bianca snapped at him, though it came out more as a plea. "Why do you need my blood? What are you going to do with the medicine?"

"Isn't it obvious?" Lanzel asked. "Your blood was changed enough to allow you to use the Ether around you. Well, I just took some of that back from you. Most of the serum bottles were destroyed. I'd hoped to use your sister to make more, but these idiots didn't understand the concept of bringing her to me *alive*. That, and from what I understand, she took a bullet for you. Such a thoughtful sister. I suppose she wanted to redeem herself after using you as a test subject."

"My sister loved me," Bianca argued. "She would have done anything to keep me safe. Maybe helping me use magic was just a way for her to—"

"You are so naive," Lanzel said. "Not everyone has a proclivity to magic. I'm sure she had some *willing* subjects, but she had to have one she could keep a constant watch on. Who better than her own sister whom she had guardianship over after her parents' death?" He looked at his hand again. When he called on the purple magic this time, it flared and snarled like a raging beast. "The senkas will rise. We used to be a great people long ago, back before, heh, *Light* magi and Hunters decided to put us in our place. There's beauty in our craft, in sacrifice. In bringing life back to the dead."

He walked towards her and bent forward, hands behind his back. She squirmed to get away from him, but the ropes didn't budge. "Tell me, Bianca. If you had the chance to see your family, to walk with them again, would you take it? You know senkas can bring people back from the dead."

"No, you can't," Bianca hissed. "You might put life back into the body, but you can't bring a spirit back from the dead. What comes is just a shadow of what they once were."

"Without proper control of the Ether, that's true. But with this newfound magic, I can raise the dead. I can do that for your sister. And for Gladus," he said and smiled kindly at her. "And I would, if you agreed to stay with me. To let me keep drawing from your blood until I can make my own elixir."

Bianca narrowed her eyes. "What about when you can make your own?"

"Then you can go free," Lanzel said as if it was the most obvious thing in the world. "I don't want you dead. I didn't want your sister dead, but, there comes a risk to employing Hunters, and unfortunately, she paid the price."

"So did Gladus," Bianca replied. "So did my parents. And so have others. How can you justify that?"

"Again, I'm not in control of what my Hunters do."

"But you sent them! It's your responsibility to keep your *pets* at bay, including your vampire. Did you know she threatened a child to get me here?" She glared at Trish who looked away. "If working with you means threatening children and families, then you can go to hell!"

Lanzel pressed his hands together. Understanding crept into his eyes, and he crouched down in front of her. "My child, I have no reason to hurt anyone if I have the thing I need most." He touched her leg, sending a shiver of disgust racing through her body. "You won't be hurt, and neither will the people you have decided to call friends. You and I will go away, and I won't go near them again. I can restore your sister *and* Gladus. I can keep this medicine hidden so that other parahumans can't become more powerful and destroy others. You can have your family back. Isn't that what you've always wanted?"

Bianca stared at him and a lump formed in her throat. She'd never had the chance to say goodbye to her sister. That, above all else, was what she wanted most. To say goodbye. To apologize for not being strong enough. She blinked back tears and tilted her head, pressing it lightly to the chair. How could she agree to go with this madman after what he'd made his Hunters do?

But how could she deny him if it meant he'd leave Henry and his family alone? She reached for her caracara for support, but she had no answers. This was beyond them both.

She bit her lip. "Prove it. Prove you can bring my sister back." She nodded to the dead Hunters. "Show me."

Lanzel smiled. "Of course. You're wise to ask." He stood up and walked towards Riccardo.

"No," Bianca said, shaking her head. "That one." She motioned to Chad with her nose. Riccardo had been the crueler of the two. Chad, at least, had seemed to have some form of honor. Maybe if he came back to life, he could help her.

Lanzel lifted an eyebrow, intrigued, but did as she asked. He stood over Chad's bleeding body and held his hand over the man's head, just above the bullet hole. "Rise," Lanzel said plainly.

Bianca could have laughed. No magic swirled around him or the room. He just stood there, hand splayed, eyes focused on the corpse.

"*Rise*," he said with more inflection.

This time, his eyes glinted and turned completely purple. Magic spiraled around his arm and hand, spreading like a web over the dead Hunter's body. Bianca leaned forward as best she could and watched the bullet slide out of the man's head and his flesh heal. His eyes closed as if on their own. Lanzel didn't speak any words of magic that she could hear, but he bowed his head and kept his hand flexed, sending more Ether into the fallen man.

Chad's fingers twitched. He lolled his head from side to side, his arm groping for his gun. But he didn't grasp it. He pressed his hands slowly on the ground and started to push himself up. He went to his knees, his eyes filled with purple magic. Lanzel held out his hand. Chad took it and rose slowly. When he turned towards Bianca, she saw a soulless mound of clay. His eyes provided open windows to something else.

Something not entirely human.

Lanzel pulled back and smiled at his creation. Chad stood slightly slumped, as if he didn't quite know how to hold himself up. "You see? I've restored life."

Bianca swallowed hard. Chad rolled his neck around slowly and righted himself. He breathed in a deep breath of air, the sound rattling in his lungs. His eyes looked beyond, as if in a different plane of existence.

She shook her head at the perversion "You've animated a corpse. It's not him."

"Who are you?" Lanzel asked the Hunter.

"Chad," the man replied in more of a hiss than his actual voice.

"What is your profession?"

"Hunter. I hunt parahumans."

"Do you know who I am?"

Chad slowly looked at Lanzel and tilted his head to the side. "Master."

Lanzel clapped his hands, giddy. "There we are. He may not be perfect, but he will obey."

Obey was all he could do, Bianca realized. He didn't move except to look at Lanzel, waiting for orders. How sad. The man was better off dead. She couldn't help but wonder if he had a family waiting for him. Did they know his profession? What would they do now that he was dead, no, a walking corpse? He breathed labored breaths that didn't sound consistent, like he couldn't decide if he should be breathing or not.

Bianca curled her lip in disgust. She couldn't let him do that to her family, but it wasn't just about them now. More than just their lives were at stake. "I don't want you to raise my sister. It won't be her. But, if you promise that you'll leave the District alone, then I'll go with you. I'll be your host, be the thing you need most."

Lanzel smiled widely and moved to her side. "You've made me so happy," he said, his eyes glinting and hungry with power. Bianca stared in terror as he lost himself to the magic. If he could animate someone, what other harm could he do to the District? "I believe I can make this promise. We should go. We don't want anyone trying to find you."

He reached down and broke the ropes wrapped around her chest and waist. He slashed the ones on her ankles with magic and freed her wrists. Bianca rubbed them gently and stood up. Her head moved sluggishly from Trish using charm on her, but she stayed upright.

Bianca watched him turn away from her. He wanted to flee before someone found them. Heh, no one wanted to claim her. She knew that. Henry would go home and try to convince his mother to help, but Haley wanted nothing to do with her. She was on her own, and she, alone, had to stop this.

So as Lanzel approached Chad and touched his cheek, Bianca moved with all the speed she could muster. She snatched Riccardo's gun off of the ground. She turned, pointed the weapon at Lanzel's head, and fired.

The bullet whizzed towards the magus.

Lanzel lifted his hand and caught the bullet in an orb of purple magic. It swirled in the air, stuck in an unending loop. The senka stared at her in disappointment then flicked his wrist. The bullet continued its track, but went after the fallen Riccardo instead. It slammed into the man's body with a squelch.

Bianca stared in horror. She fired again, but Lanzel countered each shot with his magic. He walked towards her, sending bullet after bullet back into Riccardo's body. Bianca backed up as she fired. When her spine hit the wall, she put the gun to her own head and touched the trigger. "Don't! Get away from me."

Lanzel froze mid-step. He stared at her in alarm and raised his hands. "Now, now, my dear. Let's not be hasty."

"You can't get the medicine from me if I'm dead," Bianca said, trying to stop her voice from trembling. "I'm not letting you take me, but I'm not letting you, ah!" She yelped as the gun burnt her hand. She dropped it to the ground with a clatter and grabbed her wrist. The burn remained on her fingers for a few moments then passed.

Suddenly, magical purple ropes snapped around her wrists and jerked them behind her. More tendrils hobbled her and sent her to her knees. She looked up at the senka. He frowned down at her and flicked his finger, gagging her with his magic. Her caracara squawked in alarm and tried to launch herself at him, but Bianca stopped her.

"No! I won't lose you." This madman could raise the dead. What prevented him from ripping her bird out of her head or perverting it too?

"I guess I can't trust you yet. That's a shame. I had so hoped we could work together as a team, but it seems to me that you're going to be as resistant as my little vampire pet. So be it." He flicked his finger, and the magic turned into actual ropes and a gag. Bianca fell onto her side with a muted grunt. Lanzel stepped over her and pressed his foot against her chest, pushing her onto her back and her bound hands uncomfortably. "I'll make you appreciate the life I'm giving you. You'll learn to call me master, too." He snapped his fingers at Chad. "Get her." Lanzel stepped towards Trish, shaking his head.

Bianca squirmed away from Chad as best she could, but she had nowhere to go. The Hunter bent down and grabbed her by her waist. He threw her over his shoulder and headed for the stone stairs. Bianca lifted her head in time to see Lanzel drag Trish to her feet, her wrists tethered in chains and the muzzle keeping her at bay.

Bianca lowered her head and fought back tears. She was prisoner to a monster, and a corpse, with the same crazy vampire who had helped kill Gladus. Even being on the run would have been better than this.

Chad carried her up the first few steps towards her fate. No one would ever know what had happened to her. She'd never see Henry or Kaitlyn again.

Tears trickled down her cheeks in defeat.

Chad stopped as the door above them exploded. Something snarled a second before a figure collided with Chad and sent him and Bianca tumbling backwards down the stairs.

Chapter 17
Rescue

Kaitlyn

Kaitlyn hardly thought of herself as the bravest woman or werewolf in her pack. She'd grown up the runt of the litter and been forced to submit under the rule of an overly dominant alpha male who hadn't believed in taking a single mate for life. And when his son started looking for someone to call his own, Kaitlyn had happened to be the prettiest, and the tamest. And so she and Evan became a couple.

But Kaitlyn could only stand so much abuse, both mentally and physically. He'd torn into her, shredding her hopes, her dreams, and her spirit with words and claws. She'd become a shell of herself, and only the fear of death had forced her to leave her abusive pack behind.

She'd fled and found shelter in the Purple Door District under the rule of her loving Alpha. Evan had tried to find her, but Paytah had made certain that no wolf would come near her, not even his own packmates unless she agreed to it. The wrong word, or action, from a male triggered a PTSD reaction that left her in a heap on the floor. Nick and Paytah were the only male werewolves she could handle thus far, and even some of the females scared her.

Imagine her surprise when a little bird ended up on her doorstep, needing similar help and guidance that Kaitlyn herself had needed when she'd first arrived at the pack.

Maybe they hadn't been abused in the same way, but they'd both lost something dear to them, be it family or innocence, and they were both being hunted by their demons. Kaitlyn didn't feel brave enough to fight her own, but she could fight Bianca's.

They arrived at the Eden Florist warehouse not long after Bianca's kidnapping. She did not like having Fraula and Saul with them, mostly Fraula, but at least she didn't travel alone. Paytah stood at her side, keeping a firm, comforting hand on her back. Carlos, in his golden eagle form, perched on Paytah's free arm, mighty wings folded down his back. The hallway would make it difficult to fly, but he could do more damage with those talons than with his human hands.

And of course, she had Tess. While not a wolf herself, she was pack, and that brought the same comfort as having Paytah there.

Fraula sniffed, her pale nose wrinkling above her rose-painted lips. "I smell blood down below. Freshly-spilt blood." She breathed in deeper, her eyes turning red with hunger. "A *lot* of blood. I don't think everyone will be walking away from this."

"Comforting," Paytah said dryly. He looked down at Kaitlyn and squeezed her shoulder. "Are you sure about coming with us? You can still back out."

Before Kaitlyn could reply, Fraula sighed impatiently. "If your pup is going to give us so much trouble, perhaps you should order her back home."

"Oy," Tess snapped. "Don't tell our alpha what to do, fang face."

Kat flashed sharp teeth, her golden fur bristling with anger. "*I'm not going anywhere. Bianca needs my help, and I'm not a child.*"

"You're barely over twenty," Fraula scoffed. "And you." She rounded on Tess. "Are little more than a babe yourself. You don't even have the blessings of a ward to be here." Her fierce blue eyes glinted. "When you get to be *my* age, then you can say you're not a child."

"Fraula," Saul murmured. He touched her arm and shook his head. "Not now. I can smell Trish down there. I have not met your Bianca, so I do not know her smell, but if Trish is here, I imagine Bianca will be as well."

Carlos fluffed his feathers and shifted on Paytah's arm. "*We should have called on Legion. This may be bigger than the six of us.*"

Paytah shook his head. "Little late for that now. We need to go down. Carlos and I will take the lead. Kaitlyn, you—"

Kaitlyn's ears perked as she heard the sound of gunshots down below. Before Paytah could stop her, she launched forward, jerking herself free of his hand. She heard him shout her name, but she ignored him and barreled through the entrance. She followed the scent of blood and went immediately towards a door on the right. A locked door couldn't stop a werewolf.

She slammed into it with all of her might until the wood splintered under her frame. Someone lumbered up the stairs. She growled and threw her whole weight into the man, and both heard and felt bone crunch before she threw him backwards down the stairs.

Bianca, bound and gagged, fell off of his shoulder and rolled across the floor, creating a dust plume in her wake. Kaitlyn stumbled into the room after the fallen man and took everything in in a quick sweep. A pale man with black hair stood holding a chain attached to Trish's cuffs. Bianca lay on the floor, dazed. The man she'd hit curled up, holding his stomach. And a body covered in blood lay brokenly off to the side.

Kat sensed the electrical twinge of magic in the air, and she looked sharply at the black- and violet-clothed man as he raised his hand. She dropped to the ground on instinct, just missing a blaze of light that passed over her back. Kat sprang to her feet and scrambled over towards Bianca.

"*Hold on*," Kat said. "*I'll get you out of here.*" She bit down on Bianca's wrist restraints and broke them with her teeth.

Bianca ripped the gag out of her mouth and shoved Kat back. "Watch out!"

The magic came again. Kat flattened herself on Bianca, protecting the bird with her own body. She snarled, flashing her teeth at the man until a blast of magic crawled across her face like blistering flames. She yowled in pain, her vision turning white for a moment as she fell backwards onto the ground.

Suddenly, the room filled with shouts and snarls as the cavalry arrived. She sensed a burst of magic, likely from Tess, and heard a warning screech from Carlos.

Soft hands clutched at her fur and patted her cheeks. "Kaitlyn? Kaitlyn!" Bianca shouted.

Kat blinked her eyes open and stared up at Bianca. The woman looked bruised and exhausted, but she was alive. "*You're okay.*"

"Get up," Bianca urged. "We have to get out of here."

Something smashed into the wall near them.

Kaitlyn rolled onto her stomach and saw Fraula sink to the ground, a burn mark on her shoulder. The vampire clutched the injury and hissed at the magus as he advanced on her. Saul leapt on his back and sank his teeth into the man's shoulder. He yelled in pain, until a bolt of magic filled Saul's mouth and threw him to the ground. She swore she saw one of his fangs hit the concrete near his twitching body.

Paytah had loosed Carlos at the entrance of the room. The eagle flapped towards the magic user, slicing his shoulder with his talons, while Paytah shifted into his great black wolf form. Tess kept the magus at bay with three sharp tosses of flaming orbs.

Bianca shook her head and crouched in front of Kaitlyn. "Lanzel is a senka!" she shouted. "Don't! He can use blood magic!"

"*Shit*," Tess hissed. "Kat, get her and your tail out of here *now*!"

Kat didn't hesitate. She shoved her body into Bianca, pushing her towards the door.

Paytah leapt at Lanzel's back this time, aiming to sink his teeth into the man's throat. Lanzel turned. He brandished a small dagger and sliced Paytah along the leg as he dodged out of the way. Paytah didn't even grunt as he landed, but Kat saw the blood drip from his front leg and off of the dagger. The werewolf growled and turned back to attack Lanzel again.

The senka lifted the dagger at Paytah. "Stop!" he ordered.

Paytah struggled then stopped mid-step. He blinked in surprise and looked down at his unmoving legs then back at Lanzel.

Carlos zoomed around for another attack, talons outstretched.

Lanzel glared at the eagle. "Fetch," he ordered Paytah and twitched the blade again. Paytah spun on his paws and pounced.

Carlos curled his talons in at the last second to avoid scraping Paytah across the face, but the werewolf clamped his jaw around the great bird and dragged him from the air. Carlos screeched in pain and surprise. He flapped his mighty wings and pecked at the wolf's nose until Paytah yelped and let him go.

Carlos landed in a heap on the ground. Kaitlyn smelled blood, but she could also tell that Paytah hadn't closed down on the bird to kill him. He maintained partial control, fighting the blood magic.

Tess growled and waved her hand, creating a flaming whip that snarled through the air. She lashed out at the senka. A jerk of Lanzel's wrist brought a bleeding body into the air, and the whip wrapped around that instead. Flesh sizzled. Tess banished the whip and hurled another orb of fire at the senka which he easily caught in his hand.

"You're little more than a child," he crooned and hurled the ball back, the orb surrounded by purple magic. Tess tried to block it with a shield, but the purple magic broke it, and the tainted fire caught her shoulder. She dropped to a knee with a cry of pain.

Kaitlyn pressed herself against Bianca. "*I have to help them.*"

"He'll get control of you, too, and kill you."

Kaitlyn shook her head. "*I'm not going for him.*"

Someone had to keep Paytah distracted.

Apparently Fraula thought the same thing. The vampire leapt at Paytah and brought sharp claws down on his face. He closed his eyes, but howled in pain nonetheless. Lanzel sneered and hit her with magic, driving her back. Another wave of his hand healed Paytah's wounds. "Kill her," he ordered.

Trish shouted and struggled in her chains. She jerked hard, pulling the magus off balance. Lanzel yanked back just as hard and grabbed her chin. "Would you rather I make you do it?" he spat in her face, white spittle hitting her cheek.

Paytah had no choice but to obey Lanzel. He ran towards Fraula with his teeth bared. Fraula lashed out at him again, her claws going for his face and his throat. He bodied her into the wall and pinned her to the ground with his weight. She snarled and lurched at his jugular.

Paytah caught her throat in his mouth first.

He held her there, and Kaitlyn saw the conflict on his face as he tried not to kill her. Fraula choked beneath his vicious teeth. She struck at him again and again with her claws and fist, but her hits grew weaker as his teeth closed tighter around her throat.

Kaitlyn bolted towards her alpha. "*Tess! Cover Bianca!*" She slammed into his side with all her might. He grunted and let go of Fraula, allowing his body to crumble underneath hers. Kat pounced on him and brought her teeth down around his neck, keeping him pinned, or so it seemed.

"*I have you,*" she told him. "*I won't let you hurt anyone. Don't worry.*"

"*Kat, his hold is too strong. You need to stop me.*" His voice came from a distance, as if a chasm stood between them.

Kat blinked. "*I'm not going to hurt you. You'll be okay. We just have to kill him. That'll stop it all.*"

"*Kat—*"

Lanzel threw Trish back to the ground and pointed sharply at Paytah. "I told you to kill her!" he snapped, gesturing to Fraula.

The vampire curled up on the ground, clutching her bleeding throat.

Paytah growled darkly beneath Kat, but in her mind he said, "*End me!*"

"*No!*" Kat shouted, only to yelp when he jerked his head and bit her leg. She jumped back instinctively, limping and tucking the wounded limb against her chest. Paytah bodied her, driving her closer to Bianca and Tess, before he took off after Fraula. Tess grabbed the avian's arm and pulled her back towards the doorway to get her out of the line of fire.

Saul, who had finally managed to get back to his feet, tried to intercept the black wolf. He struck Paytah along the back, but the werewolf moved faster, and he brought his mouth down around Fraula's head.

"Fraula!" Saul shouted.

Kat looked away when she heard the crunch and both Saul's and Trish's anguished cries.

Lanzel sighed in satisfaction. "I should thank you, Bianca. I wouldn't have been able to use my blood magic to take over a werewolf without your help."

Kaitlyn whipped her head around to look at the avian. "*What is he talking about?*"

Bianca's eyes had filled with furious tears. "I have something that was injected into me that allows me to use Ether. He took some of it. He can use more magic. Stronger magic. Kat, you have to get out of here. All of you, get out of here!" She tried to break free of Tess, but the magus kept a firm hold of her.

"Stop it," Tess growled and jerked Bianca towards the door.

Lanzel clicked his tongue. "No, no, little *witch*." He waved his hand, but Kaitlyn didn't know what he'd done until the man she'd knocked down the stairs suddenly launched himself at the fire magus. Tess gasped and hit him with a flaming orb, but even as his flesh burned, he kept coming for her. Tess reluctantly released

Bianca to defend herself.

Kaitlyn swallowed hard and looked at Carlos and Saul. Carlos hobbled back on his feet, but Saul wept over Fraula's body, useless. Paytah had moved away from Fraula of his own volition, mouth dripping red, and put himself as far from the others as possible.

Lanzel smiled in amusement and looked at Carlos. "Really? You honestly thought that you, an *avian*, could defeat me? Pathetic. At least the werewolf and the vampire stood a chance." He looked at Kaitlyn and sighed. "You are a pretty little thing, aren't you? Shame. I can't have you running off telling people about me." He looked at Paytah. "You. Kill her."

Paytah growled as he struggled not to obey. He dug his claws into the concrete and trembled with the stress of fighting.

Kat crouched low and looked between Lanzel and Paytah. She had to stop this. She had to do something. With Paytah under Lanzel's control, Fraula dead, Saul mourning her, Carlos hurt, and Trish bound, her odds weren't good. Tess continued battling the zombie man. Only Bianca remained free.

She swallowed and glanced back at the avian. "*Go on. I can't protect you from him.*"

"Lanzel won't let him hurt me. Kat, go. *Please.* I don't want anyone else to die for me."

Lanzel glared at Paytah. "Kill her!" he barked.

Paytah couldn't fight it this time.

He rushed Kaitlyn, even as he screamed at her mentally to run. Kaitlyn thought of Bianca's words and took a breath. Stupid... so stupid, but she hoped that it worked. She hoped Bianca was right.

"*You swear he can't hurt you?*"

"Yes. Lanzel needs me alive."

Paytah ran at her at full speed. She waited until the last possible second then dropped and rolled to the side, putting Bianca straight in Paytah's path.

Lanzel shouted in fright. "Stop!" he ordered.

Paytah skidded but still bumped into Bianca, sending them both to the ground. Bianca grunted and lay across him, keeping him pinned. If he struggled too much, he would end up hurting her.

Kaitlyn rolled to her paws and raced towards Lanzel. He raised his hand and lashed out with magic, but she expected it this time. She dodged it and started to run in a circle around him, keeping him distracted from ordering Paytah from doing anything. A blast almost hit Carlos as he waddled over to Bianca and Paytah. Kaitlyn kept running until Lanzel faltered a moment, dizzy from spinning.

She rushed him and hit him in the legs. He dropped, and she spun and brought her teeth down on his arm. She broke skin and tasted his blood in her mouth. As he cried out in pain, she forced her werewolf venom to seep into him. It would hurt him, slow him. And if it didn't kill him, it might at least eliminate his magic.

Lanzel roared in pain. He grabbed his dagger again and thrust it towards her face. She jerked to the side, but not fast enough. The blade caught the side of her throat and stabbed her flesh.

Kat howled and shook her head until she wrestled the blade from his hand. But the dagger wound burned like fire. Blood trickled out of the wound, held at bay only by the silver blade.

She whined and limped away from him.

Lanzel gripped his arm tightly with his hand. "You bitch!" he screamed at her, though it wasn't really an insult to Kat, being a female dog after all. He held out his hand towards Paytah and rasped, "Kill her now!"

Kaitlyn tried to think quickly. She couldn't stand up against Paytah for long in her condition. Even injured, his size and strength overpowered hers. She spotted a fallen gun and sent a thought to Carlos. "*Are you still able to fight?*"

"*Yes. I'm acting more hurt than I am. Trying to get close to the Senka.*"

"*There's a gun. Get that to Bianca. He can't hurt her, but she can hurt him.*"

Carlos didn't look towards the gun, but Kaitlyn knew he understood. She sent him another thought. "*Be quick. I don't know how long I can hold Paytah off.*"

"*I'll help, Sister.*" Tess's voice echoed in her head. "*Let me get rid of this garbage and I'll give the senka a good distraction. You save our alpha.*"

Paytah had freed himself from Bianca's tight embrace. He ran at Kaitlyn with intent to kill, his teeth bloody and hungry. He couldn't hold back, no matter how hard he tried. Kaitlyn accepted that. She might have to hurt her alpha to save him, but she wouldn't kill him. She wouldn't leave Rozene without a mate, or the pack without an alpha. He had a good heart. He would let her kill him if he had the opportunity, and she refused to allow it to happen.

She dodged and danced around him, using her smaller, lighter frame to keep just inches out of reach of his teeth and claws. He followed her, snapping and snarling.

"*Kaitlyn,* please. *Don't let me do this to you,*" Paytah begged.

"*I'm not leaving you in his clutches.*" She glanced over his shoulder and saw Carlos stumble and fall right on top of one of the Hunter's guns. Lanzel made his way towards Bianca, his face twisted with rage and pain. Purple magic snapped out and wrapped around Bianca's wrists, pulling her towards him.

"Let me go!" she shouted and struggled in his bonds.

"You're coming with me whether you like it or not," Lanzel spat, his voice laced with agony. He clutched his bloody arm against him.

Suddenly, the zombie man flew across the room, wrapped in a ball of fire. Tess panted, her hair sticking to her sweaty face. She advanced on Lanzel, fire crackling around her fingers. "Let. Her. Go."

"I grow tired of this," Lanzel hissed and hurled violet lightning at the magus. Tess dodged and sent a ball of fire curving around towards his side.

A swipe at Kat's face pulled her attention back to the battle at hand. She dodged again, but Paytah clawed her across the cheek. Kat stumbled and yelped when he pounced on her, knocking her to the ground. She rolled away before he could pin her and snapped at his leg. This time, she managed to close her teeth around his right paw. He jerked back with a yip and shook it out. Kaitlyn hit him broadside, knocking him sideways. But the wound sapped her strength and she stumbled.

She panted and whirled. "*Tess, keep his eyes on you*! *Carlos*! *Now*!"

Carlos got his talons around the gun. He flapped his powerful wings and lifted into the air behind Lanzel. Lanzel started to turn towards him. If he saw the gun, it would all be over.

Tess swung out the fire whip again, catching the senka around his throat. He screamed in outrage rather than pain and grabbed the fire whip in his bloody hand. Violet electricity zoomed down the Ether strand. Before Tess could let go, the power crashed into her and threw her into the ceiling.

Between the building being condemned, and the magical attacks spewing everywhere, the warehouse finally started to give in. The force of Tess's body smashing into the roof of the basement started the collapse. She fell to the ground, wood and stone crashing down around her. More timber tumbled in front of the door, blocking Lanzel from escaping.

Lanzel grabbed Bianca by the hair and started to conjure a spell that Kat imagined would let him take her far away from there.

They were running out of time.

"*Bianca*! *It's up to you. You have to stop him*!" Kat shouted at her friend. She limped towards Lanzel, snarling. He looked back at her; at the same time Paytah landed on her back and drove her to the ground. The dagger clattered out of her throat, causing blood to gush from the wound. Paytah knocked her legs out from beneath her and brought his teeth down around her throat. The heat of his breath washed over her as his mouth closed in.

"*Kaitlyn, I'm sorry. I'm so sorry. I'm trying.*"

Kaitlyn couldn't move without cutting her throat. "*I know, Paytah. It's not your fault.*"

She looked forward as Carlos threw the gun towards Bianca. Bianca saw it and caught it in her bound hands. Lanzel looked down at her. He held out his hand, wrapping the gun in purple magic. But Bianca didn't falter. She glared into his eyes.

Kat swore she saw the faint outline of a bird leave Bianca's head and crash into Lanzel's. An unearthly, tortured cry tore from the senka's mouth. He grabbed at his head, his magic on the gun breaking free.

"Get out of my head!" he screamed and turned blazing eyes on Bianca.

She pointed the gun and fired.

Lanzel's head snapped back.

At the same time, Paytah jerked his mouth away from Kat. He stood over her protectively and watched with her as Lanzel collapsed to the ground, a bullet between his eyes.

Bianca fell to her knees, dropping the gun to the ground. Carlos landed next to her and pressed his head against her arm. She stared down at her hands numbly. Her face turned putrid green before she lurched and vomited on the bloody floor.

It took Kaitlyn a moment to realize that this was probably the first person Bianca had ever killed. Her heart ached for the young woman. She wanted nothing more than to go and comfort her.

But Kat had her own problems. Her neck wept crimson blood from both the dagger and Paytah's teeth. He hadn't bitten through her throat, but he'd left more breaks in her skin. She rested her head on one of her paws and whined under her breath in pain.

Except for her whimper and Bianca's vomiting, the room fell quiet. Saul had grown still beside Fraula. He held her close, head buried against her chest. Trish, now freed of Lanzel's magic, crouched beside Saul. She still had the chains and muzzle on, but she touched the man's arm. Saul stared at her then wrapped his arms around her and pulled her close.

Kaitlyn sighed. Paytah licked her face affectionately and nuzzled her neck, checking the wound.

"*You were an idiot*," he told her. "*I could have killed you. I told you to put me down. Why didn't you listen?*"

"*With all due respect, Alpha, your order was stupid. I'm not going to kill someone who has been like a father to me. Besides, do you know how scary Rozene can get when she's mad at you? I didn't want her hunting me down for the rest of my life.*"

Normally Paytah would have chuckled, but by his grim expression, she could tell that the wound in her neck left no room for laughter. Dizziness threatened to consume her even though she lay still. "*Tess? Is she…*"

Paytah looked over to the other member of their pack. When Tess didn't move, he trotted to her and nuzzled her cheek. "*Alive, but out cold. She has a head wound and is losing blood fast. So are you. Too much. We need her awake, or we need to get you home. Now.*"

"*But, the others,*" Kat tried to say. Saul refused to move. Bianca had a fit, understandably, next to a wounded Carlos, Tess lay unconscious beneath rubble, and Paytah bore his own wounds. "*None of us are in any condition to move. And the door is blocked.*" She looked at the debris and coughed. A steady cloud of dust worked its way through the room, making it harder to breathe.

Paytah mustered a whine, torn between going to her and staying with Tess. The sound pulled Bianca's attention towards Kaitlyn. When she saw the blood, the werebird struggled to her feet and ran to Kat's side. She pressed her hands over the wound, causing the werewolf to hiss in pain.

"You're bleeding all over!" Bianca exclaimed. She looked around frantically, but she came to the same conclusion as Kat. They were trapped in a basement with five wounded parahumans, her, and a former traitor. Bianca closed her eyes tightly and then looked down at Kat. "I'll get you home. It's okay. You're not going to die down here."

Kaitlyn mustered a wolfish smile then closed her eyes. "*Don't make promises you can't keep. At least you're safe. And so is my pack.*"

"Kat, don't you dare!" Bianca cried.

Kaitlyn heard rustling, and when she opened her eyes, she saw Bianca place a rosary with a feather around her neck. Bianca touched her paw and bowed her head. "Mother, please help," she begged.

Kaitlyn blinked a few times as Bianca said her prayer. The fight had drained her, and as her blood dripped on the concrete, the world started to spin.

There came a sudden commotion as the doorway blew open, scattering more debris in the room. Through flashes of light, Kaitlyn managed to make out figures dressed in black before she passed out.

Chapter 18
Legion

Bianca

Bianca struggled to sit up, coughing through the cloud of dust. The explosion had knocked her onto her back and dazed her. Her ears buzzed. She looked down at Kat, but the werewolf fell unconscious, blood soaking her golden fur. "Kat? Kat!" she shouted and shook the wolf, but to no avail.

She squinted as flashlights stung her eyes. She saw Paytah standing over Tess, the young woman still partially covered by stone and wood. Carlos flared his wings defensively, but he and Paytah were the only ones still standing. She looked around frantically and spotted the bloody dagger that had fallen out of Kat's neck. She didn't want to touch it, but she had nothing else to protect herself and the wolf.

Bianca gripped the dagger and leaned over Kat. Talons grew on her fingers, and the feather pattern formed across her body. She reached for her caracara. Attacking Lanzel's mind had been well worth the risk, and she'd do it again for her friends. For herself.

Figures dressed in black entered the room, flashlights in their grasps. One person held up a hand and created a glowing blue ball. She pushed it into the room, and the dust started to seep into it, providing a fresh breeze and allowing the intruders to see Bianca and her friends.

It also gave Bianca a full view of the uniformed people and the silver badges on their chests.

Badges engraved with a silver infinity ouroboros and a crimson
"L."

Legion.

For a moment, Bianca forgot all about the senka who had tried
to steal her away, along with the Hunters who had killed Nora. She
stared at the new threat and rose over Kat, her heart pounding in
her chest, her bird clacking her beak in outrage. Kat's blood coated
her hands as she tightened her grip on the dagger. She stepped over
the wolf and prepared her bird.

An ebony man in the lead noticed her and raised a gun with his
flashlight. "Stand down!" he shouted.

Bianca raised the dagger.

"*Bianca, stop,*" Carlos said to her. He started to shift, returning
to his human form, except, not entirely. His arms formed in place
of his wings, but two new wings sprouted from his back. They were
the same color and shade as the golden eagle's, just bigger so they
matched his body size.

It gave her pause.

Like wolves, werebirds had two forms, their bird, and their
seraph. The latter gave them the ability to fly even as a human. Her
parents had been too young to shift, but they'd told her all about
them. So instead of launching herself at Legion, she could only
stare in wonder at Carlos as he finished his transformation and
came to her side.

"We mean no harm," he told Legion, hands in the air. He
wrapped one of his wings around Bianca and pulled her close to his
side, both restraining and comforting her. "We came to rescue the
girl here."

"Get down on your knees," the lead man ordered. "Keep your
hands up."

Carlos didn't argue. He tightened his wing around Bianca and
knelt, forcing her to kneel with him. His bird brushed her mind. "*I
won't let them take you away. It's okay, Bianca. Just stay next to
me.*"

"*But it's Legion,*" she argued. Her caracara flapped anxiously
next to his golden eagle. "*They'll put us in cells. We'll never be free
again.*"

"*Yes we will, Bianca. Please, I'm begging you to trust me. If
not for yourself, then to save Kat and Tess. They need our help
now.*"

Bianca glanced at Kat. The wolf hadn't stopped bleeding. Any fighting would waste time and bring Kat that much closer to death.

She shut her eyes. *No more death*, she thought and dropped the dagger to the ground with a clatter before holding up her hands.

"What a mess," the magus beside the lead man remarked. She looked around the room and started to count off the people. "Well, it seems our informant was off by one, but the ones still conscious are accounted for."

The lead rescue agent nodded. "Good. There's too much chaos here. We'll get this sorted back at base before anyone bleeds out." He cast a wary glance at Kat and Tess. He touched his ear with a finger. "Send Jay down here. We need a transport."

Bianca tensed again, but Carlos wouldn't let her make any sudden movements. He held her steady and glanced sideways at her. Her caracara leaned into his eagle until the bigger bird preened her head feathers. "*What are they going to do to us?*" she asked.

"*Get the information they need and help us. I promise. I know how these people are.*"

"*I hope you're right. I don't want to lose anyone else.*" She glanced down at Kat only to flinch as she heard more rubble fall near the door.

A young woman with blonde hair in a high ponytail stepped into view. She dressed in the same black attire as the others, but she also wore an elegant tie and a crystal around her neck. She took count of the room and whistled. "You like testing the crystal's use, don't you? I only have so many of these." She touched her hand to it and pressed her other fingers to her ear. "Agent 642CIR returning in three...two...one." The jewelry started to glow beneath her hand.

Carlos tightened his hold on Bianca, and suddenly the world spun.

She felt weightless, dangling in time and space. Colors flashed in front of her, reminding her of her visions until wave after wave of dizziness washed over her. She counted it a blessing that she'd been unconscious the two times Gladus teleported her.

She landed barely above the ground and grunted as her knees connected with marble flooring. The sudden light made her gasp and put her arm over her eyes. It took her a few blinks to actually see their strange destination.

The room revealed a mix of white marble flooring, black walls, and a few red planters with ferns in them. It smelled sterile like a hospital but had the cold feel of a lawyer's office. Hallways led off from the room where they'd landed. A silver reception desk with the Legion logo on the front stood near the front of the room near a single red doorway.

Three people hovered around it, two men and a woman. They seemed inconsequential except for the beautiful Muslim woman wearing a pale gold and black hijab over her uniform. She carried a file with her as she walked towards the bedraggled group, boots tapping on the floor. She took a cursory look over Bianca and her friends and glanced at the two men.

"Bring the injured to Medical Bays 3 and 4. Bodies to Morgue B."

"Yes, sir," they said to her without hesitation. They directed orders into their own earpieces and people rushed in with gurneys. In short order, Saul, Tess, Kat, and Paytah, who had remained quiet all this time, were strapped down and taken away. Lanzel, his companions, and the dead female vampire were also escorted out of the room, leaving Carlos, Bianca, and the still-bound Trish.

The vampire froze in place, her eyes wide with terror.

The Muslim woman, whom Bianca could only assume was the Special Agent in Charge, SAC, looked down at her and motioned to the woman they'd called Jay. "We'll take the vampire into the interrogation room with us as well. Bring the avian girl with you."

Carlos took a timid step forward. "Please, allow me to stay with her. She's never met Legion before. I think she was told you had a bad reputation."

The SAC lifted her chin, her hijab rustling softly. "We are neither good nor evil. We get the job done and make sure people stay safe." She sighed. "But, I will allow it. I'd rather not have to sedate the girl if she panics."

Bianca tensed. "Sedate me?"

"She won't," Carlos whispered and helped her to her feet. With agents still partially surrounding them, they were ushered into the hall.

Bianca soon lost track of where they were going. The twists and turns were disorienting. Blazing florescent lights lit the building, but with no windows she couldn't even guess where they were. Were they even in Chicago?

She gripped Carlos' hand and stuck close to him as they were brought into what looked like a regular interrogation room from cop movies. But the chairs in here had straps on them. Trish was forced down in one. They freed her of the chains, but then secured her arms. They replaced her gag with a leather strap holding thin metal bars, like something out of *Silence of the Lambs.*

Jay took a step towards Bianca, and she immediately jerked back in Carlos' arms. The woman paused then raised her hands to show she didn't have a gun. "You're injured. I have medical training. While we talk, I'd like to tend to your wounds."

Carlos squeezed Bianca's arm. "It's all right," he told her.

Bianca hesitated a long time before she finally sat down. She watched Jay cautiously as the woman pulled a bag off of her shoulder and set it on the table. A first-aid kit on wheels. Bandages, gauze, medicine, syringes, needles, sutures, and more stood out against the black fabric.

The SAC spoke quietly into her earpiece again and sat down on a chair opposite Carlos and Bianca. "I have someone with me who told us where you would be. He's going to sit with us, and then you're going to explain exactly what happened." She put a small black device on the table and touched a button. Bianca didn't hear anything, but she noticed a faint red light.

Recorder.

Before she could argue, another agent appeared with a man at his side. It took Bianca a moment to recognize him.

"Vic?" Carlos asked in surprise, his big wings flaring.

The fire magus offered a curt nod before he took a seat at the table. His eyes drifted to Bianca. "Glad to see you in one piece," he said. He sounded sincere; she hoped he meant it.

Bianca noted the dark circles under his eyes; he hadn't been sleeping.

The SAC pulled out a notepad and crossed her legs. "Let's begin," she said. "The whole story."

All eyes turned to Bianca. After everything she'd learned from Lanzel, she didn't even know where to start. She glanced at her arm as Jay tended to the area where she'd had the blood drawn. "My sister lied to me," she said. "I didn't have Hunters after me. It was a senka." And she went into the web that Lanzel had woven for her, providing every detail, even his admission to her parents' deaths, her sister's murder, and the "flu shot" that had helped give Bianca her visions.

It was like listening to a documentary while she sat in the audience. This wasn't the life she'd known or the one she'd wanted. Her sister had lied. Bianca had been used, and she didn't know how to feel about it. She wanted to be mad, but disappointment weighed heavier. Why had Nora gone down that path? How could she have thought that infecting people with this *serum* would make them better or stronger? And how could Nora experiment on her little sister of all people?

"Gladus said she would help me," Bianca said and her voice hitched with emotion. "But she didn't get the chance, because she," she pointed at Trish, "killed her."

"I didn't kill her," Trish protested. "The Hunters shot her in the head."

"You shot her in the stomach!" Bianca shouted until Carlos squeezed her hand to try to calm her down. "You struck first."

Trish set her jaw. "I didn't mean for her to die," she said quietly. "If I'd bitten her, it would have either killed her or removed her magic, which would have been worse than death for her. I shot her above any vital organs so she'd have a chance to survive. I didn't think the Hunters would finish her off. I thought they'd just leave her for someone to find!" She looked at the SAC. "I may not have liked her, but I didn't want her dead."

Bianca glared. "You could have left. You could have told her what was happening!"

"No I couldn't," Trish hissed. "The Hunters had a target on my head, and the heads of my coven members. They murdered one in front of me just to leave an impression."

Carlos grimaced. "Gavin."

Trish's anger subsided. Grief and tears filled her eyes before she looked away. "Yes."

The room fell quiet as Bianca took it in. Had the Hunters really threatened the vampire with the death of her coven if she didn't obey? She supposed she wouldn't put it past them. That sounded very much like Hunters. But why?

The ward, Bianca realized. Gladus had put up a ward around her house, and Bianca had been left in Carlos' care otherwise. They'd needed someone who could get through that barrier. Otherwise, it resembled the District market for the Hunters. No matter how hard they tried to come to the door, something forced them to turn away.

The SAC murmured to herself and wrote down a few more notes.

Carlos looked a Vic. "How did you know where we would be?"

"Tess," the magus replied. "While you were on the way there, she texted me to let me know the details. She might be part of Paytah's pack, but she's still a magus, Carlos. She feels a connection with my people. She wanted me to know what was happening in case things went south, and I took it to Legion. Which is what Gladus should have done in the beginning. Maybe if she had, she'd still be alive."

The Legion agent nodded in agreement. "That's the point of being a Violet Marshall. We need to know if there's Hunter activity in the area, or if vampires are randomly going missing."

Trish tensed. "Wait, they said they wouldn't touch my coven."

"It's not just *your* coven," the SAC replied. "Other covens and packs have come forward to tell us their members are vanishing. We're working to get to the center of this. As for now." She looked at Bianca and put the paper down. "The first thing we need to do is see if all of that serum is out of you." She held out her hand. "Let me see your arm."

Bianca shied away from it at first, but the threat of being sedated put an end to her resistant. She slowly showed her arm.

The SAC took it and opened her mouth. Two sharp fangs protruded from the top of her gums. When Bianca struggled, the woman gripped her arm harder. "I can taste magical properties in blood. It's the best way to know if you're clean. Please don't struggle. I don't want to make a mess or have to use those." She nodded to the bonds.

Bianca whined in her throat, but Carlos' hand on her shoulder calmed her enough to obey. The vampire pressed her teeth into Bianca's arm. The bite didn't hurt too badly but it still stung.

The SAC sucked on her for a few moments then lifted her head. She closed her eyes, tasting the blood as if it was a fine red wine. "Hm, there's some left. Agent," she said to Jay. "Use the blue syringe. And we'll need 2 ccs of antidote Radiant."

Jay complied, and once again a needle with a syringe that glowed blue pushed into Bianca's vein. She watched her blood flow into it.

"What is that?" she asked, gesturing to the syringe.

"Technology and magic combined," Jay replied with a kind smile. "It's supposed to help pull magical properties out of blood. Helps if, say, a magus gets too overpowered and can't release pent up magic. Or someone gets an electrical charge of Ether and needs it drawn out of them. We're kind of doing that to you now; drawing out the harmful stuff. It's just a mix of a spell and technology that's letting me do it." She stopped with the syringe half full and clicked her tongue. "I think that's all." She capped it and put it into her case. Then she drew another syringe and a vial of yellow liquid.

Bianca tensed and pulled her arm away. "What are you going to do to me?"

"It'll subdue anything we missed," the SAC replied.

"But how do you know it's the right antidote? What if it does something worse to me?"

The SAC lifted her eyebrows. "You think *you're* special?" she asked. She gave a low chuckle and wrote another note down. "*Children.*"

Bianca stiffened at the news. *I'm not the only one? Mother, how many other people were tested, and how come no one else found me sooner?* She glanced down as Jay started to push the yellow serum into her body. Her veins warmed, causing her to squirm in discomfort. A firm grip on her arm prevented her from pulling away or getting any other ideas.

When Jay finished, she withdrew the needle and wrapped Bianca's arm. "You might feel a little sleepy and flushed for a couple of hours, but it'll subside. If it doesn't, tell medical staff immediately. If the site of injection starts to turn red, swells, or you feel like you're running a fever, tell us."

"Does it normally do that?" Bianca asked warily.

Jay shook her head and smiled. "No, it's just standard procedure after giving someone a shot. Don't worry, you're going to be fine. And if you start feeling weird, just tell them to ask for Agent 642CIR and I'll come find you."

"Don't you have a name?"

The agent nodded. "Of course. I'm Legion." And with that, she packed the items away and stood. "I'll get these to the lab."

The SAC nodded and watched Jay depart before looking back at Bianca. "Without that serum inside of you, the visions should stop." She glanced at Carlos. "I assume I can release her into your care."

Carlos nodded firmly. "Yes."

"Good. But we *will* be watching." She reached for the recorder and settled back. "Your friends need time to heal. We will teleport you all back to the District once you are all healthy enough to travel. For now, I'll bring you to quarters where you can rest. You will be under guard. For all of our protection, you understand."

"Of course," Carlos agreed.

Bianca looked between them. "Before I go to the room, can I see one of my friends? I want to make sure she's going to be okay."

The woman rose and swept her files off of the table in one fluent motion. "Once everyone is out of surgery, then yes, you may sit with her. Until then, rest."

***

Bianca ventured into the recovery room a few hours later. Saul and Paytah had endured minor wounds compared to Kat and Tess who stayed in surgery for most of the night.

Bianca sat down at Kat's side and looked the werewolf over. At some point, they'd managed to help Kat shift back to her human form. She looked battered and bruised, and thick bandages wound around her neck, but despite all that, she breathed deeply. Her heart beat a steady tempo on the machine, a soothing sound after so much trauma. A Legion nurse came and went to check on them, but otherwise Bianca sat alone with Kat, at least on the inside of the room. Two Legion agents stood outside the doors.

Bianca started to doze off to the rhythmic beep when she heard Kat sigh. Her eyes snapped open, and she watched the werewolf worriedly.

Kat slowly came around. She stared at the ceiling then rolled her head to the left where Bianca rested. The werewolf studied her then gave a half smile. "Hey."

"Hey, yourself."

"Not dead, then?"

Bianca mustered a tiny grin. "You'd probably feel better if you were."

"Heh, true." Kat coughed and grimaced a little. She lifted her hand and ran it along the bumpy bandages. "Damn. He got me worse than I thought. The others?"

Bianca filled her in on Paytah and Saul. "Tess is in recovery nearby." She nodded to the bed where the magus slept. "Broken shoulder, arm, and leg, plus plenty of other wounds from having part of a building fall on her. I heard they pulled in another magus to steady her. She'll be fine, just beat up."

"Oh, she's going to be a piss ant when she wakes," Kat lamented. "At least she made it." She sighed and closed her eyes wearily. "How are you?"

"Besides stunned and angry? I honestly don't know." Bianca looked down at Kat's hand. Hers hovered near it, but their fingers didn't quite touch. "I'm grateful to be alive. Relieved that the senka and Hunters are caught. Glad to be released into Carlos' care. But everything I knew is a lie. My sister. My parents."

"Wait, what?" Kat asked and looked back at her. When Bianca didn't elaborate, she reached out and laid her hand on the avian's. "Okay. Start from the beginning."

So Bianca did. Kat stayed awake through it all and listened, her lips pressed into a grim line. When Bianca finished, the werewolf sighed and shook her head. "I'm sorry. That's…that's just shit what your sister did. I'm so sorry, Bianca." She squeezed her hand.

Bianca drank in the comfort and physical contact. "I guess it's good that I've found new people to trust. Carlos said I can stay with him, but I'd still like to, you know, come and visit?"

Kat arched an eyebrow. "Are you asking or stating?"

"I guess a little of both." Bianca chuckled. "I didn't grow up with a lot of friends, and I'm not ready to let a new one go. So. If you can tolerate being followed around by a stubborn bird, I'd like to be friends."

Kat glanced at their conjoined hands and offered a little smirk. "I think I can agree to that. For now."

Bianca didn't ask what she meant. Her cheeks flushed in response, and Kat mustered a tired, weak laugh.

They sat in silence for a bit. Kat faded in and out of consciousness, thanks to intermittent doses of morphine. When she woke the third time, the wolf grasped at her neck and frowned. "A nurse. She took the necklace you put on me. I'm sorry."

Bianca made to reply but paused when she noticed the purple jewelry sitting on a small table next to Kat's bed. She leaned forward and picked it up. Sure enough, it held her necklace with the feather. She stared at it. For a moment, she wanted to toss it aside as her sister's betrayal burned deep in her bones. But the necklace meant more than that. It connected her to the Mother. And, it was still the last remaining link to her past.

Bianca slowly put the necklace on and reached for Kat's hand again. "Just rest, Kat. You'll be home soon."

"We'll be home," Kat corrected her.

Bianca touched the necklace and took a shaky breath. "Yeah, *we'll* be home."

Chapter 19
Home

Bianca

Three days passed before Bianca and her friends were released from Legion custody. It took Tess and Kat both longer than they expected to recover, plus there was the whole paper processing mess that Bianca couldn't even begin to wrap her mind around. They were watched like hawks, and Bianca found Jay around almost every corner she turned, not that she minded overly much. Of the lot, Jay made Bianca feel the most comfortable.

When they were all released, Jay teleported them back to the District.

"I'll be around," the Legion agent told them. "A new Violet Marshall still needs to be named, and I'm going to stay here to make sure no inner fighting starts up."

Word had already been sent to Paytah's and Carlos' family. The moment everyone appeared, Rozene got out of her truck, another man not far behind, and rushed towards Paytah, Tess, and Kat. She wrapped her arms around all three, though Tess was confined to a wheelchair while her wounds healed.

"You had me worried sick," Rozene accused and kissed Kat and Tess on the head. Then she turned to Bianca and did the same, surprising her. "I'm glad you're safe," she said.

The other man, dressed in a police uniform, went to Tess and shook his head. "What have I told you about running off with your pack brothers and sisters? You're not invincible like them."

Tess smirked. "To be fair, I think I did more damage to the wall than it did to me. And I doubt the wolves would have made it out any better."

His shoulders slumped. "Tess…"

"I'm fine, Dad," Tess said. She lifted her good hand and created a fire ball in it. "See? Still a fiery pain in the ass. And besides, you said you wanted an excuse to spend more time with me. What better way than to make sure I can't get out of the chair!"

Her father rolled his eyes. "You're going to be insufferable, aren't you?"

"Oh, yeah. You think I was antsy before."

He shook his head then leaned down and hugged his daughter gently. "I was worried about you, firebug."

"Daaaaaad!" Tess complained. "Come on, not in front of the alpha!"

Paytah couldn't hide the smile from his face. "Firebug, huh? Now I know what to call you when you make me mad."

Tess gave a mock growl until her father wheeled her away. Just before they were out of earshot, she called back, "Hey, Bianca!"

Bianca jumped. "Yeah?"

"I think it goes without saying, but, welcome to the District, even if it was a shitty greeting. You werebirds definitely know how to make an entrance, don't you?" With a final wave, her father helped her to the car.

Bianca decided not to be offended by the off-handed greeting. They were safe, and that was what mattered most.

Paytah held his mate by her waist and looked at Bianca with eyes that weren't quite so red or angry. "Take care of yourself, little bird. And don't be a stranger. My door's open to Carlos. That extends to you."

Bianca inclined her head. "Thank you, sir."

Rozene offered her a smile. "I should get these two home. Carlos, take good care of her." Rozene took Kat's hand in a motherly grasp and began to lead her and Paytah away. Kat looked back and flashed Bianca a warm smile.

Bianca smiled back before turning to the avian rushing towards them.

"Uncle Carlos!" Anita cried and threw herself into Carlos' arms. "Haley and I have been freaking out. You're sure you're okay? You don't need to see a doctor?" She fussed over him, lifting his arms, checking in his mouth, and going so far as to test his temperature with the back of her hand.

Carlos laughed and caught her wrist. "Yes, Anita, I'm perfectly healthy. All I want to do is go home and see my wife and chicks." He glanced over his shoulder. "Saul? Do you need a ride home?"

The vampire stood off to the side, looking despondent. Though, Bianca thought most vampires looked that way. He raised tired eyes and shook his head. "I can find my own way home. Thank you."

Anita frowned. "It's not safe in the streets right now," she reminded him.

"I'll find my way," came the somber reply as Saul turned on his foot and walked off.

Bianca personally didn't think he should be traveling alone, considering the circumstances, but what right did she have to judge? And besides, after her experiences with Trish, she had no inclination to be any closer to a vampire than necessary.

And here her family had said werewolves were the dangerous ones.

Trish was detained at Legion for all Bianca knew, so she took comfort in knowing no vampire would attack her in the middle of the night.

She hoped.

Carlos draped his arms around Anita and Bianca and walked them towards the car. "Let's go home."

***

When they arrived at Carlos' house, they were greeted with the delicious scent of a homemade dinner. Spicy herbs tickled her nose and sweet smells made her mouth water. Bianca walked up the stairs with Carlos and Anita. She couldn't help but to bite her lip nervously.

I don't know about this. Haley tossed me out last time, she thought.

"*She did, but Carlos told you she sent him and the others to get you*," her bird reasoned. The caracara nestled in her mind, anxious, but hopeful. "*Carlos promised you could stay. That should be good enough.*"

Bianca relented. She walked through the door as Madison and Henry rushed towards them. The sight of Henry filled her with relief. He'd made it home in one piece.

"Mama, Daddy's home!" Henry shouted. He threw himself into his father's arms. Madison attacked his legs with a squeal.

"My babies," Carlos cried and kissed Henry all over his face and ruffled Madison's hair.

Haley wheeled out of the kitchen with the biggest look of joy on her face that Bianca had ever seen. "Carlos."

Anita swooped in and scooped Madison up. "Alright, niños, let your mama see your papa."

Carlos handed over Henry as well. He went to his wife and wrapped his arms tightly around her. "I didn't mean to worry you."

"I told you not to do something stupid," Haley scolded and kissed her husband's cheek.

Bianca shifted behind Carlos and looked down at the kids.

Henry went to her and grasped her hand. "I knew you'd come back."

His voice drew Haley's attention. She lifted her head and looked over at Bianca. When their eyes met, Bianca dropped her gaze. She tucked her hair behind her ear and took a slow breath hoping that Carlos hadn't been lying to her.

The room fell quiet, tensions high as everyone waited.

And then, something fluttered into her mind. A presence appeared near her caracara. Bianca opened up to the new bird. Haley's barn owl rested beside her caracara, wings tucked at her sides.

Bianca wanted to cry.

In all the time she'd been with the family, Haley had never let her feel her bird. Now, the owl stared at her with sad eyes.

"*I'm sorry,*" Haley said mentally to her. Bianca sensed her sincerity through their connection.

"*I understand why you were angry and scared,*" Bianca said. "*You were just trying to protect your family. There's nothing wrong with that. You're not the bad guy.*"

"*I was cruel to you, and I'm sorry. Avians need to stick together. You reminded me of that when you rescued my son. You didn't have to save him.*"

Bianca laughed out loud and shook her head. "*What was I going to do? Just leave him to Trish? No, I had to do something. I would have done the same for you.*"

"*I know that now.*" The barn owl flicked her wings and leaned forward, beak open as if ready to preen Bianca.

The caracara closed the gap. As the barn owl started to preen her, Bianca's eyes filled with tears of relief and joy at finally being accepted.

Haley left her bird in Bianca's mind as she spoke aloud. "Welcome home to the family, Bianca."

Bianca couldn't stop herself. She rushed forward and wrapped her arms around Haley in a fierce hug. The elder woman paused then slowly embraced her back.

"Does this mean Bianca gets to stay?" Henry asked.

Haley nodded against Bianca's shoulder. "Yes, Henry. We have a new family member."

"Yay!" both children cried at the same time.

As Bianca stood up, the pair rushed her and pounced. Bianca fell sideways onto the floor with the kids in her arms and laughed, hugging them to her.

Haley chuckled. "Come on, now. Let's eat before the food gets cold."

Bianca helped the kids to the table. Normalcy settled over her and chased away her tension. She belonged to the family.

They were just starting dessert when the doorbell rang.

Carlos frowned and got to his feet. "I wasn't expecting anyone."

Bianca swiveled in her chair as he headed out the upper door. She couldn't help but be nervous. They'd just arrived home; she didn't need anything else to go wrong.

Carlos returned several minutes later with a tall man following on the avian's heels. Bianca didn't recognize him, but a sniff told her that he was a vampire; his pale skin also tipped her off. He dressed in black pants, red shirt, and a business black jacket.

Haley stiffened. "Duke Joseph," she said coolly.

Bianca's heart jumped into her throat. *Duke?* So this was the vampire leader of the District. He did not look like the type of person she wanted to tangle with in the middle of the night. He almost reminded her of Saul who, despite going into a fight, had been dressed like the battle held no more weight than a business meeting.

"Haley," Joseph said with a slight incline of his head. "I apologize for the intrusion. I won't stay long." He made a point of clearing his throat and straightening his tie. "First, I want it known that Trish did not act under my direction. What she did was to protect the coven. Be that as it may, she will be staying with me and my wife for the foreseeable future and receiving a strict reeducation in our mannerisms and affairs."

Bianca covered her mouth to hide her disappointment that the vampire hadn't been locked up for what she'd done. It didn't make Bianca feel any safer.

"Go on," Carlos said.

"Second, I'd like to apologize to you and your family for her actions against you. She will be punished for them, and I will see to it that it does not happen again. Third, I received a call from Priest Vic that Gladus' will was read. It states that the next Violet Marshall will be Alpha Paytah."

Carlos drew in a surprised breath, but he didn't appear upset with the decision. Haley even looked relieved.

"That's good news," Carlos remarked. "Hopefully that will end all the feuding."

"We can hope," the duke replied. He pressed his lips together and shifted. "Finally, I thought it a courtesy to warn you to keep your birds close. Vampires are going missing. And Paytah mentioned that he heard from other packs that their wolves are vanishing. I don't know who is behind it, but I don't think you want your new little bird to end up in someone else's claws." He gave Bianca a look which sent chills down her back.

Carlos went to her side in an instant, his hand on her back. "Thank you for the *warning*. I will take care of my own."

"Hm." The vampire breathed out heavily through his nose. "The memorial for Gladus will be in a week at the Irish American Heritage Center. 2:00 pm sharp. Formal attire." With that, he turned on his heel and marched out of the house.

Bianca stared after him and looked at Carlos and Haley. "Pleasant individual."

"We caught him on a *good* day," Anita grumbled. "Paytah… wow."

"I'm not surprised," Haley remarked. "They were close, and Paytah does have the biggest pack in Chicago, and a great amount of support from the District." She touched Carlos' arm. "I'm glad it's not you."

"In all honesty, so am I." Carlos sat beside his wife and rested his head on her shoulder with a sigh. Bianca couldn't fault him for his relief, not after what had happened to Gladus.

She looked at the kids as they watched their parents and relief coursed through her as well. She knew the pain of losing her family; she wouldn't wish it on anyone.

Chapter 20
Time to Say Goodbye

Bianca

Bianca sat on a violet-covered chair surrounded by more parahumans than she had ever seen before in her life. Carlos, Paytah, Joseph, Vic, and the other leaders in the Purple Door District had brought along most, if not all of their groups to say goodbye to Gladus. Many had loved her and had arrived to pay their respects to the fallen magus.

It seemed longer than a week since the battle against Lanzel. Bianca managed to get settled in at the house and taught Henry regularly how to paint when she didn't need to help Haley with chores. Carlos continued looking into school for her and also making plans for her to start working at The Guacamole Grill. Anita couldn't contain her excitement at having someone else in the "family" to work with at the restaurant.

Twice Bianca went to visit Kat. The second time they stayed out almost until sunrise, just talking and getting to know one another. No fights. No deception. She needed normal in her life.

Legion lived up to their threat of checking in. Agent 642CIR, or Jay—whatever her name was—came by once to check on Bianca and to announce that she would be attending the funeral to keep the peace. The feuding all but stopped with Paytah taking on the mantle of Violet Marshall, but the tension remained amongst the parahumans. Time would tell if the community could pull together under the new VM.

Legion didn't hide their displeasure about the whole affair with the senka. Lanzel's paperwork about the Ether serum had been recovered. Bianca doubted that they had much to fear now that Legion had snatched up the information like a greedy child. They wouldn't let it get out to the public. They'd already tested that her blood remained normal. And seeing as her visions had ceased since being given the antidote, she suspected they'd leave her alone from now on.

Maybe Legion wasn't the big bad monster her parents had made them out to be.

For a moment, all seemed right with the world.

Well, not everything.

Bianca stared at Gladus' urn. The silver canister, flecked with purple, stood on a pedestal beside a table filled with pictures and items that reminded everyone of the magus. Her ward, a mixture of men and women of different appearances and skills, sat at the front of the room in a small circle around the urn. They'd taken turns talking about Gladus' kindness, her stubbornness, and yes, her incessant need to save everyone. Priest Vic had spent a long time on that part alone.

Paytah and his pack sat to one side of the room, his arm wrapped warmly around his wife's shoulders, Nick perched on his left. The alpha kissed Rozene on the cheek and rubbed her shoulder gently as she dabbed at her eyes. Tess, now in a regular chair, leaned against her father.

Joseph lingered near the back of the room with his vampires. Bianca recognized Saul's dark form sitting as far away from the front as possible. He held a small box in his hands that belonged to his deceased lover, Fraula. Trish didn't make an appearance, and Bianca didn't know if that was a good thing or a bad thing. Either way, Bianca never wanted to see the vampire again after the part she'd played both in Gladus' death and Bianca's capture.

Carlos sat in the same row as Bianca, supporting Madison on his lap. Haley held his hand and Henry's. Henry leaned against Bianca for support. He sniffled through the ceremony, so much so, Bianca wrapped an arm around him and hugged him close. As an added comfort, she sent her caracara into his mind and nestled with his red-tailed hawk fledgling.

Kaitlyn sat on her left. She'd started out with the pack, but when the ceremony began, she'd settled in with Bianca to give her comfort.

Bianca glanced at the golden-haired woman and smiled sadly. Kat smiled back and leaned over to bump her head lightly against Bianca's.

Bianca sighed as she looked around. So many parahumans, so many groups that would have torn the other apart had they not been in a neutral area. They had come here for one reason.

To say goodbye.

"She was gracious to everyone, no matter their background," Vic said beside the urn. He looked at the table. "Never has the Purple Door District seen such a dedicated Violet Marshall. Our world is a little darker without her in it. And I know my ward will always feel the emptiness that her absence has left behind." He sighed and looked towards Bianca's row. "Carlos, Father of his Cloister, said that he would like to share a few words."

Carlos stood up and handed Madison over to his wife. He touched Haley's hair affectionately then walked up to the front of the room. His mustache looked even grayer now. He had a little limp from Paytah biting him, but the doctors said that it would go away with time. The two men had already reconciled, not that Paytah had had a choice in his actions. Carlos must have been favored by the Mother. Otherwise, how had Paytah been able to fight the blood magic as long as he had?

Carlos took the microphone. "We've heard similar stories about Gladus. How wonderful she was. How she brought us all together. We all know it. I've lived in this area longer than many of you, so I've seen my fair share of Marshalls. Gladus was an amazing woman, but her heart went out to too many. She brought in the weak, the weary, and the bedraggled. But she also brought in those who would one day turn against her. She saw the good in everyone and wanted to give them a chance." He glanced at the urn. "She was a grandmother to my children, and one of my best friends. Even before her death, she brought another blessing into my family. My adopted daughter, Bianca."

Bianca blushed as several eyes turned towards her. She still didn't know what the other parahumans thought about her, but she supposed it didn't matter. Her cloister provided enough support.

Carlos went on. "She was taken from us cruelly, but I think we should be comforted to know that she died doing what she loved; protecting people. She was selfless in more ways than one, and I'll never forget her for that." He cleared his throat and gripped the microphone a little harder. "With that, I would like to turn this over to the new Violet Marshall. Alpha Paytah."

A slow, respectful clap rippled through the room as the werewolf rose and walked over to the microphone.

Bianca watched Paytah take Carlos' place. The only ones who didn't clap quite as vibrantly were the vampires and the werecats, though Joseph made sure to show his support. She glanced at Paytah until Kat's hand found her knee.

"He wanted this," she whispered to Bianca. "Gladus has been grooming Paytah for a while to take her place. The fact that she named him in her will as her chosen replacement is probably what made the others not fight it."

"Better him than Joseph," Bianca replied quietly. "After what Trish did, I don't think I'd trust him to keep people in check."

Kat nodded in agreement.

Paytah looked around the room and spoke in his deep, soft voice. "I know that it was difficult for some of us to accept a new Marshall. It's not an easy job, dangerous, too. But I thank you for giving me your trust. I swear to do right by Gladus and honor her memory by welcoming in those who need help." He glanced at Carlos.

"But I will also keep a watchful eye to make certain those same people don't later turn against us. Gladus' home will remain part of the Purple Door District and will be used as temporary lodging for new people." He touched the urn delicately. "I've decided that the house will remain the same. It has comforted others for years, and I think by leaving it untouched, it will keep Gladus alive in our memories just a bit longer. With that being said, I invite you to dine and celebrate her life. Give yourselves the opportunity to meet other members of the District. Thank you."

He put the mic back on the stand. People started moving quickly and swept to the bar at the back of the room to get a drink. A buffet had been set out; food donated by The Guacamole Grill and other District establishments.

Bianca stood up and glanced at Kat. "I want to go talk to Saul for a moment. I'll meet you at the urn?"

Kat tilted her head, but she nodded. "Of course. Take your time."

Bianca brushed her arm then headed towards the back of the

room. Vampire eyes followed her path as she walked towards Saul. He sat with his head bowed, one thumb brushing lovingly over the box. "Saul?" she said softly.

The dark vampire looked up. There were no tears in his eyes, but they were puffy and red.

"I wanted to say thank you," Bianca murmured. "Thank you for helping to rescue me. I'm so sorry for what happened to Fraula." She glanced at the box.

Saul looked down as well and gripped it. "She always said she wanted to die fighting. I just didn't expect it to happen at the jaws of one of our District members. Much less our new *Marshall*."

Bianca stiffened. "Paytah had no choice. He was being controlled by the senka."

"Heh," Saul chuckled bitterly. "And yet he managed not to crush his own wolf's neck. Or Carlos. Strange that he only had to sacrifice one." He glanced at Gladus' urn, and when Bianca followed his gaze, she realized he had his eyes on Kat. "Be careful around your new *friends*, bird. You might be in their jaws next."

Bianca looked back to him, but Saul had vanished. She caught a glimpse of his coat tails as he left the room. Her shoulders slumped and she brushed her hand through her hair, tugging it a little in distress. Once he finished grieving, he'd come to his senses.

Maybe.

She folded her arms and walked slowly through the room. She found Vic standing alone, a cocktail in one hand. He stared down at a few pictures of Gladus, his left hand tucked in his pocket.

"I don't blame you, you know," Vic said upon her arrival. "For what happened to Gladus. She knew what she was doing when she brought you in."

"But, the vision—"

"Not all visions come true," Vic said and glanced at her. "And who knows how real they actually were? You could touch the Ether, but you couldn't control it. It's not like you wanted her to die." He chuckled. "Though, if you ever tasted some of her healing tonics, maybe you would have."

Bianca uttered a little laugh before sighing. "I'm sorry that you lost her."

"She was really fond of you, you know. She hadn't taken that kind of interest in someone for a long time. I know you're living with Carlos now, but, I would like to invite you to dinner with the ward sometime." He smiled at her. "I'd like to get to know the little bird who caught our Gladus' eye."

The invitation surprised her, but Bianca warmed up to the magus more. "I'd love that."

Vic touched her shoulder then gestured over to the urn. "Go on. You should say goodbye, too."

Bianca bit her lip as she walked towards it. Gladus' name was etched into the metal surrounded by violet swirls that reminded her of the magus' magic.

She touched the cool metal with the tips of her fingers. "I'm sorry," she whispered. "All you wanted to do was help me, and you died because of it. I'll try to carry on your work and help the new people who come in." She smiled faintly to herself. "Thank you for helping me find a family."

A hand settled warmly on her back. She glanced at Kat as the werewolf took her hand in hers.

"She wouldn't blame you. You shouldn't blame yourself."

"I just wish I could have been braver to save her. Brave like you."

Kat laughed, shaking her head. "I wasn't brave. I was an idiot, as you so fondly reminded me. I'm lucky I didn't get myself or anyone else killed. I don't think Paytah is going to let me hear the end of it." She squeezed Bianca's hand again. "I just didn't want anything to happen to you."

Bianca looked sideways at her. She closed her hand around Kat's and rolled her eyes. "Just when I thought I was starting to become a normal avian again, *you* had to enter my life. So much for just friendship." She leaned against Kat and rested her head on the woman's shoulder. "Thanks for wanting to protect me. Let's take this slow, though, okay? I just got back on my feet."

"Of course." Kat kissed her hair gently. "This is the first time I've been out around this many people. I'm still trying to find my ground, but I think you can help with that."

Bianca smiled. It would be nice to help someone else for a change.

"Bianca?"

Bianca turned and blinked in surprise as Paytah walked towards her. He gave Kat a look, noticing their conjoined hands, but then shrugged it off and looked down at the werebird. "Carlos and Haley mentioned that you're trying to get into art school. Even though you missed the first semester, I have a few connections that might be able to get you in at the beginning of the next one."

"S-seriously?" Bianca gaped at him. "You'd do that?"

"Gladus wanted you to find your place here. I can at least see to it that I help fulfill her last wish."

Bianca could have cried. Not only would she be able to still paint with Henry, she could finally go to school. Her visions might have stopped, but her love for painting hadn't. "Thank you, Paytah. I start working at The Guacamole Grill on Monday so I can save money that way."

"Good." He patted her arm then gave Kat a stern look. "You never do anything easy, do you, pup?"

"No. Are you going to stop me?" She lifted her hand, still wrapped around Bianca's.

Paytah rolled his eyes. "No. Though I expect you to show up at pack meetings from now on. If you can come out of hiding to be with *her*, then you can interact with the rest of your pack."

"Deal." Kat winked.

Bianca settled her head back down on Kat's shoulder as Paytah walked away. She stared at the urn again and touched the pedestal. "Thanks, Gladus."

They stood together for a time before they wandered to the back of the room to grab food and drink. Bianca reached for lemonade until she sensed eyes on her. She looked around and spotted Jay standing off to the side of the room. The woman had been there the entire time, but she seemed capable of vanishing and reappearing with the drop of a hat.

Jay walked towards her and slid a bag off of her shoulder. She wore her black uniform, but this time she dressed in a skirt with flat shoes.

Bianca groaned. "You're not taking more blood samples, are you? Not now."

"No, no, we're done with that for the time being," the woman replied. She pulled a silver canister out of the bag and presented it to Bianca. "I went through your files, and through your sister's. Legion was the one who found her and took down her records. We have everything we need." She nodded to the canister. "We thought she belonged with you."

Bianca almost dropped the plate in her hands. Kat quickly took it from her as she reached for the canister. When she turned it over, she saw her sister's name engraved in it. Small wings and feathers were etched around it. Bianca clapped a hand over her mouth and looked up at Jay. "This... She's here? With me?"

Jay nodded and offered a sad smile. "Family stays together, right?

Bianca nodded through her tears. She held the silver tin against her chest and hugged Nora as if she stood right there with her. Her caracara keened loudly in her mind and wrapped her wings around an invisible canister. Closure. She finally had closure.

Jay touched her arm then passed her off into Kat's embrace. "Good luck to the both of you."

Bianca couldn't even muster the words. She leaned against Kat and held her sister in her arms. She looked around at all of the parahumans surrounding her. Werewolves spoke with vampires. Avians chatted with magi and felines. They were like a big family.

And for the first time since Nora's death, Bianca embraced the feeling of *home*.

About the Author
Erin Casey

Erin Casey graduated from Cornell College in 2009 with degrees in English and Secondary Education.

She attended the Denver Publishing Institute in 2009 and has been a recruiter ever since. She is the Communications and Student Relationships Manager at The Iowa Writers' House and one of two Directors of The Writers' Rooms, a non-profit corporation that focuses on creating a free, safe environment for writers no matter their experience, gender, background, and income. Just like in her book, community is very important to her.

An advocate for mental health, Erin's written and published several articles on the Mighty, specifically about anxiety and depression.

She's also a devoted bird mom.

When not volunteering and working, she's writing

LGBT/urban/medieval YA fantasy and sharing her literary journey on Instagram and Twitter. One of these days, she might actually get some sleep.

Learn more about The Writers' Rooms:
www.thewritersrooms.org
Learn more about The Iowa Writers' House:
www.iowawritershouse.com

Follow Erin

Website
www.erincasey.org

Amazon
amazon.com/author/erincaseyauthor

Goodreads
goodreads.com/erincaseyauthor

Instagram
@erincaseyauthor

Facebook
@erincaseyauthor

Twitter
@erincasey09

Wordpress
erincaseyauthor.wordpress.com

Patreon
patreon.com/erincasey